BRIAR PATCH

BRIAR PATCH

Linda Sole

This first world edition published 2011
in Great Britain and in the USA by
SEVERN HOUSE PUBLISHERS LTD of
9–15 High Street, Sutton, Surrey, England, SM1 1DF.
Trade paperback edition first published
in Great Britain and the USA 2012 by
SEVERN HOUSE PUBLISHERS LTD.

British Library Cataloguing in Publication Data

Sole, Linda.
  Briar patch.
  1. Great Britain – History – Victoria, 1837–1901 – Fiction.
  2. Great Britain – Social life and customs – 19th century –
  Fiction. 3. Domestic fiction.
  I. Title II. Series
  823.9'14–dc22

ISBN-13: 978-0-7278-8088-8 (cased)
ISBN-13: 978-1-84751-388-5 (trade paper)

All Severn House titles are printed on acid-free paper.

Severn House Publishers support The Forest Stewardship Council [FSC],
the leading international forest certification organisation. All our titles that
are printed on Greenpeace-approved FSC-certified paper carry the FSC logo.

Typeset by Palimpsest Book Production Ltd.,
Falkirk, Stirlingshire, Scotland.
Printed and bound in Great Britain by
MPG Books Ltd., Bodmin, Cornwall.

Prologue

'Something is wrong with our Carrie.' Ellen Blake shaded her eyes as she stood at the kitchen window. 'I told you to keep an eye on her, Dick. You know she isn't safe out on her own.'

'I can't watch her and do my work,' Dick muttered. 'Pa sent me down to the bottom field with the cows. Carrie followed. I sent her home but you know what she's like – it's not my fault if she wanders off in a daydream. The girl is soft in the head and it's no use denying it, Ma.'

'Our Carrie isn't like other girls. I wish the good Lord had made her ugly for then her foolishness wouldn't matter so much – but she is beautiful and the lads stare at her. She hasn't the sense to know what they're after.'

'You worry too much, Ma.'

Dick was at the deep stone sink pumping water to wash when his mother opened the back door.

'Come away in, Carrie,' she scolded. Then, on a different note: 'What's wrong, love?'

'He hurt me, Ma.' Carrie's sobs brought Dick's head round sharply. He grumbled about having to watch out for her when he was at his work but in his heart he loved her. She was vulnerable and a little lacking up top but her beauty and her sweetness of character made her a favourite with everyone. 'I didn't want to do it – but he forced me.'

'Forced you to do what, Carrie?' Dick saw the tear to her bodice and the mud on her long skirts. Moving swiftly towards his sister, he grabbed her wrist. 'Who was the bastard that hurt you – and what did he do to you?'

Carrie yelped in fright. She was sixteen; a lovely girl with hair the colour of ripe corn in sunlight and wide, greenish-blue eyes that always held an expression of wonder or bewilderment. She had no reason to be frightened of her eldest brother, though at seven and twenty he was tall, broad-shouldered and powerful.

'The squire.' Carrie's face was streaked with dirt and tears but

Dick could see the red mark on her cheek. 'He was riding his horse through the wild meadow. I asked him why he was there because that's Pa's land. He dismounted and pushed me down on the grass and then he did it . . .'

'What did he do?'

'Ma . . . Don't let our Dick hurt me. I didn't mean to let him . . .' Her eyes widened as she stared at her mother. 'Will I have a baby, Ma? Da will kill me if I bring shame on him – he said so.'

'The filthy bastard.' Dick took Carrie by the shoulders, shaking her until she started sobbing again. 'What did he do to you, girl? Did he rape you? By God, I'll kill him for what he's done.'

'You sound like your pa. Sit down and have your meal, Dick. Whatever is done is done. You can't change it and who would take Carrie's word against Squire Thornton?'

'Everyone knows what he is. He gets away with it time and again. No one stands up to him – but this time he has gone too far.'

'You don't know what he did.' Ellen caught hold of her son's arm as he started for the door. 'Where are you going? You can't touch him, Dick. Squire is too powerful. He has men working for him who think they rule this county.'

Dick met her eyes defiantly. 'I'm going to kill him, Ma – and damn the consequences.'

'Violence never helped anyone. If you do this you'll have to run and where does that leave me? You know what your pa is like and Tom can't stand up to him the way you do.'

'I'm going after him, Ma, and you can't stop me – this time the bastard is going to pay.'

'Dick, please think. Mebbe nothing happened. Carrie's all right, just a bit frightened. Come back. Please don't leave us alone with your pa.'

Dick wasn't listening. The anger had been smouldering inside him for a long time: anger at his sister for being the way she was; anger at the world for the injustice he saw around him every day; and anger at himself for bowing his head to his pa.

In the yard outside, Dick saw the long-handled axe he had used earlier for chopping wood and picked it up. His face was grim as he set off across the low-lying fields which lay between

Thornton's land and his father's farm. The squire coveted their land because of its access to the fast-flowing stream that ran through it and bordered the wild meadow. It petered out to a thin trickle by the time it reached the squire's land, which meant that all the water for the stock and much of what was needed elsewhere had to be pumped from various wells Thornton had sunk. During the previous hot summer some of his wells had run dry but the stream on their land had kept flowing, even though it had been sluggish during the drought.

'Sell to me, John Blake.' Thornton had made a generous bid for the land at the time. 'You have barely enough acres to support your family, man. With the offer I've made you could settle elsewhere – perhaps buy an inn or more land. Send your eldest boy to me and I'll give him a cottage and a job in the stables.'

Dick frowned as he recalled his father's reply. John Blake's curses had made even Dick blush and he was used to his father's foul language. Since then they had heard nothing but Thornton was not a man to take such insults lying down.

'Damn him for a coward and a rogue!'

What kind of a man took his revenge on a defenceless girl? Everyone knew that Carrie was a little slow in her mind. The doctor said it was because she'd been too long in coming when Ma gave birth.

'I'll kill him. I'll kill the bastard if I swing for it.'

Dick's anger festered as he strode through the fields, most of which were pasture for the squire's herd of prime Herefords. He was trespassing but he didn't care. What kind of a man would take advantage of a girl like Carrie?

Anger carried Dick swiftly towards the large sprawling manor house that had belonged to Squire Thornton's family for more than three hundred years. Added to over the centuries, it was a hotchpotch of styles ranging from Jacobean to the Georgian facade that the squire's grandfather had built. As he saw the grey stone walls rising ahead of him, Dick hesitated and for a moment his mother's words came back to his mind.

Please don't leave us alone with your pa.

It would be hard for her but it couldn't be helped. He took a firmer grip on the handle of the axe and strode on. When he reached the front courtyard, Dick saw a group of gentlemen standing outside. The squire was one of them. They were all laughing in the wintry sunshine – Thornton as carefree as the rest. The rogue hadn't an ounce of conscience.

'Damn your black soul to hell, Thornton!'

Dick raised the axe above his head and charged towards the men. At first they seemed unaware but then they turned to look at him. He saw their stunned expressions and the fear in their faces as they scattered. For the first time in his life he felt powerful. He had always been a labouring man, forced to bow his head and obey orders. These rich men rode by on their horses and splashed mud over him, hardly seeing him; he was nothing, dirt beneath their hooves – but they were seeing him now.

He heard the screams and shouts but his mind was focused on only one thing. Thornton must die. The squire had turned to look at him, incredulity in his eyes. He alone of them all stood his ground. Once, Dick would have admired that but the red mist in his brain shut everything out but the desire to kill.

'What do you want, Blake?'

'Revenge for my sister,' Dick said and smashed the blade of the axe against his head. Thornton went down like a stone, blood spraying everywhere. Dick felt a moment of triumph before the shot made him crumple to his knees and then fall flat in the dirt beside the body of the man he had just killed.

One

'Philip, you are a mean beast. I could never marry Mr Rushden and you know it.' Roz Thornton flashed blue eyes at her brother in the way that had half the young men in the county running after her. 'Mama said there was no need for me to marry until I was sure I really liked someone.'

Philip Thornton stood up and took a turn about the large well-furnished sitting room. The dark mahogany furniture belonged to a more elegant age and had not been replaced by the heavier pieces that were popular these days. At three and twenty he was four years older than his sister, an attractive man with reddish-brown hair and dark eyes. He did not have his father's build, being leaner and shorter by a head. For a moment he gazed out of the window at the wide expanse of lawn beyond the terrace and the shrubbery.

'That was then and this is now, Roz. Father left things in a muddle. We ain't exactly done up, but there are debts. We can't afford the money for a London season for you or me come to that – I may have to go somewhere to find an heiress. I wasn't cut out to be a farmer.'

'No, you weren't.' Roz smiled up at him teasingly. 'I'm not sure you are fit for anything but visiting your clubs and playing cards with your smart friends.'

'Hang on, Sis,' he protested. 'I'd have jumped at a commission in the army but Father said I had to come back from college and learn to become the squire. I escaped to London for long enough to discover its delights – then he got himself into this mess.'

'Is it so very terrible here? Papa always enjoyed hunting and shooting, and we had parties all the time last year.' Roz arched her pretty brows. 'Why did Dick Blake have to kill him like that and spoil everything? I know Papa used to – well, he didn't behave just as he ought, but Carrie Blake? How could he!'

Roz had always been a little in awe of her powerful, rather loud father. He'd been a handsome man, larger than life with dark hair and grey eyes. Squire Thornton had laughed a lot, hardly noticing his daughter until her sixteenth birthday when he'd taken to pinching her cheek and telling her she was his beautiful puss. 'It was all so horrid. Goodness knows what that Blake man might have done had Higgins not shot him. We might all have been killed.'

'You weren't even there.'

'Mother and I were about to go out to the landau. It was our day for visiting. Another few minutes . . .' she broke off and shuddered.

'Dick Blake wouldn't have harmed you. I knew him a little and respected him. He wasn't like his foul-mouthed father. People said he took after his mother. Ellen Blake is the daughter of a vicar. She's a quiet, well-spoken woman. Everyone wondered why she married Blake but it was probably because Dick was on the way.'

'Really! You shouldn't say such things to me.'

'Don't be a fool, Roz. You'll be married in a year or so at most and then you'll find out what men are all about.'

'I'm not sure I care to be married. It sounds rather sordid.'

'And you sound like Mama. You mustn't let her ruin your life, Roz. Father might never have been a paragon, but he told me she was always cold. He had to look elsewhere for his pleasure, and I can't blame him for that: men have needs.'

'Do you think there is any doubt?'

'I don't know. She claimed it was Father who raped her – and there's no doubt she's having a child. She must be eight months gone at least.'

'Father has been dead for more than seven months.'

'Exactly. Anyway, what I wanted to tell you before we got into all this is that I have invited friends to stay with us over the Queen's Jubilee.'

'Oh yes, we must celebrate.'

'It would look strange if we didn't. We've been in mourning long enough.'

'It would be such a shame not to celebrate Victoria's fiftieth year on the throne. She married Prince Albert when she was very young and she was so happy but then he died and she's been alone all this time. Do you think she wants all these celebrations for the Jubilee?'

'I imagine her ministers have forced her to come out of seclusion. A queen has her duty, Roz – and so have I. This place needs a fortune to run it and it's my duty to find an heiress who will marry me. At the moment the bank is letting us run, but once things get sticky the money people won't want to know. My advice is to find yourself a husband while you can. Rushden was hinting that he fancied you.'

'I can't bear the way he looks at me.'

Roz was aware that Harry Rushden liked her, but despite his owning one of the finest estates in the country, she had no desire to be his wife. He might be wealthy but he was not her idea of what a husband should be.

'Harry is no different from any other man and he really likes you. If you tried you could probably wrap him round your little finger. If you're not careful you might get left on the shelf. Especially if things go badly with the estate.'

'I have grandmother's legacy, Philip. You know she left three thousand pounds in trust until I marry or reach my twenty-fifth birthday.'

'Three thousand isn't a fortune, and you won't like living in the dower house with mother.'

'You wouldn't ask us to move to the dower house?'

'My wife won't want you and Mother living here. Mama has already asked me about the future. Unless you want to settle down to obscurity, make the most of your chances before then.'

'I'm not going to marry Rushden.'

'I'm not forcing you, Roz. I just wanted you to know what's going on.'

Roz smoothed her white leather gloves over her fingers. Now that she no longer needed to wear black she had chosen a round gown of grey cloth with a matching pelisse trimmed at the hem with red braid. Roz's bonnet was trimmed with scarlet ribbons that tied in a bow at the side of her face.

It was a warm afternoon towards the end of May and she was walking to the village with a basket of Cook's pastries for the vicarage. Mama had always been a generous woman and she saw no reason to mend her ways, despite her son's drive for economy. Philip spoke of being careful with money but he was planning three days of celebrations for the Queen's Jubilee. He had invited some London gentlemen down to make up a shooting party and there would be a small dance at the hall on the second evening. On the day of the Jubilee itself the tenants and labourers would be invited to a feast in the grounds.

'We ought to do something for the village folk. If we provide the food and ale the vicar will take care of the sports and entertainment. We can give a few prizes and I'll make a speech.'

'I wonder that you consider we have enough money for such things.' Lady Thornton had been annoyed with her son at dinner the previous evening. 'Why waste what we have?'

'Father would have done something of the kind – and we have to keep up appearances if Roz and I are to make good marriages.'

'Really, Philip. I suppose you can do what you wish – but your sister will do very well at the dower house with me.'

Roz was not sure that she would be happy to live in the dower house with her mother. It was small by the standards of Thornton Hall, having no more than three family bedchambers and two for guests, besides the attic rooms for the servants. They would have just a cook and a parlour maid to look after them and perhaps a woman from the village to come in and clean. She would be constantly in her mother's company with nowhere she could escape to when she wished to be alone.

Besides, living so close to the hall she would be constantly reminded that she was no longer the daughter of the squire but merely Philip's sister. She wasn't sure if she would be able to keep her horses and the thought of parting with them made her wretched. Yet what were her alternatives? She had the accomplishments expected of young ladies but her skills were not exceptional. It seemed she had a choice between marriage and living at home with her mother.

Seeing a large rambling bush covered by the blooms of wild roses, Roz stopped to admire and to pick a small posy. She held the posy to her nose but the perfume was faint. About to move on, she discovered that her skirt had caught on a thorn. In her efforts to pick the flowers she'd become entangled in the briars.

'Hold still a minute, miss,' a man's voice said and she jumped. Intent on her task, she had not noticed his approach. 'If you pull it the material will tear.'

'Oh . . . thank you.'

She blushed as her rescuer took hold of her skirt and carefully untangled it. His hands looked brown and there was dirt beneath the fingernails. He was dressed in the clothes of a farm worker, his shabby breeches tucked into long buckled boots and a dark brown waistcoat over his wool shirt. A handsome man, his hair was dark brown and touched his collar, curling slightly in the nape. As he smiled at her she saw his eyes were what some people called hazel.

'There, you're free now.'

'I'm not sure how I became so entangled. I dare say it was reaching for the best roses.'

'It's a pity to pick them. 'They'll die before you get home.'

'I was going to give them to Mrs Allen at the rectory. Mama sent some pastries – and I thought the roses would be nice as an extra gift.'

His gaze narrowed, as if he'd just realized who she was. 'Well, I am sure she will be pleased, but it's still a pity to pluck them – nature's bounty is for the pleasure of all who see it and the rose hip is much prized for syrup by the poor folk who gather them.'

'Oh, I hadn't thought of it like that.' Roz felt uncomfortable. She was of course on common land but had not given a thought as to who might own the roses. His manner had become cold, accusing. 'I'm sorry.'

He continued to stare at her but didn't answer, merely nodding curtly before he walked away.

What a rude man! Roz felt her embarrassment fade to be replaced by annoyance as he disappeared round the bend.

Raising her head defiantly, Roz walked on. She didn't know who the young man was and she had no wish to find out.

Tom Blake frowned as he saw Carrie standing in the lane between their land and the common. It bordered the squire's land and the wild meadow Thornton had coveted. She had her hands on her stomach and was smiling in the vague way she often did.

'What are you doing here? You should be at home helping Ma with the chores.'

Carrie turned her dreamy eyes on him. She walked towards him, a look of content on her face.

'It's such a lovely morning, our Tom. I thought I would meet Dick. He'll be coming home soon, perhaps today.'

'I've told you a dozen times, girl. Dick has gone. He won't be coming back.'

'He will one day. He told me so himself,' Carrie said. 'I know you put him in that box in the ground but he won't stay there for ever. He'll come for me one day.'

'If he does you'll be dead.' Tom hadn't the heart to be cross with her. Carrie had caused so much trouble but she didn't understand.

Carrie walked with him as they crossed the wild meadow. Tom had been to the village and was not sure what had made him take the shortcut across Thornton land after leaving Roz Thornton. Had he been seen by one of the keepers he would undoubtedly have been challenged and perhaps threatened. Following the news of Dick's death, Tom's father had gone after the keeper who had shot his son down like a dog. He'd given him a thrashing and, had someone not pulled him off, might have killed Thornton's man. He'd spent six months in Norwich prison for the assault while Higgins had got off and been praised for saving the lives of other men present when the squire was murdered. The injustice had not improved John Blake's temper and since his return from prison a month ago he had done little but sit about the house or yard, drinking and cursing.

Tom didn't take much notice of his father's curses, dodging the blows he dished out and keeping out of his way as much as possible. It was easy enough to keep busy since most of the chores fell to him now that Dick was gone. The ache inside him was still deep and he had grieved for his brother, living with the anger and frustration by working until he was exhausted.

His mother kept the house as spick and span as ever, cooking and cleaning as she too fought her grief. She and Carrie fed the chickens, collected eggs and took the scraps to the pigs. However, Ellen was too busy to help with the milking and Carrie was so big that she normally only pottered about the house and yard with her hands over her stomach and that foolish look on her face.

Tom turned his head to glance at his sister. What had made her walk this far? By the size of her she might give birth any day now. If she gave birth before another month was out it would mean – Tom's thoughts veered away from the unthinkable. If Carrie had lied to them about the squire raping her, Dick had died for nothing!

John Blake had slapped the girl about the face a few times when the news broke that terrible day, but Tom's mother had surprised him by standing up for the girl. He knew she loved Carrie, as he did, but she had too much to do and snapped at the girl too often these days. Yet she'd protected her from her father.

'You leave her alone, John. She didn't know what she was doing. It was that devil up at the hall that shamed her – and his keeper that killed our Dick. If you want to take your temper out on someone, go after them up there.'

For perhaps the first time in his life John Blake had done what his wife suggested and spent six months in prison for his pains. Since his return he had not ceased to remind her that she'd goaded him into going after the keeper. Whenever she said it was time he did some work he coughed and blamed his illness on his treatment in prison.

Tom thought of the girl who'd caught herself in the briar patch.

He knew Roz, of course. There couldn't be a man in the county that hadn't noticed Squire Thornton's daughter. She had been pretty enough when she was a girl, but seeing her close to for the first time in years, Tom thought her beautiful. Her complexion of cream and roses was something only a girl who had been delicately reared would have and her eyes were the colour of a summer sky. Her hair had a silken sheen and there was something fine about her that proclaimed her a lady. Girls of his class had fresh, sun-kissed skin and Mary Jane Forrest had freckles across her nose and cheeks.

Mary Jane had been making eyes at him of late. He'd thought once that she was after Dick but recently she had smiled at him in church. Tom knew he had only to ask and she would let him kiss her, but he wasn't sure if he was ready to settle.

Besides, the anger and bitterness inside him was too sharp for him to go courting just yet.

The thought had come to him when he was freeing Miss

Thornton's skirt that he could push her down on the earth and do to her what her father had done to Carrie. It would humble her pride and serve the family right if she got caught with his bastard. Yet even as he'd thought of it, he had been angry at himself. He was not going to stoop to the old squire's level. The girl hadn't done anything wrong; there was no crime in picking a few wild roses, even though he'd implied otherwise.

'Don't tell Ma where I went this morning.'

Carrie's plea made Tom turn his head to look at her.

'Why not? What have you been up to?'

'I just went for a walk – but Ma told me to stay in the yard. She'll be cross if you tell her.'

'I'll not split on you, Carrie, lass.'

She smiled, and Tom felt a moment of doubt. They were all used to thinking of Carrie as being simple but the look in her eyes made him suspicious. Had she been fooling them all this time? Where did she go on her walks, and was she always alone?

'You're good to me,' Carrie said and reached for his hand, her fingers curling about his. 'You and Dick are always kind to me – not like Pa. Ma gets cross but she loves me. Pa hates me.' Her wide eyes opened, innocent and free of guile. 'What have I done to make Pa hate me, Tom?'

'It isn't your fault, Carrie. Ma and me will protect you from Pa – but he's not a bad man, except when the drink is in him. Just do as Ma tells you and everything will be fine.'

Two

The hall was overflowing with people and all the activity made Roz feel more alive than she had since her father's funeral.

The family had been in mourning for months but now they were going to celebrate Queen Victoria's Golden Jubilee. All over the country people had been putting up the flags and holding street parties; the potteries had been turning out commemorative ware as fast as they could for weeks. Having purchased quite a few mugs, plates and jugs showing the Queen's portrait, Philip had given them as prizes for the games the vicar was organizing the next day.

However, the dance was this evening. Roz was looking forward to wearing a pretty new gown and flirting with the gentlemen her brother had invited for the occasion. A party of men and women had come down from London for a few days, and it was this that had lent excitement to the evening ahead. Roz thought that two of the young men were attractive. Philip had said they were both wealthy and single.

'You should grab one of them while you have the chance,' he'd told her.

'Please do not be vulgar,' she'd replied, but she was excited about the dance.

'Have you finished the flowers?'

Roz turned to look as her mother came into the small back parlour. 'Yes, Mama. The gardeners sent them early. Philip said his friends from London were to have breakfast in their rooms. They won't show themselves before noon.'

'Well, we were all quite late last night,' Lady Thornton said, her gaze going over the arrangement on the small table in the window. 'You have just the right touch with flowers.' Her expression was expectant. 'Now, tell me, what did you think of Mr Harcourt? I thought him charming.'

'Yes, Mr Harcourt is charming, Mama. I liked him – but Captain Richmond is so amusing.'

'His eyes are too bold. You could not trust him. Since your brother insists that you marry sooner rather than later, my advice would be to get Mr Harcourt if you can.'

'Mama, please do not seek to influence my choice. I hardly know either of them. They are Philip's friends. Mr Harcourt is certainly kind but I have had no occasion to think he is interested in me.'

'Well, you know the alternative. I should not have wished you to marry just yet but we shall not be able to entertain often at the dower house – and if Philip cannot persuade Miss Richmond to marry him, he might lose everything.'

'Hush, Mama,' Roz said and glanced over her shoulder. 'Supposing someone heard you? Besides, how can you be sure that Philip means to ask her?'

'Use your intelligence, Roz. She's not the most beautiful girl in the world but she *is* the only heiress your brother has invited. I know for a fact that she has ten thousand of her own and her aunt is rich and may give her something when she marries. Philip showed her some attention last night, and I think you will see that he is in earnest this evening.'

'If he truly loves her I suppose . . .'

'What has love got to do with it? Your brother has responsibilities.'

'Yes, I know. Poor Philip. I like her but she is rather . . . homely, wouldn't you say?'

'She will make him an excellent wife. I hope you will be as sensible when the time comes.'

'Yes, Mama.'

'Well, go up and change into something pretty. I need to speak to Cook about supper for this evening.'

Roz left the room. Sometimes her mama made her want to scream but she was a well brought-up girl and thus far her rebellions had been small.

Looking out of the landing window, she sighed. It was a pleasant morning and she would rather be out riding than making conversation with Miss Richmond. Roz wondered what kind of a life her brother would have if he married her, but he seemed to know what he was doing and Julia seemed nice enough – if a little dull.

Roz supposed that she was what this house party was all about really. If Julia Richmond hadn't consented to come her brother might not even have bothered to hold the dance this evening – and that would have been a shame, because Roz was looking forward to it.

'You look charming this evening, Miss Thornton,' the tall, fair-haired gentleman smiled down at her. 'Beautiful might be a better word – and you dance delightfully.'

Roz gazed up at Robert Harcourt as their dance ended. He was attractive enough in a pale, slightly insipid way, with a gentle manner that might have drawn her to him had she not seen Captain Richmond.

'You flatter me too much, sir. I do not think I am beautiful, though Mama says I am pretty.'

'You're too modest. Yet your mirror must tell you the truth every time you use it.'

'We shall not argue over it, sir. I thank you for the dance. I enjoyed myself – but now I see my next partner approaching.'

'Ah yes, Richmond – all the ladies adore him. Be a little wary, Miss Thornton.'

Roz hardly listened. Her eyes were on Paul Richmond and her heart was racing. He was so handsome with his lean, chiselled features, black hair and dark eyes that looked silver sometimes in the candlelight. She wouldn't have dared to tell her mother, but she had been drawn to him from the moment they had met. Marriage had seemed distant, something she must do eventually if her brother had his way, but now she felt breathless, on fire with the need to be in his arms.

'Miss Thornton – or may I call you Roz? At last we can dance together. You have been doing your duty as the hostess and I have been passing time.'

'I saw you dancing with Miss James. Polly is a very pretty girl.'

'Pretty, yes.' He snapped his fingers. 'Pretty girls are two a penny. You are something more . . .'

'Am I?'

'Surely you know it? Philip told me half the men in the county have been after you for ages.'

'Perhaps, but I do not care for any of them; they are dull and have no conversation but hunting, shooting or the land.'

'We are all predators at heart.'

Paul's laughter was husky. The way he looked at her was hungry, speculative; almost as if he saw her as his prey – something to be hunted. Then his hand clasped hers in a masterful grip as he led her towards the dance floor and her heart seemed to slam against her chest.

It was a dream. Surely she could not feel this wonderful. Nothing on earth could ever feel as good as dancing with Paul Richmond. His hold was firm and yet light as he guided her round and round in a dizzying succession of circles.

He pressed her hand as their dance ended. 'I want to talk to you alone – not tonight; we should be missed. Perhaps tomorrow.'

She inclined her head. Excitement curled through her and she gave her hand reluctantly to the next man to claim her. She was so lost in her dreams that she hardly knew she was dancing with Harold Rushden until he spoke.

'Our families have been close for many years.' His deep voice recalled her from her dreams. 'Because of that I believe you will not be offended if I drop a word of warning in your ear, Miss Thornton. That fellow Richmond is not to be trusted. I should not approve of a man like that being in company with my sister.'

'Jane has been married for a year.'

'So she has,' Rushden agreed and looked pleased with himself. 'I arranged a suitable match for her and she was grateful to me. She is very happy and settled in Yorkshire with her husband.'

'I am glad to hear it, sir.'

Roz held her tongue on the matter of Captain Richmond. She did not wish to argue with her partner in the middle of the dance floor.

Her reticence left him with nothing more to say on the subject and he proceeded to tell her about the new wing he was building at Rushden Towers. Since he had spoken of little else for months, Roz was able to listen, smile and transfer her thoughts back to Captain Richmond's intriguing remark.

He wished to speak to her alone. Just what did he mean? Surely a gentleman would not say such a thing to a lady unless he had marriage in mind?

'Will you enter the archery contest tomorrow?'

Roz recalled her wandering thoughts as the dance ended.

'Oh . . . I'm not sure,' she replied and glanced up at him. 'I hadn't considered it. After all, I've won for two years in a row and it seems fair to let others have a chance.'

'It would be a pity not to show off your skill. Jane always admired you. She had no talent in that direction at all.'

'It is hardly a requirement for marriage or running a home. I dare say I should have done better to work at my sewing or my music.'

Rushden murmured a denial, bowed his head and left as yet another partner approached Roz. She took his hand, allowing him to lead her back to the dance floor, but her thoughts remained with Paul Richmond. Her gaze moved round the room, seeking him out.

He seemed to have left the ballroom, and it was not until Roz went upstairs to tidy her gown an hour or so later that she chanced to see him leaving the room of one of their married guests. The lady was in her mid-thirties, a friend of Lady Thornton's and staying without her husband. Paul was pulling at his waistcoat and she noticed that his cravat was not as pristine as it had been earlier.

He did not notice Roz because he turned away to the right as she approached from the left, heading for the wing occupied by single gentlemen. He'd had no business to be here on this landing at all. Feeling shocked, she remembered Mr Rushden's warning earlier. Now she understood what was implied.

Roz hurried to her own room and washed her face in some cool water left in the jug on her washstand. Seeing Paul come from the lady's room had made her feel hot all over. She was not such an innocent that she could not guess why he had gone there. Similar things had happened during house parties on more than one occasion in the past. Mama had instructed her to ignore what went on.

'Gentlemen will be gentlemen, Roz. Papa keeps his affairs away from the house, but if a married lady and a gentleman wish to . . .' Lady Thornton shook her head. 'I do not approve, but it happens. One cannot dictate to one's guests, my dear. Discretion is all.'

She must ignore what she had seen. Gentlemen had affairs and ladies pretended they did not know. These things had nothing to do with marriage. Young girls of good family married for a home and the lifestyle they had been reared to expect.

Raising her head, Roz went back down to her guests. However, some of the glow had gone. Paul Richmond was not all she'd thought him.

Perhaps her mama was right. She might do better to encourage Mr Harcourt.

Roz spent the following morning arranging flowers and helping her brother oversee the arrangements for the fete that afternoon. She wished she might go for a good gallop on her horse but Philip asked her to set out a stall with the prizes for the children.

'Shall you enter the archery contest this year?' he asked as he inspected her work later.

'I thought it would be better if someone else won this year.'

'I'm giving a prize of twenty guineas.' Philip eased his neck-cloth. 'The truth is I can't really afford it, Roz – but Father always gave a generous prize. If you won I wouldn't have to part with the money.'

'Philip! Surely things are not that bad?'

'Well, I could pay if I had to but . . .' He shrugged. 'It was just a suggestion. Paul Richmond is entering so you probably wouldn't win anyway.'

'Are you saying I couldn't beat him?' For some reason her brother's suggestion pricked her pride. Paul Richmond had flirted with her and then gone upstairs to the bedchamber of a married woman. 'I think I'll enter after all. It will be interesting to have some competition for once.'

'Good. I should like to see you take him down a few pegs, Roz. He's a conceited devil. I shouldn't have asked him to stay if it were not for his sister. She wouldn't have come on her own.'

'Are you going to ask her to marry you?'

'I like Julia. She doesn't make a chap feel as if he has to be clever or flatter her all the time. I think we might be comfortable together.'

'Is that truly all you want of life?'

'I've never been in love, Roz. Julia's money would put things straight. I should like to buy more land and make the estate prosper. Land and respect – they're worth more than love, don't you think?'

'Perhaps. I'm not sure. I suppose if it is what you want . . .'

'If Julia marries me you might have a London season after all. I thought of taking a house in town. You could stay with us sometimes.'

'I should like that,' Roz said impulsively and kissed his cheek. 'I hope you get what you want – and I wish you happiness.'

'You'd better go and change for luncheon. Roz . . . be careful of Paul Richmond. I know he is charming but you would be better off with Harcourt – or Rushden. He keeps hinting that he's interested.'

'Of the two I would prefer Mr Harcourt. If it isn't urgent I would rather wait for a while before I decide. Besides, I doubt whether Mr Harcourt will ask me. He hasn't shown any sign of being interested.'

Roz watched the children's games for the first hour or so. She presented prizes for the sack race and the three-legged race and then wandered off to where the targets were being set up. Because not everyone owned them, bows and arrows were provided and there was never a shortage of entrants, though most entered for a laugh and were knocked out in the first round. A small queue had formed already and she saw Paul Richmond checking out one of the bows. She walked towards him, a smile on her lips.

'I see we are to be rivals,' she said. 'Tell me, are you proficient at archery, sir?'

'I am good at anything I choose to do, Miss Thornton.' His dark eyes held a hint of mockery as he met her gaze. 'Are you hoping to best me?'

'I have won for the past two years.'

'I wasn't here then.'

'No, that is quite true.'

She faced him proudly for a moment before turning away. She saw that another man had joined the group waiting for the contest to begin. Her brow furrowed as she recalled the rude man in the lane. He became aware of her scrutiny and glanced at her, the hint of a challenge in his eyes. Roz turned away just as her brother came up to them.

'We are almost ready to begin,' Philip said and then swore softly. 'What the hell is he doing here? I should have thought he and his family would have had the decency to stay away this year.'

'Who are you talking about?'

'The man looking at the bows is Tom Blake – Dick Blake's younger brother.'

'Oh . . .' Roz's throat caught as she realized Tom Blake was the man who had rescued her from the briar patch. No wonder his behaviour towards her had turned so cold that day – he must have guessed who she was. 'He shouldn't have come here. Is his sister with him?'

'Who knows? I haven't seen her.' Philip scowled. 'I can't stop him entering. It would cause a scene.'

'Just ignore him. It doesn't matter, Philip. You mustn't do anything that might upset Miss Richmond.'

'No, you're right. I am going to ask her to marry me this evening after dinner.'

'I hope it all goes well for you. People are waiting. You'd better start the contest.'

Philip walked off to call the competitors together and the contest began. Roz was one of the last to shoot so she stood watching the others. Most of them entered each year and one or two seemed to have improved, their arrows hitting the inner rings regularly, but only a couple managed to hit the centre circle.

She tensed as Paul Richmond took the bow he had selected and fitted his arrow. He drew the string back and then let the arrow fly, hitting the top of the centre circle. His second arrow hit just inside the bottom of the circle and his third was just outside. A little burst of applause followed what had been the best performance thus far.

Roz watched two others but neither did any better. Then she took her bow and stepped up. Her first arrow hit just inside the circle, her second slightly nearer the centre and her third just above the top of the bullseye. She retired to enthusiastic applause and then Tom Blake took her place. She watched with interest as he loaded his arrow and fired. The first arrow hit the middle of the centre circle, the second was just below it but the third was just wide.

Most of the other archers were eliminated at this stage. Paul

Richmond, Tom Blake, another local farmer and Roz stepped up for the second round. Standing back a little further from the target, Roz went first and all three arrows hit the inner circle. Paul Richmond followed her example but his were just off centre, the farmer missed completely and then Tom Blake stepped up. He fired three arrows in quick succession and they all hit the centre circle, each nestling close to the other. The applause was muted because everyone was aware of the history between the two families.

Seeing the look of disgust on Paul Richmond's face when he was eliminated gave Roz a quite unworthy feeling of satisfaction.

'Congratulations, Mr Blake,' she said as he offered his hand. 'I have scarcely seen better shooting. Can you do it for a third time?'

She took the hand he offered because it was tradition that the last two shook hands before the final round. She observed that his fingernails were clean this time and his boots shone instead of being caked with mud.

'I hope to prove a worthy opponent, Miss Thornton. Would you like to go first?'

'I think you should,' Roz said and stood back. 'Good luck, Mr Blake.'

His eyes narrowed for a moment and she thought he was angry. He shot very quickly again, the first two arrows dead centre but the third just clipping the outer line of the bullseye.

'You can beat the cheeky bastard,' Philip said, coming up behind her and speaking in a low voice. 'Teach him a lesson, Roz.'

Philip's neck was flushed red and he looked angry. He would hate it if he had to hand the prize over to Tom Blake.

She approached the line, loaded her first arrow and fired. It hit dead centre and her second followed it. She was about to fire again when she saw a girl go up to Tom Blake and reach for his arm. Carrie Blake looked as if she might have her child at any moment. Her hair was lank with grease and hanging about her face and her dress was stained, yet she had a pleased smile on her face.

It was wrong that any man should have used a girl like that and left her to take the consequences.

Roz took aim. Her third arrow hit the bottom circle and a little groan went through the watchers.

She stood back, lowering her bow.

'Mr Blake has won,' she said in a voice that carried to her brother and everyone else standing nearby. 'Give him the prize, Philip.'

Philip shot her a murderous look, as if he knew that she'd pulled her arrow deliberately. She saw Tom Blake approach and accept the small leather purse of gold coins. He turned and faced the watching crowd.

'This is for Carrie, because it's owed,' he said in a ringing tone and walked deliberately to his sister. He took her hand and clasped it, leading her through the crowd, who parted to let him go.

'What was all that about?'

Roz turned to look at the man standing just behind her. Paul Richmond seemed to have got over his sulk, perhaps because she hadn't won.

'Oh, nothing,' she lied. 'Just something local.'

'Your mother sent me to tell you tea is ready. Shall we go in and leave the local bumpkins to their fun?'

'Yes, why not?'

They strolled towards the house. Roz wasn't certain why she had pulled that arrow – except that Carrie Blake hadn't deserved what had happened to her.

Three

'Where did you get all this money?' Ellen Blake looked at the gold coins her son had just poured on to the table in front of her. 'You haven't stolen it, Tom?'

'Tom won the archery up at the hall,' Carrie answered for him. 'He said it was for me, didn't you, Tom?'

'Aye, for you and the baby.' Tom didn't smile. 'It's time we got some things ready. By the look of you it won't be long now.'

'I've still got the cot your pa made me,' Ellen said. 'And there's the shawl and christening gown, though she'll need new cloths to bind the babe.'

'Well, this money is for her. I won it for Carrie – it was owed her, Ma.'

'Yes, it was owed. If your pa sees it he'll go mad, Tom. He won't have Thornton money in his house.'

'Put it away where he won't see it. Carrie will need a new dress or two when she's had the babe.'

Ellen got up and put the money into a teapot on the dresser. She was proud of her blue and white set and scarcely used it.

'It will be safe there for the moment. Your pa took half the egg money and went off to the pub. I dare say he'll be the worse . . .' Her words trailed off as Carrie screamed and clutched at her belly. 'What's wrong? Is it the baby, lass?'

Carrie's eyes were wide with fear. 'It hurts, Ma. I never thought it would hurt like this.' She doubled over, arms wrapped around herself. 'Ma, it hurts bad.'

'Having a bairn always hurts, lass. It will get worse before it gets better. Go out in the yard and walk about a bit. Mebbe it will bring it on sooner.'

'I don't think there's a need for that, Ma. Look at her. Her waters have broken.'

Carrie wailed with fear as the water wet her gown and ran down her legs to make a puddle on the floor.

'Am I dying, Ma? Will you put me in a box in the ground like you did Dick?'

'Don't be so soft,' her mother said. 'If you're that far on we'd better get you upstairs. Can you help her, Tom? She's in such a state. I don't know what she expected.'

'Carrie doesn't understand any of it, Ma.' Tom took Carrie's hand. 'Come on, lass. I'll help you. I'll stay with you while the baby is born.'

'I thought it would be like when the calves come. I've seen them and it all happens quick and easy.'

'Not always,' her brother said. 'You're not to blame. You never had a choice.'

'I wanted a baby.' Carrie clung to his hand. 'I thought it would be easy.' She doubled up again, crying out in pain. 'It hurts, Tom. It hurts so bad.'

'I'll get you to bed before you give birth on the floor,' Tom said and swept her into his arms. Carrie didn't know what she was saying. She'd been raped. She'd said so the day she came home with her dress torn. It was the squire that had taken her down against her will. And yet for all her supposed foolishness she seemed to know how babies came.

What went on in his sister's head that none of them knew of?

'Roz, just a minute.' Philip stopped her as she came downstairs that evening. 'Did you let Blake win this afternoon? You rarely miss that badly. It was as if you meant to do it.'

'And if I did?' She looked at him defiantly. 'What he said afterwards – don't you think it was just? Carrie was owed something.'

'How can you say that – after what her brother did to Father?'

'He paid for his crime and without a trial. If our father raped Carrie he deserved to be punished. I'm not saying Dick Blake should have killed him, but someone should have given her recompense for what Father did – now at least a part of the debt is paid.'

'Money I couldn't afford.' Philip glared at her. 'I just hope Julia says yes when I ask her – or you may soon wish you had that twenty guineas.'

'You weren't going to give it to me, remember?' Roz turned

away and went into the drawing room where the remaining guests had gathered before dinner.

Most of their visitors had drifted away after tea. Mr Harcourt, the Richmond brother and sister and one or two others would be leaving the next day.

Roz knew their future depended on Miss Richmond saying yes to Philip's offer. Julia was pleasant but quiet and thoughtful. Had she any idea what kind of a marriage it would be? For a moment Roz felt concern for her. Philip was not the easiest of men. She hoped Julia would not let him bully her too much.

'I hope you have enjoyed staying with us, Miss Richmond?' she asked as she joined Julia by the window.

'Yes, I have. Do you think you might call me Julia? I think you are very lucky to live in a house like this, Roz. Paul sold our estate after Papa died, because he much prefers living in London. I stay with an aunt as much as possible but it would be nice to have a country house again.'

'I am sure you would always be welcome here. What did you think of the fete?'

'I thought it was wonderful. The children loved their prizes. I understand a local farmer won the archery – and you were second?'

'Yes.' Roz saw her brother coming towards them. 'The fete is just one of the things we do each year. Mama always sends flowers for the festival in the church and we make things for the church bazaar, of course. But here is Philip. He will take you into dinner.'

'May I take you in this evening, Miss Thornton?' Paul Richmond asked from behind her. He lowered his voice as she accepted his arm. 'We haven't had that private talk yet.'

'I am sure I do not know what you mean, sir.'

'Meet me in the summer house before you go up this evening and I'll tell you.'

'That would be most improper of me, sir.'

'Call me Paul and come anyway. You might find life a little more exciting if you step over the line now and then, Roz.'

He pulled out a chair for her and went off to discover where he was placed. Roz was glad he was not sitting beside her; his hints had been too particular. Did he think she was easy like the lady who had entertained him in her room? Mrs Madison had departed early that morning, declaring that she must return to town. Perhaps that was why Paul had become more determined in his pursuit of Roz.

She would not give him the satisfaction of being one of his flirts. She smiled at Mr Harcourt, who was her dinner partner for the evening.

'I hope you have enjoyed your stay, sir?'

'Yes, very much. You did very well in the archery, Miss Thornton.'

'I was beaten by a worthy winner.'

'Were you?' His gentle eyes were on her face. 'I know about the Blake family, Miss Thornton. One of your neighbours told me what happened. It was common knowledge locally at the time, of course, but the scandal was hushed up and I didn't know the sister was with child until this afternoon. I am sure she needs the money more than you do.'

Roz couldn't look him in the face.

'Philip has done his best to put all that behind us. It wasn't his fault.'

'You bear no shame for what your father did and nor does your mother or brother. Yet her brother was right – she did deserve that or more. What you did was just.'

'Thank you.'

He meant to be kind but she felt uncomfortable. Mama and Philip had always blamed Dick Blake for the scandal he'd caused, Philip dismissing their father's behaviour as something men did and unimportant. For the first time the enormity of her father's crime came home to her.

Roz was old enough to think for herself but she was accustomed to accepting what her mother and Philip told her. Mr Harcourt had made her aware of an unpleasant truth.

Somehow she felt guilty, as if her father's shame were her own. She had thought she might try to encourage Mr Harcourt's intentions. Now all she wanted was for the meal to be finished. He seemed to understand her feelings and did not speak to her again.

'I have a headache, Mama,' Roz told her mother when the ladies left the gentlemen to their port. 'Would you mind if I did not stay to take tea?'

'If your head truly hurts you may be excused. Say goodnight to Miss Richmond before you go up.'

Roz did as her mother asked and left the drawing room. However, instead of going up to her room she decided that she needed a walk in the fresh air. It was a pleasant evening and she walked slowly in the direction of the summer house. Still trying to come to terms with her feelings over what her father had done, as seen through the eyes of Mr Harcourt, she had forgotten that Paul Richmond had told her to meet him there.

The summer house had been built by Roz's grandfather and was really a folly, shaped to resemble a Roman temple with pinkish marble columns and a domed roof. She sat down on the steps leading to the sitting area, where plush-covered settees had been placed for the convenience of guests.

Roz did not go inside but sat staring at the way the moonlight turned lawns, bushes and trees to silver. She sighed, feeling lost and hurt without really knowing why. Perhaps she just didn't like facing the truth about her father.

'You came early. I had to make an excuse to get away.'

Roz looked up, startled by the sound of Paul's voice. He must think she had come to meet him.

'I didn't come here to meet you. I was thinking about something and forgot.' She rose to her feet and tried to pass him but he caught her upper arm, his fingers pressing into the soft flesh. 'Please let me go.'

'Don't be shy, Roz. You know why you came here as well as I do. I've seen it in your eyes when you look at me.'

He pulled her hard against him, bent his head to look down at her for one moment and then kissed her. It wasn't the kind of kiss some of her admirers had given her in fun but a fierce, demanding possession of her mouth. She placed her hands against his shoulders and pushed, but he wouldn't let go. Roz kicked at his shin and he cursed, breaking his hold. She ran from him but in a moment he was after her. He caught her about the body and they struggled; then Roz felt his weight bearing her down. She was on the grass and she could feel a stone pressing hard into her right shoulder.

'Stop it. No, please don't,' she cried as his hands pulled her skirts up and she felt his hand pushing between her legs. 'I don't want you to do this. Please, I beg you, let me go.'

'Bitch,' he said and bit her neck. 'Keep still or I'll hurt you. You've been leading me on since I got here. I'm going to have you whether you want it or not.'

'No, please no . . .' Roz's sobs were lost as he ravaged her mouth. She fought him for as long as she could but he was too strong and determined. And in the end she just lay there and let him do what he wanted. All the time the thought kept running through her head that this was what her father had done to Carrie Blake.

'Here, give the baby to me,' Ellen said as her son held the tiny girl up for her to see. The child cried lustily, still covered in its mother's blood. 'You're a fine man, Tom, lad. I've not seen a midwife do better than that and I've helped at a good many births.'

'I had to turn her. I've seen the vet do it for the cows a good many times and once when he didn't get here in time I did it myself.'

'Well, now you've delivered your own niece,' Ellen said. 'You should be proud of yourself, Tom.'

'Is she all right, Ma?' Tom's gaze was on the tangled sheets, which were heavily stained with blood. 'I'm not a doctor. I may have hurt her inside.'

Ellen bent over her daughter and stroked her hair. Carrie gave a little moan and her eyelids flickered.

'The bleeding has stopped. She's tired out but she'll sleep for a while and then I'll give her the baby to feed.'

'Give the bastard to me. I'll get rid of it same as we do the cat's brood in a pail of water.'

'John Blake, you should be ashamed of yourself,' Ellen said, rounding on him. 'Carrie's daughter may be a bastard but children bring their own love. You'll not lay a hand on her while I have breath in my body.'

'Get it out of the house, then. Take it to the workhouse. They'll know what to do with the brat.'

'How you can stand there and say such things about your own grandchild I don't know,' Ellen said. 'Listen to me, John Blake.

If you harm this babe or give her away, I'll leave you and so will Tom and Carrie. See how you like fending for yourself.'

'I can hire a woman to do for me and men are ten a penny in the yard.'

'Then find yourself someone to work all hours for the pay I get,' Tom said and put his arm around Ellen's shoulders.

'You shut your mouth or I'll shut it for you.' John scowled at his son. 'You're brave all of a sudden, ain't you?'

'I'm not afraid of you, Pa. Dick thought I was a coward but I prefer a quiet life. I don't want to argue with you, but lift a hand to Ma or Carrie and I'll make you beg their pardon on your knees.'

John Blake spat on the floor at his feet. 'Damn the pair of you. I don't know what it's coming to when a man's no longer master in his own house.'

He stomped out. For a moment there was silence and then Tom spoke.

'He won't do anything, Ma. He's all bluster and threat these days. Pa relies on us to work the farm and not many would work for him. Everyone knows what a temper he's got on him.'

'Aye, I know it.' Ellen shook her head over the baby in her arms. 'I'd best clean her up and Carrie too. Then she'll need a feed. I can manage here now, Tom. You get off to the milking, lad.'

He put his arm about her, kissing her cheek. 'Don't worry, Ma. I'm here. I'll protect you all.'

'It would have been better if Dick were here too. There's too much for one to do. You work all hours.'

'I can manage for the moment.'

'What you need is a wife to help you,' Ellen said. 'Choose a strong girl who can give a hand with milking and churning the butter.'

'I'll think about it,' Tom said to please her and went down the stairs. His father was sitting in his chair by the fire, a mug of home-brewed ale in his hand. He muttered something as Tom went past but he hardly heard. He was thinking about the girl that he had seen earlier that day at the fete.

Miss Thornton's first two arrows had been perfect – why had she missed so badly with the third? Tom was almost certain she had let him win. She must have seen Carrie, because she'd hesitated before she fired wide.

At first he'd toyed with the idea of refusing the prize money, but then he'd remembered what that bastard had done to his sister. The money was owed to Carrie. Dick had brought his fate on himself. He'd been angry and he'd lost his temper; that wasn't Tom's way. If Dick had spoken to him first, they might have settled it like gentlemen. They could have had the law on Thornton and made him pay – a lot more than the twenty guineas he'd won at the fete.

Why had Miss Thornton done it? He'd thought her proud and cold like the rest of her family, but now he wasn't sure. One thing he was certain of was that she was lovely and he hadn't been able to put her out of his mind since the day he'd freed her skirt from the thorns. A rueful smile touched his mouth. Miss Rosalind Thornton was way out of his league. If he married at all, it would be best to follow his mother's advice. A lady like the Thornton girl was too perfect to be brought down to his level.

'What do you think you're doing?' Philip's eyes went over Roz, taking in her stained gown, the tear to the lace at her neck and her pale face. 'What happened? You've been crying – Roz, tell me!'

Roz was trembling, her eyes reflecting horror.

Philip took hold of her arm, giving her a little shake. 'For goodness' sake, tell me. It's no good just staring at me like that – I can't help you if you don't tell me.'

'He raped me,' she said, her voice breathy and no more than a whisper. 'I went for a walk to the summer house. He followed me and he . . .' she choked on a sob and stopped. 'I fought him, Philip. I promise you I didn't give in willingly. He was too strong.'

Philip's fingers dug into the flesh of her upper arm and she winced. 'Was it that Blake fellow? Damn you, Roz. You shouldn't have encouraged him here by letting him win.'

'It wasn't him.' She raised her eyes to meet his. 'It was Paul Richmond. You brought him here – so what are you going to do about it?'

'Richmond? Are you sure?'

'Of course I'm sure. Do you think I dreamed it up?'

'Damn and blast him to hell. Will he marry you?'

'I wouldn't have him if he were the last man on earth. Did you hear what I said – he raped me, Philip. He hurt me and humiliated me – just like our father raped Carrie Blake. I want him punished. I'm going to take him to court and see him go to prison for his crime.'

'You can't.' Philip stared at her in horror. 'You can't say anything about this to anyone, Roz. Think of the scandal. Would you really want to stand up in court and give evidence? You'll be ruined.'

'I'm ruined now. Can you think of something better? Are you going to kill him the way Dick Blake killed Father? I would rather go to court. I'm not afraid. I did nothing wrong.'

'He'd say you were willing – that you'd met him there because you wanted to . . . Besides, we can't do any of this, Roz. If you say one word to anyone else, Mama – anyone – I'll be finished. Julia has just promised to marry me. If you make a fuss about this she will change her mind. The scandal will ruin my chances of finding another heiress.'

'What about me? What of my feelings?'

'You have to keep quiet. He'll be leaving in the morning and Julia will go to her aunt's for a few weeks. Stay in your room until they've gone and you won't have to see him.'

An icy chill seeped through her. 'Is that all you can think of – what it means to you? Don't you understand that I've been humiliated? I can't ever marry – and I might already be carrying his child.'

'Why can't you marry? Rushden wants you. I'll send him a note in the morning and he'll come over and ask you.'

'You really have no idea what I feel, do you?' Roz said bitterly. 'You don't care about anyone but yourself. I pity Julia; she seems lovely and is the complete opposite of her brother. She doesn't deserve you.'

'You breathe a word of this to her and I'll kill you.'

Roz looked into his eyes. 'Yes, I think you would. Well, I shan't spoil your plans, Philip – but don't send for Rushden. I couldn't face him without throwing up.'

'Please yourself,' he said and shrugged. 'Just remember he's ready to marry you but don't leave it too late. If you're carrying a child you'd be best married sooner than later. I shan't help you if you bring shame on us.'

'I'm not the one who should be ashamed,' Roz said and moved away from the door. Her hand on the latch, she turned back. 'You are just like Father – selfish and careless of others. One of these days I'll pay you back for this, Philip. Not now, not yet – but when the time comes you will know.'

Four

Roz looked at herself in the mirror. It was strange that she didn't look any different. Ten days ago she had been reasonably happy, confident, sure of her place in the world. Now she was someone else: a girl's whose self-esteem had been taken away by a careless brute. Nights of weeping into her pillow had left her feeling numbed and angry.

Did Carrie Blake feel this way? Everyone said the girl was not right in the head – but she must have been even more bewildered and hurt, because she didn't understand what was happening to her. Roz felt sick as she pictured the scene and felt Carrie's pain; it was the same pain and humiliation that she felt.

Men like Paul Richmond deserved to be whipped naked in the market square; they should be publicly humiliated, made to do penance for their crimes.

It wasn't going to happen. Paul Richmond had got away with it because Philip cared more about saving his own skin than defending her honour.

What honour? She was ruined, dirty, someone's cast off. Paul had raped her and then stood over her laughing.

Roz had risen to her feet. 'Why?' she'd asked. 'What have I done that you should hate me?'

'What makes you think I hate you? You're no better than any other woman.'

'Was it because I beat you at archery?'

He hadn't answered at once but a nerve had flicked at his temple and she'd sensed she was right. She had committed the cardinal sin of making him look foolish, in his own eyes at least – and then she'd deliberately lost to Tom Blake.

'Your brother may have pulled the wool over my sister's eyes but she has to sell herself because she's too damned ugly to find anyone who really wants her. I've put you in your place, sweet Roz. You'd better marry the country bumpkin who runs after you like a dog with his tongue hanging out. Shed a few tears on your wedding night and he'll never know the difference.'

Roz had turned away. He hadn't tried to stop her as she'd ran towards the house. She had wondered why he'd done nothing to prevent her from telling her brother what had happened, but he'd known Philip would let it go.

He must have guessed that things were dicey with the estate. Richmond knew what Philip was after and Julia had probably guessed the truth. She wanted a house in the country and a quiet life. Philip must seem kind and gentle to her but she hadn't yet discovered how selfish he was.

Roz looked at the small pile of clothes on her bed. She'd heard that Carrie Blake had given birth on the night of the fete. There were some pretty things: lace blouses and underwear that Roz didn't need and a blue dress that should fit Carrie. She'd added a string of coral beads, a matching pair of earbobs and a paisley shawl.

Would Carrie accept them from her? The gift was late and perhaps too little, but it was all she could do to show how sorry she was. Roz hadn't understood until now. All the shock and anger had been against Dick Blake for killing her father. Now Roz understood her ordeal only too well.

Roz could hear a meadowlark trilling in the sky above her head and caught sight of rabbits munching on the lush grass. A herd of Herefords was out in the pasture, enjoying the spell of good weather rather than huddling together in the pen as they did throughout the winter. She'd never had much to do with the home farm as a girl because her mother said that ladies didn't, but she'd enjoyed seeing the young calves and the lambs in spring. She hadn't wanted to know what happened to them when they were taken off to market.

She'd been too sheltered, too pampered. Had she not been so shocked by Mr Harcourt's remarks about her father's behaviour she would not have gone walking alone that night. Well, she'd had a rude awakening. The reality of life had jumped up and smacked her in the face.

What was the good of weeping over spilled milk? She couldn't undo what had happened. She was what her mother would call a fallen woman. It was unlikely that she would make a good marriage now because any man that asked her must be told the truth.

Roz suddenly saw the huddle of buildings ahead of her and realized that she'd reached the Blakes' farm. The house was so much smaller than the hall, though it looked to have several bedrooms and was substantial. The farmyard was at the back. She could hear a cock crowing and other animal noises coming from the rear and there was a strong smell from the cowshed. At the front was a small garden where vegetables grew amongst a variety of herbs and roses. Someone liked flowers, but the garden had mainly been used to grow food.

Roz walked up the path to the front door and knocked. The answer was a while in coming. When she heard the sound of a bolt being drawn, she realized that the family probably used the back entrance. The door was drawn back warily and a woman's face appeared round the side.

'Mrs Blake? You don't know me. I'm Roz Thornton and I've brought some things for Carrie – just a few clothes and a string of coral. I wanted to say . . .'

'Who asked you to come here? Take your charity and go back where you belong, Miss Thornton. My Carrie doesn't need your cast-offs.'

'Of course you're angry. I am very sorry for what happened to your daughter. If my father did what Carrie claimed, he deserved to be punished – though it was a pity your son didn't go to the magistrate instead of killing him.'

'A pity, was it? The pity of it was my Dick was daft enough to go after him in front of everyone and get shot for doing something that needed to be done. Your father was a disgrace to his name. My Carrie wasn't the only one to suffer at his hands.'

'I understand your bitterness. If I could I would do more but most of these things are unworn. I thought Carrie might like them.'

'You thought wrong. Get off my land and take your blood money with you.'

Roz flinched as the door was slammed in her face. She ought to have expected something of the sort but that didn't stop her feeling humiliated. She turned back the way she had come, smarting at the injustice of the way she had been treated. It wasn't her fault Carrie had been raped and given birth to an illegitimate baby.

'Miss . . . wait a bit . . .'

At first Roz ignored the cry and kept walking, but when it was repeated she stopped and glanced over her shoulder. She was surprised to see that Carrie Blake was running towards her, her long hair streaming in the breeze. Now that her body was no longer big with child, Roz could see how lovely she was – and how young. How could her father have raped her? Her eyes closed as she recalled her own humiliation. What must this girl have felt?

'Miss . . .' Carrie gasped. 'Ma shouldn't have spoken like that to you.' Her gaze went to the bundle Roz had wrapped in the paisley shawl. 'That's pretty – is it for me?'

'Yes. I brought you several things, including this shawl – but your mama would not allow me to give them to you.'

'Ma's sharp sometimes.' Carrie's eyes lit up like a child's in a sweet shop. 'Will you still give me them things, miss? You ain't mad at me, are you?'

'No, of course not. I'm sorry my father did that to you – and that you had a baby. I know these things don't make up for what he did, but I thought you might like them?'

Roz handed Carrie the bundle. The girl dropped to her knees and untied the knot, examining the contents with cries of pleasure. She looked up at Roz.

'Are all of these for me?'

'Yes, of course. I haven't worn most of them, Carrie. The beads are coral and given to me by an elderly aunt years ago. They are worth a few pounds if you wished to sell them.'

'No!' Carrie held on to the beads fiercely. 'I ain't never going to sell them. I shall wear them under my dress so Pa doesn't see them and take them off me.'

'Will your mother let you keep the things, Carrie?'

'I'll hide them safe. She won't know. No one knows where I hide my treasures.'

Mrs Blake had made it clear she regarded the gift as charity and rejected it, but Carrie must have heard and followed. Roz hadn't the heart to refuse her and surely it could do no harm.

'Well, you know best.' Roz paused, then: 'I should like to see your baby one day, Carrie. Is she as pretty as you?'

'Ma says she's perfect, better than me.' Carrie raised her head and looked Roz in the eyes. 'Folk say I'm daft but I know what goes on, miss. I wanted a baby of my own and I've got one. Pa wants to give it away but Ma won't let him.' She gathered her things. 'Thank you for these, miss.' She hesitated, then: 'I take Milly for a walk in the mornings sometimes and I go down to the wild meadow. I could bring her tomorrow.'

'Would you do that?' Roz smiled. Perhaps Carrie was a little simple but she certainly wasn't stupid. She liked her dreamy look and the smile that lit her eyes from inside. 'I should like to see her if you don't mind, Carrie.'

'I'll bring her tomorrow,' Carrie promised. 'Thank you for the things, miss. I've never had pretty bits like them beads and the lace.'

'You are very welcome.' Impulsively Roz moved towards her, kissing her on the cheek. 'I shall walk to your wild meadow at this time tomorrow.'

'Bye then, miss.' Carrie seemed to be looking beyond Roz and her eyes had lost their animation, becoming vacant as she stared into space.

Roz realized that she had switched off. She walked away, glancing back a couple of times. Carrie was still standing in the same place, clutching her bundle in her arms. Roz understood why people thought she was daft; she wasn't really, just different.

Some of Roz's anger had drained out of her but now she felt empty and lost. The future seemed grey and endless. What was she going to do with the rest of her life?

At least she was luckier than Carrie. Yet Carrie hadn't seemed resentful. She'd said she wanted a baby, which struck Roz as a little strange. Somehow that didn't fit with her story of being raped, but perhaps she only felt like that now she had the child. Her emotions must have been all over the place these past few months.

Roz would not have to face the same humiliation. Her womanly flow had started six days after the night she'd been raped. Had she been carrying Paul Richmond's baby, she might have killed herself. Her mother would never have forgiven her for bringing shame on them.

It was going to be hard living with just Lady Thornton for company. The move to the dower house would happen while Philip and Julia were on their honeymoon. Before that there was the wedding.

'We shall stay with Julia's aunt for a few days,' Lady Thornton had told her daughter the previous evening. 'Lady Mary is giving Julia a wedding reception as a gift. I had thought they might prefer to have the wedding here, but apparently Julia's aunt wants to have it at her home.'

'That's kind of her, Mama – and will save you the trouble.'

'As if I should grudge anything I do for my children. However, Julia is anxious to oblige her aunt and naturally Philip agreed. I shall arrange for our things to be moved while we are away and we'll return to the dower house.'

'I suppose we couldn't let the dower house and take a house in Bath?'

'Whatever are you thinking about?' Lady Thornton looked down her long nose. 'I couldn't possibly afford to live in Bath. You must make up your mind to a quiet life at home with me – or find someone to marry.'

'No one has asked me,' Roz reminded her mother. 'I might have said yes had Mr Harcourt shown any interest – but he'd heard about Carrie Blake and I dare say he did not wish to be associated with our family.' His disapproval had made her uncomfortable at the dinner table.

'Philip told me that her brother had the effrontery to enter the archery contest. He says you let him win the money – did you?'

'I might have done. She was owed something.'

'I do not know how you could say such a thing. After what happened, they should never have attended the fete. Philip should have sent him away instantly.'

'Do you not think that might have caused more scandal?'

'Please do not contradict me. Allow me to be the judge of what is proper.'

Roz let the argument go. Her mother would be angry if she learned that Roz had taken Carrie some clothes and the coral beads, but there was no need for her to know. Mama seemed to have put the blame entirely on the Blake family, though surely she must have known her husband's reputation. It seemed that her irritation was saved for her daughter, though Roz had no idea what she had done to deserve it.

It was nearly time for luncheon. Roz quickened her step as she reached her home. She was almost at the door when a gentleman came out, a smile on his face as he saw her.

'Miss Thornton. Your mama said you had gone for a walk.'

'Yes. It was such a lovely morning.'

'I know you like to walk and to ride.' Harold Rushden hesitated. 'Lady Thornton tells me you are moving to the dower house after the wedding. You will find it very quiet, I think?'

'Yes, I dare say we shall. We must hope that Julia will invite us to dinner or a card evening now and then.'

'Someone as lovely as you shouldn't be hidden away. As you know, I spend part of the year in London or Bath – if you married me you could hold your own evening parties whenever you wish. Without meaning to brag, I'm thought of as quite a respectable and wealthy man, Miss Thornton – or may I call you Roz? As my wife, you would be the mistress of two houses and have your own horses and rig.'

His proposal was so unexpected that for a moment she couldn't find the breath to answer.

'Are you asking me to marry you, Mr Rushden?'

'Yes, of course. Forgive me for being so clumsy. I'm a plain-spoken man, but I care for you – always have. I should be happy if you would take me.'

'I hardly know how to answer you, sir. I was not expecting a proposal.'

'Your brother knows my feelings. I thought he would have told you.' His dark eyes were intent on her face. 'I know you're not in love with me. If you could bring yourself to be a proper wife to me, I would be satisfied with kindness and courtesy, which is what you'll get from me, Roz.'

The words of refusal were on the tip of her tongue. She had no right to accept his generous offer even if she wanted to marry him and in her heart it was the last thing she wanted. Yet what was she going to do if she refused him?

Roz studied her suitor. His features were heavy, his nose short and his jaw square, eyes closer together than she liked, but he was strong and healthy. He had a fine estate close by – and a townhouse. She would be able to live in London for several months a year. It was the life she had been taught to expect.

'This has taken me by surprise, sir. Would you allow me a little time to consider?'

'Take all the time you want,' he said and a look of relief spread over his face. 'I thought you would turn me down flat.'

'I'm grateful and . . . honoured that you asked,' Roz said. 'If I give you my answer after Philip's wedding, will that be soon enough?'

'Aye. Your brother invited me to the wedding but I shan't come. I'll send a gift and leave it at that – I won't badger you for an answer, Roz – and if it's no I'll understand. You might have done better if your father hadn't come to a sticky end. I've country manners and I ain't no oil painting.'

'You shouldn't put yourself down,' Roz said and offered him her hand. 'Just because some of our friends have fancy manners and live in town it doesn't mean they're better than you.'

'Aye, well, I thought that fellow Richmond might have turned your head but he's no gentleman, Roz.' He held her hands between his big ones for a moment then released her.

'When we return I shall send word.'

'I'll know when you're back.' He walked on to where a groom stood ready with his horse.

Roz turned her head and watched him mount and ride away. Once upon a time she had thought she would rather remain unwed than marry him, but she had expected to have several offers. Now her chances were practically nil because her father had left the estate in such a desperate situation.

Would it be wrong to marry him?

Roz wondered what he would say if he knew what had happened to her on the night of their ball. Philip had said she wouldn't be believed in court. Harold Rushden might think she'd invited trouble by going for a walk alone at night.

Her heart told her to reject his offer but her head warned that she might not get another chance to escape from her mother's scolding.

Roz saw Carrie as she approached the meadow the next morning. The grass was high but the girl was sitting on the bank above the stream. Her child lay on a shawl on the grass beside her and the girl was chewing the end of a grass stalk and staring into the distance. She didn't appear to notice Roz until she spoke to her.

'I wasn't sure you would come. May I see the baby?'

Carrie turned her dreamy eyes on her and smiled. 'Hello. I brought Milly to see you, miss. Ma is glad to get us out of the way for a bit. I'm more of a hindrance than a help to her.'

'I'm sure that's not true.' Roz said sat down on the dry grass. The child had lovely fair hair just covering her head and the bluest eyes she had ever seen.

'She has your hair and eyes,' Roz said, slightly disappointed. She'd hoped for a sign, something that would confirm the identity of the baby's father. 'You must be proud of her, Carrie.'

'She knows what you say to her. She sucks my finger and cries when she wants feeding. Ma showed me how to change her cloths. I look after her myself.'

Carrie's pride was obvious. Roz touched the tiny fists and smiled. 'I'm glad it turned out so well.'

Carrie picked up the child and put her into Roz's arms. Milly burped and then seemed to smile. Roz stroked her cheek with her finger.

'She really is a darling, Carrie.'

'She likes you,' Carrie said. 'She knows you're her aunt. I had an aunt once but Ma said she died – that means they put her in a box in the ground like Dick. Maybe she'll come back one day. Dick is coming back. It might be today. I come to meet him most mornings.'

'She isn't my niece, she's my . . .' Roz frowned. 'The squire is dead, Carrie. Didn't they put Milly's father in a box in the ground?'

Carrie's laughter was soft and low. ''Course not. Squire isn't in the ground. He comes riding this way sometimes, but he hasn't been by for a few days. I shall show him Milly when he comes. He'll give me a shilling for her.'

Roz felt cold all over. Carrie had a pleased smile on her lips but it wasn't one of guile or maliciousness. Roz didn't think she was lying or making up tales.

'Do you mean Squire Philip, Carrie?'

The girl turned her bland gaze on her and nodded. 'Aye, your brother, miss. You be Squire's sister – and he be Milly's pa.'

'Did my brother hurt you, Carrie? Did he force you?'

Carrie stared at her for a moment, then: 'He said to tell me ma it was force. Said it was best to say Squire and not his name. He promised he would look after me if I did what he said.'

Roz felt the sickness rise in her throat. She got hurriedly to her feet and walked away before she said something she might regret. The girl hadn't known what she was doing or realized the consequences – but Philip had known.

Roz stared at her reflection in the mirror, feeling shame and disgust. How could her brother have seduced a girl like Carrie and then blamed the consequences on his father? He'd shown no signs of guilt or remorse over his father's death.

It should have been Philip lying in the family crypt. Roz knew that if she'd gone to her father and told him what Paul Richmond had done he would have thrashed him. Philip had made her keep quiet because he wanted to marry Paul's sister to save his own skin.

What would Julia think if she knew the truth? He deserved that Roz should tell her before the wedding – but would Julia thank her for revealing what kind of a man Philip really was?

Roz's anger had carried her home but now she just felt sick and ashamed. The plans for the wedding were moving ahead and if Julia jilted Philip now he would probably lose the estate. His creditors had given him time because he was marrying an heiress.

He ought to be punished but he wasn't the only one who would suffer. Roz's mother would be homeless and Julia would be shamed in her turn. She didn't have the right to pull down this house of cards, Roz decided.

One day she might find a way to punish Philip, but to vent her anger on others would be spiteful – and she only had Carrie's word for it that Philip was the father of her child. She'd lied at the start and caused a double tragedy. Had she told the truth her brother might have thrashed Philip and made him pay some-thing for her child. He had been angrier than he might have been because Squire Thornton was known for taking down innocent girls. Carrie's child might not be of the old squire's getting, but that didn't mean he was washed clean of all sin. If Roz's father hadn't raped Carrie, he'd done it to others. His reputation had sealed his fate. Dick Blake had seen red and acted in a blind rage – but he might not have been so furious if he'd realized Philip was to blame. Especially if he'd known that Carrie was willing.

There was a bitter taste in Roz's mouth. Philip had caused all this wretchedness with his selfish behaviour. He hadn't wanted to own up to what he'd done and so he'd persuaded Carrie to lie.

Because of Philip, her father was dead and everything that followed had stemmed from the double tragedy. If Roz's father had still been alive his bank would not have decided to call in his debts – and that meant Paul Richmond might never have been invited to the ball.

How could she go to Philip's wedding? Roz felt she would be sick if she looked at him – but would her mother allow her to stay at home alone?

'Not go to your brother's wedding?' Lady Thornton stared at her in disbelief. 'Think what people might say – and the offence it would cause to Julia.'

'You could tell Julia I wasn't well.'

'You would have me lie to her?' Roz felt the severity of her mother's gaze. 'I don't understand you. Why do you wish to miss such a happy occasion? You may well meet Mr Harcourt at the wedding, Roz. You wanted to visit Bath – if you married Mr Harcourt you would be able to go where you please.'

'I doubt he will ask me.' Roz raised her head to meet her mother's gaze. 'Mr Rushden has made me an offer. I've promised to give him my answer when we return.'

'Mr Rushden?' Her mother's expression of displeasure faded instantly. 'Now that would be suitable, Roz. I hope you intend to say yes?'

'I think I may – but I need time to think. If you would let me stay here, I could be alone and consider my answer.'

'If you are in two minds you should accompany me to Julia's aunt's house. Lady Mary has many friends. You might meet someone more suitable, Roz.'

Roz sighed inwardly. She should have known that her mother would insist. If she knew the reason her daughter wanted to stay home she would be horrified – and yet she might still decide that they had no choice but to carry on as if nothing had happened.

Five

'Roz . . .' Philip caught her arm as she tried to pass him in the hall at Julia's aunt's house. 'You've been giving me the cold shoulder since you arrived this morning – you're not still angry over what I said, are you? I was thinking of you as much as myself. The scandal would've ruined you.'

Roz flashed him a scathing look. 'You don't think that's already the case?'

'Mama told me Rushden has spoken to you. You should take him. He's always been mad for you.'

'Perhaps he won't be so interested when I tell him the truth.'

'Don't be a fool, Roz. He doesn't have to know – if you're clever.'

Roz felt a rush of vomit to her throat.

'I'm not as proficient a liar as you.'

'What do you mean?'

'Do you really want to know?' She faced him then, blazing with anger. 'We'd better go into the study. You might not want anyone else to hear this.'

Philip looked at her uncertainly, then turned and walked into the study. Roz followed and shut the door behind her.

'I've seen your daughter, Philip. She looks very much like her mother at the moment but babies change as they grow. Once her hair gets darker she will look more like you.'

'What the hell are you accusing me of? Why should that girl's child resemble me rather than father?'

'She told me, Philip. I gave her some clothes and a string of beads. She brought the baby for me to see – and then she told me. You said she should tell her mother the squire had raped her but it wasn't like that, was it? You lay with her and you gave her presents – but when she told you she was carrying a child you didn't want to be bothered so you told her to lie. Dick Blake didn't murder our father, you did.'

Philip looked green, but then he recovered and glared at her. He grabbed her by the wrist.

'Breathe one word of this to Julia or Mother and I'll kill you.'

'You told me before. If I don't say anything it is for Mama's and Julia's sake.' Roz refused to flinch even though his fingers were digging into her flesh. 'You're rotten to the core, Philip.'

'You made all this up to get back at me because I wouldn't let you sue Paul Richmond.' Philip's top lip curved back in a sneer. 'Who would believe her now? Or you, either? You went with Paul Richmond and then tried to say he'd raped you. I am certain he would back me up.'

Roz's eyes met his defiantly. 'You can threaten me all you like, Philip – but take care how you murder me. You might not be able to blame my death on someone else. Mama might lose her home if the truth came out now so I shan't tell – but you'll never be easy in your mind, because one of these days I'll find a way to make you pay for what you've done.'

'The bitch asked for it,' Philip said. 'She was always following me around, smiling the way she does. She knew what I was after and she wanted it.'

'Carrie probably wanted a baby. People say she is stupid but she knows enough to understand how babies are made.'

'Damn the scheming bitch to hell,' Philip muttered and released Roz's wrist, flinging away from her. 'Father wouldn't have remembered whether he'd had her or not. There was hardly a farmer's daughter in the district that he hadn't taken down. No one ever bothered to come after him before so why did that damned fool Blake have to kill him? Had he demanded compensation Father would have paid him.' For a moment regret flickered in Philip's eyes. 'You can't blame me for Father's death.'

'You are responsible for his death and Dick Blake's. I ought to shame you before the world but I'm not going to – yet.'

'Be careful, Roz. I could break your neck with my bare hands.'

'Yes, you could, but you'll have to be careful, Philip. You don't want to hang. I shan't go walking alone while you're around.'

'You think you're so clever.' His eyes narrowed. 'What do you want?'

'You disgust me, Philip, but Julia doesn't deserve to have her life ruined and Mama would never recover from the scandal.

You're safe enough for the time being, but one of these days I'll pay you back for Carrie – and me.'

'Mother would never believe you.' Philip was grinning now. 'Carrie is soft in the head and she lied – if you were out of the way there would be no one to touch me. You'd best watch your back, Roz. I don't like being threatened.'

'At least we know where we stand,' Roz said. 'You've covered your tracks for now, Philip, but you'll get caught out. Some people would believe Carrie. Mud sticks. You might save the estate but you wouldn't enjoy being cut by your neighbours. You cheated and lied to save yourself. If that became known you would be finished.'

'I ought to shut your mouth for good.' He took a threatening step towards her.

'I wrote a letter, Philip. It is somewhere safe. If I die violently it will be sent to the right people.'

His hands balled at his sides. He wasn't sure whether to believe her or not but he was uncertain, frustrated.

'Accidents can be arranged,' he muttered. 'You'd best marry Rushden. If you're still here when I get back from my honeymoon I'll make you wish you'd never been born.'

'I've wished that a thousand times.' Roz lifted her head. 'Treat Julia decently or you may be the one wishing you'd never seen the light of day.'

Philip swore, strode to the door and went out, slamming it behind him. Roz stood where she was. She was shaking now and a feeling of nausea washed over her. She had made an enemy of her brother but she hadn't been able to control her feelings. He deserved to be punished, yet she couldn't tell anyone. It would bring the whole family tumbling down. She would have no home and no chance of a decent marriage; her mother would be devastated and so would Julia.

She was caught in a briar patch and whichever way she turned she couldn't break free. Worse, there was no one to rescue her this time. Roz had called her brother a coward but she wasn't much better. Yet what could be gained from ruining all their lives?

'You look lovely, Julia,' Roz said and kissed her cheek. Julia was wearing a gown of ivory silk. Plain but elegant, it suited her well as frills and lace would not. She actually looked pretty with her hair dressed softly and a satin bonnet with a tulle bow and veil. They were in Julia's bedchamber and almost ready to go down. 'Philip is very lucky. I'm not sure that he deserves you.'

Julia looked at her with her doe eyes. 'I know he isn't in love with me, Roz. I didn't expect to be married and I'm grateful that Philip offered. He needs my money and I want a home and children. If I have those I don't mind about the rest.'

'You won't care if he goes off to London and leaves you at home?'

'Father left me more than the ten thousand pounds,' Julia replied. 'I have another twenty in trust for my children and the income is secured to me for life. Philip can't touch it unless I agree. My lawyer refused to change the terms of Father's will. Philip may spend the ten thousand if he wishes, and then I'll have the purse strings.'

Roz wondered if Philip understood that she wasn't the meek little woman that she seemed. There was more to Julia than any of them had guessed and Roz glimpsed a strong will behind the mild manner.

'My brother is stubborn and he has a temper. Be careful, Julia.'

'I'm not pretty like you,' Julia replied and patted the large, creamy pearls at her throat. 'I think these are more appropriate than diamonds, don't you?' She smiled at Roz. 'I've never screamed or had tantrums, Roz. Yet I usually get what I want in the end. Philip didn't want to take me to Italy for our honeymoon, but that is where we're going.'

'Well, I wish you luck,' Roz said and smiled. She was beginning to like Julia more each time they met. 'If you live at the hall I shan't be far away.'

'I've already told Mama that I want you to think of the hall as your home, Roz. You must visit me every day and dine with me often. I am hoping we shall be friends.'

'I'm sure we shall, though I may not be at the dower house for long. I may be getting married soon.'

'To Mr Rushden?' Julia nodded as if she'd expected it. 'I think he loves you, Roz. You are lucky, because he is devoted to you.'

'Yes, I think he cares for me.' She gave Julia a wry smile. 'If you're sure you want to marry my undeserving brother, we'd better go down. Everyone is waiting.'

Philip and Julia were greeting their guests at the reception. Roz looked at the array of expensive gifts set out at one end of the long room. Julia's family had given her some wonderful things: jewellery, silver and there was a card that said her uncle had bought her a small house in Bath.

Roz's gaze went back to the happy couple. Philip had a smile of satisfaction on his face. No doubt he was congratulating himself on catching such a prize. Julia's family was wealthy and her aunt had already hinted that she would be leaving her fortune to her favourite niece.

Julia seemed content. How long would it be before the veil was stripped and she saw Philip for the selfish brute he really was?

'Miss Thornton, I hope you are well?'

Roz turned her head and looked at the gentleman who had spoken. 'I am quite well, Mr Harcourt. I wasn't sure if you would be here today.'

'Julia is a cousin of sorts, though distant. I am fond of her in my way. I hope your brother intends to look after her, Miss Thornton. I should be most distressed if she had cause to regret her marriage.'

'I think Julia has few illusions, sir. She seemed to think that she would be satisfied with her bargain.' She looked into his eyes, challenging him. 'I do not think she is quite the doormat some might believe.'

'Julia has a mind of her own,' Harcourt agreed. 'It's when Philip begins to understand her that the trouble may start.'

'You do not approve of our family, do you?'

'Now what makes you think that, Miss Thornton? Your mama is a very respectable lady – and you are both brave and beautiful.'

'Brave? Now where did that come from, I wonder?'

'Perhaps I am more observant than you imagine, Miss Thornton. I believe they are going to toast the bride and groom. This is not the time for revelations. Another day, perhaps . . .'

Roz watched him walk away. What could he have meant?

She turned her head as her mama came up to her.

'Well, that all went off nicely, do you not think so? Julia looks lovely. She will make Philip a good wife.'

'Yes, I expect so. I hope she will be happy.'

'I am sure she will be content with a home and family, as I was.' Lady Thornton's gaze was hard and direct. 'What did Mr Harcourt have to say to you?'

'Nothing very much, Mama. I think we must follow everyone into the dining room or we may miss the toasts.'

'Julia has been given some lovely gifts. It is an elegant and lavish reception. Just think what you would have missed had you not come.'

Roz made no answer, joining the flow of guests heading for the dining room. She took her place and glanced across the table at Mr Harcourt. Just what did he know that he thought ought not to be revealed on such an occasion?

Could he have guessed what had happened to Roz near the summer house that night? Had Paul Richmond told him?

Roz went up to her bedchamber as soon as the bride and groom had left for their wedding trip. They would be away for at least eight weeks, perhaps longer, which meant that Roz might be married before she saw her brother again.

Philip had looked directly at her just once during the reception. The menace in his eyes had chilled her. Roz had threatened to make her brother pay one day, but it was unlikely that she would act on her words. She'd let her chance slip to reveal him as a cheat and a liar – and perhaps Julia would not have thanked her if she'd spoken out. Roz was leaving for home in the morning and then she would have to give her answer to Harold Rushden.

Should she tell him about the rape? A part of her wanted to confess it all, but she wasn't sure she had the courage. If she confessed he might not want to wed her – and the truth might come out. Roz couldn't face the thought of people whispering behind her back. She was caught fast and there was no way to escape without hurting herself and others.

A knock at the door just as she was about to retire made her pause. When she opened the door she was surprised to see Julia's aunt.

'Lady Mary. I wasn't expecting you.'

'How could you when I have only just made up my mind? May I come in?'

'Yes, of course.' Roz moved away from the door. 'Julia looked lovely today and she seemed happy.'

'Yes. I believe she will make the best of her marriage. She has always loved children, you know.'

'Yes, I see.' Lady Mary knew more than she was prepared to admit. She was a tall lady with white hair and at that moment elegantly dressed in a rose silk dressing robe that carried the scent of lavender. 'You have something to say to me?'

'Now that Julia is married I expect to be alone most of the time. Not that I am lonely for I have many friends – but Julia spoke highly of you. I am thinking of travelling abroad for the winters in future and I wondered if you might like to see something of the world? I should pay all your expenses and give you an allowance for pin money and clothes.'

'Travel with you?' Roz was stunned. 'I really do not know what to say, ma'am. We hardly know one another and . . . I have received an offer of marriage.'

'Ah, then I must congratulate you. I had heard that you would be living in the dower house with your mama and I thought – but no matter. Forgive me for disturbing you at this late hour, but I may not be up when you leave.'

'It was a generous and thoughtful offer.' Roz hesitated and then leaned forward to kiss the lady's soft cheek. 'Had I not promised to give my answer I might have accepted your offer, but I think my future is set.'

'I wish you happiness, my dear.' Lady Mary walked to the door and then turned to look at her. 'Should you change your mind you may write to me. Goodnight, Roz.'

'Goodnight. Thank you.'

Roz stared at the door as it closed behind her. For a moment she was tempted to go after her and tell her she had changed her mind. Yet what purpose would it serve? A year or so spent travelling with Lady Mary would be pleasant, but then she would have to return to her home. If she missed her chance to marry she might never get another one.

★　　★　　★

Roz felt some regret as she took her leave the next morning but the decision was made. She was to return to the dower house with her mama and then she would marry Mr Rushden.

They had been travelling for more than an hour in silence when Roz's mother looked at her across the carriage.

'Your brother has informed me that he is reducing the size of his stables. Once he and his wife return to the hall we shall have to give a day's notice if we require the landau. I must hope that my friends will visit me often.'

'I am sure Julia would not refuse you if you asked for it to be at your disposal one day a week.'

'I hope you are going to be sensible, Roz? If Philip denies you stabling for your horses you will not be happy. I am sure I did not expect him to be so ungenerous.'

'I suppose Philip feels he has to use Julia's money to the best advantage.'

'Your father would have managed somehow without all this economy. My jointure is so small that I cannot afford to set up my own stables. If you married Rushden he might do something for me – at least allow me the use of a carriage.'

'Yes, I dare say he might,' Roz agreed. She smoothed the fingers of her gloves. There was no point in putting it off any longer. 'If Mr Rushden still wishes to marry me I shall accept him.'

'Well, of course he will.' Lady Thornton nodded her approval. 'He isn't quite what I should have liked for you but in the circumstances you are lucky to have this chance.'

'Yes, I suppose I am.'

'I can hardly afford to support myself, Roz. I thought Philip would allow me something from the estate but he insists I must manage on six hundred pounds a year.'

'Many people have far less, Mama.'

'I dare say they may but it is not what I have been used to.'

'You have more clothes than you can possibly need, Mama. Especially since you are to live quietly.'

'It is all very well for you, Roz. You will have a wealthy husband. I dare say I shall be invited out sometimes. I cannot wear the same old clothes for ever.'

'I shall ask Mr Rushden if he will make you an allowance.'

'I do not want charity. If your brother thought of his mother more I should not need to ask.'

It was best not to answer. Roz had no idea what Philip had said to his mother to bring on this tirade, but it had obviously upset her. Lady Thornton continued to grumble at intervals throughout the journey home.

Roz smothered her sigh. Her mother's temper had surely never been this fractured? If the choice was between marrying Harold Rushden and years of listening to her mother's complaints, she had best take him as soon as possible.

'I came as soon as I heard you were home.' Harold's expression was expectant as he looked at her. 'Do you have an answer for me, Roz?'

'My answer is yes,' Roz said. 'Yet there is something I ought to tell you . . .'

'Whatever it is, it doesn't matter.' He came towards her, hands outstretched. 'I dare say I know a lot more than you think, lass. I've held back because I wasn't sure you would take me, but I love you. I've wanted you for years. I had the house done up for you, even though you hardly gave me a glance – but I hoped you'd notice me one day.'

Her throat caught. 'I don't know what to say . . .'

'You've no need to say anything more. I'll take care of things now, Roz. You'll want for nothing – and I'll see your mother is comfortable.'

'Philip says she can only have the carriage once a week . . .'

'I'll buy her one of her own and pay for its stabling. Anything you want, lass. You've only to ask.'

'You are too good to me, Mr Rushden.'

'Call me Harold, lass – or Harry if you'd rather.'

'I like Harry, if I may.' Roz was suddenly shy because the look in his eyes came close to adoration. She ought to tell him about Paul Richmond but she couldn't bear to see that look of love turn to disgust. 'You may kiss me if you wish.'

'Aye, I wish,' Harold said and moved closer to her. He hesitated, then bent his head. At first his mouth was soft as it touched hers, then he made a little groaning sound and pulled her closer, his kiss becoming more passionate, demanding. Roz flinched as a memory flashed into her head. He looked down at her anxiously. 'Forgive me, Roz. I'm a bit on the rough side for you, but I'll never hurt you.'

'I know that,' she said and slid her hands up behind his head. Closing her eyes, she pressed her lips to his and banished the humiliating memory to a corner of her mind. 'I promise I'll be a good wife, Harry. I'll be all you could want. I promise.'

Regret swathed through her and she wished she could go to him as an untouched virgin, but she couldn't change what had happened. She must just pray that he would never find out.

'I'll call Mama. She is hoping for good news, Harry.'

'Aye, so was I – and I've got it.' He smiled and the doubts vanished from his eyes. 'I'm a happy man and the sooner we're wed the better. We'll have the banns called for when your brother comes home.'

'Why wait for Philip?' Roz looked up at him. 'He is my brother but there isn't much affection between us. We could have a small party here before the wedding and then give a reception at your home and perhaps a dance after our honeymoon – if that would suit you?'

'It would suit me fine. Call your mother, lass. I'll be paying for the wedding. My people will put on a good show for us, Roz. Your mother can enjoy herself shopping for new clothes for you both and she needn't worry about the bills, because I'll be paying them.'

'We can manage our own clothes, Harry. You mustn't allow Mama to take advantage of you because she will if you let her.'

'Aye, she can try.' He laughed. 'Money isn't a problem, lass. All I want is for you to be happy.'

'I shall be. I am happy.'

Roz went to the door to call for her mother. She was feeling better than she had for a while. Marriage to Harry Rushden might not be as bad as she'd feared. She didn't love him but she respected him and perhaps she would learn to care one day.

'You've made me happy by saying yes.' Harry grinned like a young lad given his first pair of long trousers. 'We'll do all right together, Roz. You'll see.'

Six

'Where are you off to this fine day?' Mary Jane Forrest stood deliberately in his path, looking up at him with a challenge in her green eyes. She was a pretty girl, her freckles more prominent than ever after the hot days of summer. Her long red hair was loose on her shoulders; she wore it tucked behind her ears and large gold loops in her ears. Tom thought she looked like a gypsy in her bright red skirt and white blouse low cut at the neck.

'I've been to the market,' he replied. 'Now I'm going down to the stream to fetch the cows in for milking.'

'I could give you a hand if you like?'

'Now why would you want to do that when you're all dressed up and looking as fine as a princess?'

'You're mocking me, Tom Blake.' Mary Jane pouted at him. 'I thought you liked me and I'm wearing my best things just for you.'

'Just for me, is it? Now why would that be, Mary Jane Forrest?'

'You know I like you, Tom.' Mary Jane tipped her head to one side. 'There's a dance at the village hall this Saturday. Will you take me?'

'If I take you folk will say we're courting.'

'What if they do? It's time you had a lass of your own to help you. Everyone says it.'

'Do they now?' Tom's mother was always on about him finding a girl to help her about the place but he was annoyed that others should gossip about his private life. 'Do you know what the girl who marries me would be taking on, lass?'

'Of course I know. I like your ma and Carrie is a lovely girl – bit soft and dreamy but she's all right.'

'I thought you liked our Dick?'

'I did a bit, but I liked you too. I hadn't made up my mind then, but now I have. It's you I want, Tom Blake.'

'You're a bold one, Mary Jane.'

'Your ma told me if I waited for you to make up your mind I'd wait for ever. You do like me, don't you, Tom?'

'I like you,' he said. 'You forgot about my pa – you know he's drunk most of the time these days?'

'He wouldn't bother me. Pa sometimes gets drunk on a Saturday night but Ma says to ignore him.'

'My father isn't funny when he's drunk; he's not like yours, Mary Jane. If you want to give me a hand with the cows I'll not refuse you. I'll take you to the dance on Saturday, but I'm not promising anything more – do you hear me?'

'Not yet.' Her eyes sparkled with mischief. 'I'm going to get you, Tom Blake – you just see if I don't.'

'Mebbe you will, and mebbe you won't.' He laughed as she walked beside him. 'You'll have to tuck that fine skirt up when we take the cows into the milking sheds or you'll get cow muck on it.'

'After a look at me legs, are you? If you're good I'll show you more than me legs one day, Tom Blake.'

Tom nodded but didn't answer. She was a bold lass but he hadn't heard that she was easy. Mary Jane thought too much of herself to go with anyone that asked her. She was making her position plain enough and had given him something to think about but he was in no hurry.

'Did I see Mary Jane Forrest in the yard earlier?' Ellen asked that evening. 'Gave you a hand with the milking, did she?'

'She offered so I let her.' Tom washed his hands at the sink. 'I'm taking her to the dance in the village on Saturday.'

'Made up your mind, have you?'

'It's just a dance, Ma. I'm not planning on getting wed just yet.'

'You know I could do with a hand here, Tom. Carrie is useless these days. She's off across the meadows most afternoons. I've seen her wearing fancy clothes, even though she thinks I'm too daft to know. That girl up at the hall gave them to her. I sent her away when she came calling but Carrie must have gone after her.'

'Miss Thornton came here? When was this?'

'Before her brother's wedding.' Ellen sighed. 'I suppose she meant well. What happened to Carrie – it wasn't her fault. I sent her away with a flea in her ear.'

'That's not like you, Ma?'

'I know, but I just lost me temper. Carrie doesn't need charity.'

'No, but it wasn't meant that way. Miss Thornton just wanted to show she was sorry.'

'You speak as if you know her.'

'Not to say know her. I've only met her twice. She was pleasant the day I won the prize at the archery. Shook hands with me and wished me luck in the final round.'

'As long as you remember that she isn't of your own class, Tom.'

'What do you mean by that?'

'Your pa would never have her here – not that she'd come.'

'No, she wouldn't so you're wasting your breath, Ma.' Tom wiped his hands. His gaze travelled round the large kitchen. It was clean and there was a fine oak dresser set with blue and white china, a scrubbed pine table and chairs and two rocking chairs, one either side of the inglenook. 'This house isn't a hovel, but not what she's used to at the hall.'

'She'll be living in the dower house with her ma now. Bit of a comedown for her, I'd say.'

'Well, that's where you're wrong, Ma. Everyone in the village knows that Miss Thornton is marrying Mr Harold Rushden from Rushden Towers. He's richer than the Thorntons ever were. He isn't county gentry like her family, but his father left him a pretty penny and he hasn't wasted it.'

'Getting married, is she? She's done well to get Mr Rushden. He's a decent man.'

'Aye.' Tom turned away from her. 'Where is Pa?'

'I think he slept in the barn last night. He came in for a mug of tea earlier but wouldn't eat a thing.' Ellen sighed. 'If he goes on like this he will kill himself. Can't you talk to him, Tom? He won't listen to me.'

'I've tried, Ma. The last time he threw an empty beer jug at me. He was bad enough before Carrie had the baby, but now he drinks all the time.'

'He hates the baby but she's lovely, Tom. I swear she understands every word I say to her.'

'Mary Jane would help you with her, Ma. I know Carrie loves the baby but she has no idea to look after her.'

'Your sister is very possessive of her child. She insists on changing her when she's here and she's not too bad at it – but then she'll

go off for hours and leave me to cope with her and the chores.
It's like she just forgets everything.'

'Yes, I know.' He hesitated, then: 'Mary Jane will say yes if I
ask her.'

'Well, that's up to you. I can't force you to wed but I need
help here.'

Tom sat down at the table while his mother served him with
a large helping of stew from the pot that hung over the fire. She
kept the stew going for days, adding vegetables or meat to bulk
out the gravy.

'Aren't you having any?'

'I'll wait until Carrie comes home. There's no use waiting for
your pa; he may not turn up until the morning.'

Tom was thoughtful as he ate the meat, which was so tender
that it almost melted on the tongue. His mother was a good cook
and he knew she was finding it hard to cope with so many chores.
He owed it to her to make up his mind. Mary Jane was a lovely
girl and he'd be a fool to let her slip between his fingers.

For a moment he saw a girl's face as she watched him free her
skirt from the thorns of a wild rose. Tom smiled wryly.

Roz Thornton was far above him. He'd always known it but
a man could dream. As long as he knew it was a dream it didn't
harm anyone. Roz wasn't for him. In a few weeks she would be
married and it was time he stopped dreaming and got on with
his life.

Roz sighed impatiently as she waited for the seamstress to pin
the hem of her wedding gown. It was too good a day to waste
indoors being fitted for a dress. She wanted to ride out and enjoy
the last of the summer. Soon the drenching rain would turn the
fields to mud and she might be forced to stay indoors for days
at a time.

'How is that now, miss?'

The seamstress sat back on her heels to look at her handiwork.
She took a few steps about the room, feeling the little train at
the back of her gown trail easily behind her.

'Much better. I can walk without tripping over the hem now.
Thank you for all your hard work, Mrs Mitchell. You've done
very well.'

'I'm glad you're pleased. You're one of my favourite clients.'

Roz turned so that the seamstress could unhook the bodice and slipped it forward, letting the skirt fall to the ground so that she could step out of it. Mrs Mitchell's assistant rushed forward to scoop it up and smooth the white silk with reverent hands.

'I'll have it ready this time next week. Will it be convenient to call at the same time?'

'Yes, thank you. That will give you another week should we need any last-minute alterations.'

'Yes, miss.'

The seamstress and her assistant gathered up their things and left. Roz changed into her favourite riding habit of soft blue and made her escape down the back stairs before her mother could stop her. She walked swiftly through the park that separated the dower house from the hall, making her way eagerly to the stables.

'Good morning, Miss Thornton.' Roderick, the head groom greeted her with a smile of welcome. 'Shall I saddle Dancer for you?'

'I thought I might take Rascal out this morning.'

'I'm not sure that's a good idea. Your brother doesn't like you to ride his horse, miss.'

'Well, he isn't here so he won't know, will he?' Roz arched her eyebrows. 'Rascal needs exercise. I'm doing my brother a favour by taking him out.'

'If you're sure you can manage him. You know he can be a handful at times.'

'I'm sure.'

Roz's dark honey-blonde hair was loose on her shoulders, a playful breeze blowing strands of silk across her face. She tucked it back behind her ears and waited for the groom to lead out her brother's favourite horse.

'Thank you. Don't look so anxious, Roderick. If anything did happen I should tell Philip I took Rascal without your knowledge.'

Roderick shook his head and stood back, watching her as she mounted using the block and then rode out of the stable.

Roz felt the gelding's restlessness and put him to a canter. Rascal pulled at the reins impatiently, wanting to be given his head, but Roz held him in until they reached a stretch of open grassland. Once she let him go he set off at breathtaking speed, his hooves flying over the expanse of green. Roz's hair streamed behind her and she laughed, excitement racing through her body. This was living; this was freedom she'd needed after hours of listening to her mother ranting on about the wedding and her duties as a wife.

The amount of visiting Lady Thornton thought necessary combined with choosing materials and having fittings for her new gowns was tedious. Roz could have put up with all the congratulations and the smiles and chatter but her mother never ceased to grumble about their reduced circumstances. She'd accepted Harry's offer of a chaise and pair and took full advantage of anything he sent her as a gift, but then complained to Roz that she hated charity. Not that she ever said a word out of place to him. When he visited she was all sweetness and light. It was Roz who had to bear the brunt of her complaints.

Lady Thornton had scarcely allowed them to be alone together since the engagement was announced. Harry was busy but whenever he came to visit Roz's mother kept him talking. Roz had discovered that she liked Harry but she wasn't in love with him. Was liking enough for a good marriage or was she making a terrible mistake? She couldn't wait to leave home but would she regret it one day?

Lost in her thoughts, Roz was on the steep hedge before she realized. Belatedly giving Rascal the order to jump it, she felt his refusal and tried to grip with her knees but he pulled up short and then reared up in protest, dislodging her. She fell to the ground and hit her head, letting go of the reins. For a moment the gelding pounded the ground with its hooves, narrowly missing her head, then turned and raced back across the grassland the way they had come earlier.

Tom saw what happened but, at the other side of the field, he was too far away to do anything. He raced towards the spot where the rider lay on the grass, her eyes closed. Falling to his knees beside her, he bent over her, stroking her forehead and then gently feeling for damage.

'Miss Thornton. Oh, God. Please don't be dead. Please be all right . . .'

'What . . .' Roz's eyes flickered open. 'What are you doing? Take your hands off me.'

'I was trying to help. Your horse refused the hedge. What on earth did you think you were doing trying to jump at that late stage?'

Roz glared at him and sat up, grimacing. 'I feel dizzy. Roderick warned me not to bring him and now he will think I couldn't manage Rascal.'

'You could have been killed or seriously injured.' Tom stood up and offered her his hand. She took it but gasped and swayed for a moment, falling against him as he caught her and held her close. He could smell the light perfume she wore, like summer flowers, and his senses reeled. His throat tightened and he felt an urgent desire to kiss her. Fortunately she recovered and moved away. 'I thought you were going to faint. Sorry.'

'I should have fallen had you not caught me. I'm not badly hurt but I feel a little dizzy and I'm shaken.'

'I'll help you. If you will lean on me, I'll take you home.'

'Not to the dower house, not yet. I have to find Rascal. My brother will be furious if anything has happened to that horse.'

'My house is nearer. You're on my land here. Why don't I take you there for a while? I'll find the horse and bring it back to you. You should ride him again straight away if you can.'

'I'm not afraid of a tumble.' Roz smiled suddenly. 'You are very kind. Will your mother mind if we go to your house? I'd like to sit down for a little while – and if you could find Rascal for me that would be wonderful.'

'Don't worry about my mother, Miss Thornton. She was upset when you brought those things for Carrie but she didn't mean to be so rude to you.'

'I saw Carrie afterwards, and the baby. She is lovely – just like your sister.'

'Aye, she is, but Ma says she's much brighter.'

'Your sister isn't stupid, Mr Blake. She goes off somewhere in her mind now and then but that doesn't make her mad.'

'You've seen more than most,' Tom said. 'I'll give you my arm, miss – but if you feel faint tell me and I'll carry you.'

'My head is clearing now but I'd still like to sit down and perhaps drink some water.'

'Ma will give you one of her cordials. Work wonders, they do. Years ago they would have burned her as a witch.'

'They didn't burn witches in this country, they hung them – but sometimes they burned the bodies afterwards to stop the evil spirit returning.'

'Fancy you knowing that,' Tom said. 'I read about Joan of Arc. They burned her as a witch but that was in France.'

'Yes, it was.' Roz had taken his arm and the touch of her hand made Tom very aware of his body's urges. 'Do you like reading history, Mr Blake?'

'I read whatever I can get my hands on, miss – when I have the time. It's not often because there's always a job to do these days.'

'Losing your brother must have been terrible for you.' She hesitated, then: 'I am so sorry for what happened. I know you must hate our family.'

'I don't hate you, miss. I know it wasn't your doing.'

'No, not mine.'

Tom noticed the hesitation. 'If there's something on your mind you'd best say it.'

'I'm simply ashamed that a member of my family could use your sister so ill – and I wish that keeper had thought before he killed your brother.'

'It's a wonder you don't hate us.' Tom turned his head to look at her. 'Dick killed your father. He shouldn't have done it. I'd have done it differently – gone through the courts and demanded compensation for Carrie. Your father should have been made to pay but he didn't deserve to die.'

'No, my father didn't deserve it – a thrashing might have sufficed.'

'Aye, well, that's water under the bridge. We're at the yard now, miss. It's muddy. Shall I carry you to the door?'

'I've had mud on my boots before, Mr Blake. I think I can manage.'

Tom nodded. 'Mind your step then because it can be slippery.'

As they approached the back door it opened and Tom's mother stood watching.

'What's happened, Tom?'

'Miss Thornton took a tumble from her horse on the common. I brought her here to rest while I find her horse.

She asked for a drink of water but I promised her one of your cordials.'

'Aye, come in, lass,' Ellen said. 'You'll be shaken and needing something to steady your nerves a bit. Will you sit by the fire and have a glass of my elderflower wine?'

'Thank you so much. Your son has been very kind, Mrs Blake.'

'Aye, Tom's a good lad. He's got more sense than my elder son – God rest his soul.'

'It was a tragedy for us all, Mrs Blake. I am truly sorry for what my family did to yours.'

'I'm away to find the horse.' Tom turned back as the women disappeared into the kitchen and closed the door.

He felt the tightness in his stomach ease. Holding Roz Thornton in his arms, inhaling her delicate perfume and being so close to her was something he wouldn't forget in a hurry. He was a damned fool to let her get under his skin, but if he were truthful it had happened the first time he spoke to her.

She was above his station, and besides, she was going to be married in a couple of weeks. He had to put Miss Thornton out of his mind and think of something else. Mounting his own horse, he set off across the common. Hopefully he would find the wretched beast that had unseated her before it damaged itself or returned to the stables. She didn't want to confess she'd come off to her brother's grooms.

Tom admitted to himself that he'd fallen in love with a woman he could never have. He was a fool but he'd get over it. Mary Jane was willing, even eager to wed him. Once she was his wife he'd have better things to do than moon over Roz Thornton like a lovesick calf.

Roz reined in her horse and turned to look at the man who had insisted on accompanying her back to the hall.

'I can manage now. How can I thank you?'

'I need no thanks, miss. Just make sure you watch how you go in future.'

'I don't think I'll ride him again. Besides, I shan't be here much longer. You know that I am getting married soon?'

Why had she told him? Was it because for a few minutes as he'd held her she'd felt something between them? No, that was stupid. His brother had murdered her father. The gap between them was too wide to be breached. Yet she'd felt the need to make him aware of her marriage – why?

'It's common knowledge in these parts. I wish you every happiness.'

'Thank you.' Roz sighed. 'I'm not sure I'll be happy but I may be content.' She urged her horse forward at a walk, then glanced back. 'I'll take some books to the farm, Mr Blake. You can return them to the dower house when you wish – keep them as long as you like.'

She thought he shook his head but she had already made up her mind to select some of her books for him. He said he read anything but he probably did not have access to some of the latest novels. She would take him Mr Stevenson's *Treasure Island*, something by Henry James and of course George Eliot's *The Mill on the Floss*, which she had just read for the second time herself.

As she rode into the yard Roderick came hurrying out to take the bridle as she dismounted. She saw him checking the horse for injury and smiled inwardly. She was fortunate that Tom Blake had caught the horse for her. If Rascal had returned to the stable alone and injured she would have found it humiliating.

Smiling, she nodded to the groom and set off for the dower house. She had been away longer than she intended because Mrs Blake had been talkative and she had felt it would be rude to rush away even when Tom returned with the horse.

She had enjoyed herself. The farmhouse kitchen was large and clean. Roz suspected it was cleaner than the kitchen at the hall and there had been a lovely smell of herbs and baking. Sitting in the rocking chair by the inglenook, Roz had been reluctant to leave. She thought that if she'd been Ellen Blake's daughter she would have been content to stay at home.

Laughing at her own thoughts, Roz shook her head. Her future was set; to change things now would cause unnecessary hurt and scandal. Besides, what changes were open to her? The smile faded as Roz faced reality. She had escaped for an hour or two but nothing had changed.

★   ★   ★

'Do you think I'm pretty?' Mary Jane asked as Tom brought her a glass of lemon barley. 'Jack Dawson was here a minute ago. He wanted me to dance but I said I was with you.'

The village hall was not large and crowded with men and women: some young couples and others who had come as a family for a Saturday night treat. The noise of laughter and children's voices could be heard above the fiddler and Mrs Swindon banging away with more enthusiasm than skill on the pianoforte.

'Well, I brought you here, but you can dance with anyone you like.' Tom gave her a brooding look. 'You're pretty, Mary Jane – the prettiest girl here, but I've promised nothing. You're free to dance with Jack if you want.'

'Don't be so sharp, Tom,' Mary Jane said. 'You know you're the only one I want.'

Tom drank deeply of his beer. It was his third that evening. He couldn't shake off his feelings of loss and regret. Mary Jane was here and willing. He only had to say the word and she'd do anything he asked. It was ridiculous to lie in bed at night with his body and mind on fire with need, thinking of Roz. Sometimes he let himself dream of kissing her – of taking her. Tom wouldn't take her in a hurry the way his mates took girls down behind the riverbank. Silk sheets and Roz in a white gown of lace . . . Tom brought his thoughts back to the present. Mary Jane was looking at him oddly. He put his empty glass down.

'This one is a barn dance. I can do that – give me your hand.' She hesitated and he arched his brow. 'Do you want to dance or not?'

'I want to dance – but you know what I want more, Tom Blake. I want you to wed me.'

'Well, mebbe I will,' he said and grinned at her. 'You be nice to me later, Mary Jane, and we'll see.'

'I'll be good to you,' she said and giggled. 'You'll be bound to marry me then, Tom Blake – or your ma will take her stick to your backside.'

Tom smiled and pulled her close to him, whispering in her ear. She giggled and nibbled at his neck. Tom felt his body respond. She was pretty and tempting – and she was available.

Seven

'You look beautiful.' Lady Thornton dabbed at her eyes with a lace kerchief. 'I am so proud of you – and so pleased you've found a decent man to marry.'

Roz kissed her cheek. 'Harry says we shall be away for about three weeks. I think he is taking me to Paris but I'm not certain. Philip should be home before then so you will have Julia for company.'

'It won't be the same as having you,' Lady Thornton said and sniffed. 'Mr Rushden says I shall be welcome at the Towers whenever I wish. You will invite me to stay sometimes, Roz?'

'Of course, Mama. I think we should go down now. I don't want to keep Harry waiting at the altar.'

'You are happy about this?' Lady Thornton laid a gloved hand on her arm.

'Why should I want to change my mind?' Roz lifted her head. 'You can visit your friends or us whenever you wish, Mama. If you're lonely you could take on a companion.'

'I suppose so.' Lady Thornton smiled but Roz saw regret in her eyes.

Picking up the spray of white lilies and roses that Harry had sent for her, Roz gathered her long skirt for the slow walk down the stairs. In the hall several servants, relatives and friends had gathered. Her uncle, Matthew Rooke, looked up at her and smiled. He was her mother's elder brother: white-haired, gentle and a bachelor, he lived alone in a house filled with dogs and clocks, which he loved in equal measure.

'Beautiful,' he murmured as she reached him. 'I never expected this honour, m'dear. Philip should have given you away, but I'm glad you chose me.'

'Harry didn't want to wait – and I would rather it was you.' Roz took his arm. 'Your gifts are much appreciated by us both.'

'I wanted you to have something nice for yourself as well as the silver candelabra.' He nodded as she showed him that she was wearing the pearl and diamond bracelet he had given her. 'You won't be forgotten when I've gone, m'dear.'

'I would rather have you than anything you might leave me. You've always been a second father to me – and someone I can trust.'

Her uncle patted her hand. 'I've told your mother she can come and stay with me if she's lonely, but I doubt she will.'

'That was kind of you, uncle.'

'Well, I felt I ought to ask, but truth to tell I'm used to my own ways and I dare say Amelia is the same.'

Roz laughed softly. They went out to the waiting carriage. The sun was shining but there was a definite bite to the air. Roz shivered and her uncle glanced at her in concern.

'Are you cold, girl? Do you want to send for a shawl before we leave?'

'I shall be fine. The breeze is a little cool but once we're in the carriage it will be warmer.'

'Might be cold in church,' her uncle warned but she took the groom's hand and climbed into the carriage. Matthew followed and gave the order to move off.

Roz waved to the servants who had waited outside to see her off. Many of them had come down from the hall for the occasion and her mother had given orders that a celebration should be held for the servants at the hall. Yet her mind seemed to be wandering, skittering here and there like spring lambs. She couldn't stop thinking about Ellen Blake's kitchen – how warm and comfortable it had been, and Tom Blake holding her when she felt faint. He was one of the most attractive men she'd ever met – apart from Paul Richmond. A shudder went through her and she hastily blocked out the memory of that night.

'I told you it was cold.'

'I'm not cold, uncle. Just a little nervous.'

'Rushden is a decent fellow. He'll be good to you. If he isn't you let me know and I'll sort him for you.'

'Harry loves me.'

Would he know that he wasn't the first with her? Roz had tried not to think about it but the guilt had stayed at the back of her mind all this time. She ought to have been honest with Harry, even if he had claimed whatever she told him wouldn't matter.

The carriage was drawing to a halt. When it stopped, her uncle got out and then offered his hand. She climbed down, shaking her skirts out and glancing about her. Several people were outside the church and she heard cries of good wishes. A man was standing slightly apart from the others. She wanted to wave and smile at Tom Blake but somehow she couldn't manage it. He inclined his head to her, then turned and walked away. Roz felt cold all over. Her uncle offered his arm as she hesitated. For a moment she wanted to run away. She wanted to run after Tom Blake and ask him to take her far from here, somewhere she would be safe and warm.

'Anything wrong, m'dear?'

'No, uncle. Everything is fine, thank you.'

She took his arm and walked into church as the organ started to play.

'You are so beautiful, Roz,' Harry said and lifted his champagne glass to her. 'I know I've been saying the same thing ever since we left the church, but I can't believe my own luck. I kept thinking you would change your mind.'

'I was scared on the way to church,' Roz admitted. 'Don't put me on a pedestal, Harry. I'm just a woman.'

'You're the woman I love,' he replied and touched her hand as she toyed with her wineglass. 'I feel blessed – honoured. I'll be good to you, lass.'

'Yes, I know.' Roz sipped her champagne. Her eyes moved round the room. There were more guests here than had come for Philip's wedding, most of them Harry's friends and relatives. 'I need very little – but I do want to be a good wife.' She lifted her eyes to meet his. 'Please believe that, Harry.'

'Aye, I know.' He looked thoughtful, as if sensing her apprehension. 'We'd best circulate, Roz. We'll be leaving soon and I've hardly spoken to some of our guests.'

'Yes, of course. I'll throw my bouquet for the young girls.'

Roz walked across the room, stopping now and then to greet people and exchange kisses before reaching the table where her mother and a few of the ladies had gathered earlier to join in the toasts and gossip.

'I'm going up in a few minutes, Mama. I'm ready to throw my bouquet now.'

'Stand on the stairs and do it,' Lady Thornton said and then called out to some young girls loitering nearby. 'Roz is going to throw her bouquet, girls.'

Some of the ladies and a group of giggling girls followed them into the magnificent entrance hall. Roz walked up three of the wide stairs then tossed her bouquet over her shoulder and turned to watch. The girls were laughing and jostling with each other and Miss Mary Jenkins caught the bouquet, laughing in triumph as she held it up for everyone to see.

'I'll be married next,' she said.

'I'll come up with you, Roz,' Lady Thornton said, a suspicion of tears in her eyes.

'Yes, of course, Mama.'

Rushden Towers was not the medieval fortress its grand name suggested but a rather ugly Victorian house, square and unappealing. However, Harry had built a new facade of a long porch with elegant pillars and an imposing front door. He had also planted an avenue of ornamental cherry trees which softened the approach.

Roz had visited her new home with Harry a few days before the wedding and he'd given her a tour and shown Roz her own apartments, which were adjacent to his.

'This looks very smart,' Lady Thornton said as she followed Roz inside the suite of sitting room, dressing room and bedchamber.

'Harry had most of the house refurbished recently. Do you like the more modern style, Mama? I think I do – though there are too many knickknacks in here. I shall put a few of these ornaments away once I've settled in, but I don't wish to offend Harry by doing it all at once.'

'Too many frills and tassels,' Lady Thornton said. 'I dare say you will teach your husband to have better taste, Roz. You can't make a silk purse out of . . .' She faltered as she saw Roz's look. 'Harry is a gentleman; I shan't say otherwise but some of his family . . .'

Roz frowned at her mother. 'Harry's grandfather bought the farm and his father was a farmer too, but he was sent to a good school and he is as much a gentleman as Philip – perhaps more so. I like the house, though I may change things a little in time.'

'I am sure Harry will tell you to rearrange what you like,' Lady Thornton said and picked up a solid silver pot from the dressing table. 'Everything is good quality – and this has your initials on it, Roz.'

'Harry is very thoughtful and generous.'

'Yes, he is.'

A maid knocked and entered. She dipped a curtsey to Roz and asked if she could help, coming to assist with the hooks at the back of her bodice.

'Thank you, May,' Roz said as she took away the beautiful silk wedding dress. 'You can help me with the carriage gown and leave me to finish.'

'Yes, ma'am.' The girl looked shy. 'The master says I'm to come with you and look after your things – if that pleases you, Mrs Rushden?'

'I'm very happy to have your services, May. I'm sure we shall get on well.'

'Thank you, ma'am. Is there anything else you need?'

Roz looked at the bed where her hat, gloves and reticule had been laid ready. 'I believe you have thought of everything.' She unclasped the bracelet from her arm but left on the pearls at her throat. 'Please put this in my jewel case and take it with you when you go down.'

'Yes, ma'am. I'll take good care of your things.'

'I am sure you will.' Roz smiled as the girl picked up her jewellery case, placed the bracelet inside and locked it, giving the key to Roz. She slipped it into the reticule and the girl left. Roz fitted the hat at a jaunty angle. It was green velvet with curling black feathers which set off her travelling gown of emerald green trimmed with jet on the fitted jacket. 'Will I do, Mama?'

'You look just as you ought.' Her mother kissed her cheek. 'Be happy, Roz.'

'Yes, I think I shall.'

Roz nodded and then gathered up her things and went out. Some of the guests had gathered in the large hall and were waiting to greet her with cheers as she went down to them. Her gaze paused for a moment on a gentleman she had seen only briefly when he congratulated them after the wedding. She was a little surprised that he had actually come, though she knew Harry had invited him and he had sent them a set of fine Derby porcelain for dinner and dessert. He inclined his head and she did the same, and then Harry was moving towards her.

'Roz, lass,' he said. 'You look more beautiful than ever – are you ready to leave?'

'Yes, of course.' She took his hand, glancing back at her mother. Lady Thornton was sniffing into her kerchief and being comforted by Uncle Matthew. 'Uncle, Mama, thank you both. I shall see you very soon.'

Harry led her outside to the carriage. They were greeted by a group of mischievous children who showered them with rice and rose petals. Harry sheltered her, laughing as he helped her inside the comfortable carriage. She leaned forward to wave as the guests crowded outside to see them off.

'The reception went well,' Harry said. 'I'm a sociable man, Roz. We'll entertain our friends often in the future, but I'm glad it's over for today. I wanted to be alone with you.'

'We shall be alone for the next three weeks.'

'Apart from May, my man, and the grooms,' he agreed. 'I dare say we'll meet people when we're in Paris. You guessed that was where I meant to take you?'

'You spoke of my buying clothes in fashionable houses. I thought you might mean Paris. You do know I already have several new gowns?'

'Aye, but nothing compared to what you deserve, lass. I may be a bit rough about the edges despite going to Cambridge, but you're a lady and I know what you're due. Besides, I'm going to enjoy spoiling you.'

'Are you?'

'We'll stop at a decent hotel for the night and take the ship tomorrow afternoon. I think you'll enjoy Paris, lass.'

'Oh yes, I want to explore. Have you been before, Harry?'

'My father sent me on a tour there after I came down from Cambridge. I missed the fens and the mists of England and couldn't be doing with all that sunshine – but I dare say I shall like it better this time.'

'Because I'm with you?'

'Yes.'

'Come here, Harry.'

'I didn't want to crush your dress.'

'My dress doesn't matter.'

He lurched across the moving carriage and landed on the seat beside her, laughing as he half fell against her. 'Now see what I've done. I'm a clumsy oaf.'

'You're a kind, generous man, Harry Rushden, and I'm glad I married you.' She gazed up at him. 'Why don't you kiss me?'

'If I start I might not know when to leave off.'

'We are married.' She leaned towards him, taking his face between her hands. 'I'm not made of porcelain, Harry. I shan't break if you touch me.'

'You're all I ever wanted,' Harry said and drew her close. 'You know I love you, Roz.'

'Yes – and I'm beginning to be fond . . .'

His kiss cut off the words before she could finish.

Roz closed her eyes and shut out the bitter memories of the night she'd been raped. Harry was her husband and she had to smile and welcome him to her bed, as if she were the innocent girl he thought her.

Roz had never before felt as nervous as she did now. She had dressed in a beautiful lace peignoir and stood with her long hair flowing about her shoulders, looking at her husband. She caught her breath as he moved towards her, reaching out to draw her into his arms.

'Harry, I must te—' she began but his arms were about her and his mouth was on hers. His kiss was so hungry, so demanding that she couldn't breathe, let alone speak. He bent and swept her off her feet, carrying her towards the large bed where he placed her gently amongst the fresh linen sheets.

'I love you, Roz. It doesn't matter.'

It was too hard to say anything when her heart was hammering in her chest. The last time a man had been this close he had hurt her, tearing at her like a mad beast. Harry's gentleness as he loved her was breaking her heart because she couldn't respond as she ought.

She didn't love him, even though she was grateful for his consideration. Her fingers stroked the back of his head but although she didn't recoil from his touch, she couldn't give him the response he wanted. She felt empty, frozen. Afterwards, he lay with his head against her breast for a moment or two before rolling on to his back, staring up at the ceiling in silence for what seemed an eternity.

'Who was it?' he asked at last.

'I'm sorry. I did try to tell you.'

'Who was it, Roz?' Harry took hold of her arm, his fingers digging into her flesh. 'Tell me!'

Roz shuddered at the memory. 'Paul Richmond. He raped me on the night of the ball. Do you hate me because I married you without telling you?'

'No, I don't hate you.' Harry rolled off of his side of the bed and started to dress. 'If you'd told me I should have killed the bastard but I would still have married you.'

Roz sat up against the pillows, her knees drawn to her chest. 'Just now – I couldn't . . .'

'I didn't expect much, but I would have waited for a while if you'd explained. In the carriage you kissed me. I thought . . .'

'Kissing is all right but the rest – I just kept thinking of what he did. He hurt me. You didn't, Harry. In time perhaps I'll do better.'

'Yes, perhaps.' She saw the disappointment and hurt in his eyes. 'Why didn't Philip go after him? The bastard shouldn't have been allowed to get away with what he did to you.'

'He wanted Julia's money. If I'd made a fuss he would have lost any chance of her. In time he might have lost the hall and my mother would have had to leave her home.'

'Is that why you wanted the wedding quickly? Are you carrying Richmond's bastard?'

'No.' Roz got out of the bed and touched his arm. 'I swear I'm not having a baby, Harry. I know I ought to have told you but I was afraid of hurting you.'

'Didn't you realize that I would find out?' Harry moved away and stood in front of the window. 'What do we do now? It was bad enough wanting you and knowing you didn't want me when we weren't married, but this is even worse. You're my wife and you can't bear to have me touch you . . .'

'I didn't want to reject you. I just couldn't feel anything. In time things will get better.'

'Will they?' Harry turned to look at her, cold accusation in his eyes. 'Do you think I'm made of stone? Do you imagine I want to make love to a woman who lies there like a dead thing? I'm not that insensitive.'

Tears welled in her eyes but she held them back. He was so angry – but who could blame him? 'You didn't force me. I just . . .' She shook her head because there was nothing she could say. 'I wish I'd told you.'

'Yes, it would have saved a lot of bother. At least I would have known exactly what I was letting myself in for. But I loved you and thought that you had at least some feelings for me. I had no idea I make your flesh crawl – I should have known that it was too good to be true but I couldn't see past your pretences. What a fool I've been!'

'Do you want a divorce?'

'And have every man in the county laughing behind my back?' He glared at her. 'You married me and you'll stick to your bargain, Roz – but there'll be no marriage in the true sense. I'll play the devoted husband in public but I'll find my pleasure elsewhere.'

'I'd hoped we'd have children, a proper home life.'

'Well, you'll have to pray there's a brat on the way,' Harry said bitterly. 'You wanted children. I wanted a loving wife. We shall both go short – but you'll have a home and the money. I dare say that will content you.'

'Won't you give me a chance? If you're patient I'll learn to do what you want.'

'I don't want you to pretend for me.' He walked towards the door. She grabbed at his arm but he threw her hand off. 'Go back to bed, Roz.'

'Please don't leave me like this. We are married. I'll learn to be a proper wife to you, Harry.'

'I've told you I don't want that,' he said. 'I thought you would at least be warm and giving in bed and that I could make you love me in time – but I don't think that's going to happen, is it? I'm going to find somewhere else to sleep. In Paris we'll have separate rooms.' Harry looked so hurt. Roz knew that she had spoiled everything. He wasn't a cruel man but what she'd done by not telling him about the rape before they married was unforgivable. Perhaps later, when it didn't hurt so much, he might understand that she, too, was hurting.

'We're still going to Paris?'

'Of course. As far as the world is concerned, we're the perfect couple. I shan't trouble you at night and you won't question where I go when I stay out late.'

Roz stared at the door as he went out and closed it with a snap. She sat on the edge of the bed, silent tears running down her cheeks. She'd never wanted to marry him, but recently she'd begun to respect and like him — now he despised her.

Eight

'You look as if you've found sixpence and lost a crown.' Ellen rolled out the shortcrust pastry she was making. 'Why the long face, Tom? You've asked Mary Jane to wed you so why look so miserable? Surely you haven't changed your mind? It took you long enough to ask her.'

'Don't nag me, Ma. I've something on my mind and its naught to do with you so best not ask.'

'If you won't tell me, you won't. See if you can find your father. He didn't come in last night. I don't know where he's getting the money to drink so much.' She went to the dresser and took down her best teapot, giving an exclamation of annoyance. 'The lid has been chipped – and half the money's gone. The thieving wretch! You won that for Carrie.'

'She doesn't want for much.' Tom frowned. 'The harvest was good this year. We'll have money left over after the seed and stores are bought for the winter. I'm going to start an account at the bank in Wisbech when I drive in next time. It's time we put the money somewhere safe until we need it.'

'Your pa doesn't hold with banks, Tom. He remembers when there was a run on them and a lot of folk lost their money.'

'The bank I'm talking of is solid enough. Besides, I earned the money and there's no need for him to know. I want to save the surplus for the future – for all of us.'

'I'm not sure. It's your pa's farm . . .'

'And he'd let it go to rack and ruin. It's my management that has brought the extra in and I'll decide how it's spent. The Rushden family started out as farmers and look at them now – worth a fortune. We need more land. I've got my eye on ten acres of pasture. With that I could increase the beef herd and that will bring in more money for next year. I could double our acreage in a few years.'

'And how are you going to manage more land and stock? You'll need to bring them in to feed through the winter.'

'Aye, I know, that's why I thought I'd wait until the spring to buy. I can build another pen next year and I'll hire some spring grass as well and keep our hay for the winter.'

'You're full of big ideas, lad – but your pa will have something to say to all this.' Ellen thumped the pastry down on the table.

'That pastry will be as heavy as lead the way you're going,' Tom teased and earned a glare from his mother.

'You're not mooning over the Thornton girl, are you?'

'That's a daft thing to ask. She would never look at me – and I've asked Mary Jane to wed me. I'm away down to the wild meadow. If I see Pa I'll send him home.'

He went out without glancing at his mother. She was right; he was mooning over Roz. He hadn't been able to get her out of his mind since he'd seen her outside the church. She'd looked so beautiful and he'd wanted to snatch her up and run off with her. A wry smile touched his mouth as he thought of her likely reaction if he'd tried.

Yet for a moment she'd looked scared, as if she wished she could run away and not marry the man waiting for her. In his dreams, Tom found her weeping and lost in the meadows. In his dreams, she ran into his arms and he loved her in the long sweet grass while a lark sang in the sky high above their heads. In his dreams he was a successful man, wealthy enough to give her the home she deserved.

Tom's thoughts were rudely interrupted as he saw his father walking towards him. Lurching might be a better word because John Blake was drunk, muttering and grumbling to himself. When he saw his son he yelled something abusive and then, before Tom could reach him, pitched forward and fell to the ground.

'Pa.' Tom raced towards him, turning him over on his back. His father was muttering but something was wrong. He had been drinking because the smell of whisky was on him, but his mouth seemed to have dropped on one side and his face was screwed up. 'Pa, wake up. I'll get you home. You need to be in bed.'

His father didn't answer, making unintelligible sounds and dribbling from the side of his mouth. Tom suddenly felt anxious. He bent down and lifted his father under his armpits, his strength easing him up until he could lift him in his arms and over one shoulder. John Blake was still heavy despite starving himself for weeks. It was a huge burden for any man to carry and Tom was staggering under his weight by the time he reached the house, but his mother saw him coming and had the kitchen door open before he got there.

'Put him on the sofa, Tom. Is he drunk?'

'I think he's had a stroke,' Tom said. 'I'll saddle the horse and go for the doctor. He was trying to get home when I found him.'

'Yes, fetch the doctor. Your father's not been himself lately but he's still my husband. I don't want him to die just yet.'

'He's as strong as a mule. He'll be all right,' Tom promised as he headed for the door. 'I'll be back before you know it.'

'He's had a stroke,' the doctor confirmed after making his examination. 'It was lucky you saw him, Tom. With rest and care, I think he will pull through this time, but we shan't know the damage for a day or two. He may have lost the use of an arm or a leg or it might just be his speech.'

'He couldn't speak properly when I found him,' Tom said. 'If I hadn't gone that way he could have lain there for hours.'

'Well, keep him in bed and watch him for the next day or so. If he has another seizure it might finish him; otherwise he'll probably live for a while yet.'

'We'll do our best,' Tom promised and led the doctor back down the stairs to the kitchen.

'How is he, doctor?' Ellen looked concerned as she took a tray of jam tarts from the oven. 'I dare say he'll want a lot of nursing?'

'He will need watching for a while, and if he pulls through he may lose the use of some of his limbs. I was telling your son he'll need a lot of care.'

'Yes, but who's to be up and down them stairs a dozen times a day?'

'You'll have to make Carrie do her share,' Tom said. 'I'm off to bring the cows up for milking, Ma.'

'Well, I'll leave you to it.' The doctor put his hat on and went out.

'Tom, you know I can't manage alone,' his mother cried in desperation as the door closed behind the doctor. 'It's no use saying I should make Carrie do more because she will sneak out when my back's turned – besides, John won't have her near him.'

'She can help milk the cows if I watch her,' Tom said. 'If I can get my chores done quicker I'll see to pa when I get back.'

'You're making a rod for your own back. It's time you were married. Ask Mary Jane about setting the banns and bring her back here.'

'It's hardly fair to expect her to take care of Pa. I may have to take on an extra man sooner than I thought.' Tom frowned. 'I suppose it's the only way. I'll speak to Mary Jane at the weekend, but I'll be looking for an extra pair of hands to help in the yard at the hiring fair.'

'You please yourself but you'll have to do something sharp, because I can't do all the work here and nurse your pa alone.'

'I doubt you could lift him.'

'Will he need everything done for him?'

'The doctor said he may recover but at the moment he doesn't seem to be able to move the left side of his body at all.'

'He's going to be a burden to us all, Tom.'

'Ma! You don't mean that. You're just tired and worried. I should've done something about hiring an extra man before.'

'I'll still need someone to help in the house, even if you help with your pa.'

'I've said I'll speak to Mary Jane,' Tom said. 'But she'll want a couple of days away at least. You can't expect her to come straight back here and start on her wedding night. So I'll get a local man in and perhaps one of her sisters will help you out in the house until we get back.'

'I came here on my wedding night, aye, and started work the next day. I don't know where you get your fancy notions, Tom Blake – wedding trip, indeed. That kind of nonsense is for the gentry.'

'Well, my wife is getting two days and three nights in a hotel somewhere at the sea. We'll go on the train and stop somewhere nice.'

'Where will your grand ideas end, I wonder,' Ellen grumbled as she got on with the supper. 'I can hear the cows. You'd best away to the milking.'

Tom inclined his head and left the kitchen. He didn't know where the idea of a trip to the sea had come from either, but it was in his head now and he was determined not to give it up.

The farm had prospered because since Dick's death he'd been able to run it as he pleased, and he had coins jingling in his pocket. He would take Mary Jane to a hotel on their wedding night and then they would have a trip to the sea. Tom wasn't sure how much it cost to stay in a hotel, but he would manage it somehow.

Ellen stood in the bedroom doorway and stared at her husband. She would never have wed him if she hadn't got caught with Dick. The night she'd lain with John Blake in the meadows she'd had too much drink at the harvest supper – and she'd been suffering from rejection. Squire Thornton had come visiting at the rectory too often for it to be on church business. He had flirted with the rector's pretty daughter, stealing a kiss whenever he could get her away from her mother's watchful eye.

Ellen had fallen in love against her better judgement. Even in those days the squire had acquired a reputation, but he hadn't been married then and she was a gentleman's daughter, even if her father had no money. Ellen didn't see why the squire wouldn't wed her, but she resisted giving him his way and then, just before the harvest service of thanksgiving, she'd learned that he was to wed a girl with a fortune.

It was in a fit of pique that Ellen had drunk too much cider and given herself to John Blake in the meadows. She had regretted her marriage many times over the years, but with Dick on the way she'd had no choice. Her husband was snoring, his mouth hanging open. She thought the doctor had given him something to make him sleep. Her first reaction when Tom brought him home was that she didn't want him to die, but how long would it be before she was wishing he would never wake up? She laughed at Tom's plans for the future, but her younger son was eager to make a better life for them all and she wouldn't say no to having a little time to herself. Tom was a great reader and she'd borrowed some of the books Miss Thornton had brought for him, snatching a minute here and there to read a few pages herself.

There would be no leisure time for either of them if they had to wait hand and foot on John Blake. He'd have them up and down the stairs a dozen times a day. She walked closer to the bed, staring at the spare pillow lying beside him. He was suffering. Life couldn't mean much to him now. It might be better for everyone if he were dead. If she picked it up and held it over his face . . . the thought made her go cold all over.

As if he could read her mind, John opened his eyes and looked at her. He didn't speak, just stared at her in a way that sent shivers down her spine and then closed his eyes again. Any feeling of guilt she had fled. If she'd ever cared for him he'd killed her feelings long ago, just as he'd destroyed her hopes.

If looks could kill she'd be the one in her grave.

'Call the banns this Sunday?' Mary Jane's eyes lit up. 'I thought you wanted to wait – what made you change your mind?'

'I shan't lie to you, Mary, lass. Me pa is playing up like the very devil, ever since he came to his senses. Ma won't expect you to see to him but she needs help in the house. I'll be doing as much as I can myself, but even if we take on a girl temporarily as well as a yard man there will be more than she can manage.'

'So it's another pair of hands you want,' she said and pouted. 'I thought perhaps you liked what we did the other night and couldn't wait to be wed?'

'I did and I do want to wed you, lass – but I want you to be sure. You need to know what you're letting yourself in for. It's not a life of ease and luxury I'm offering.'

'It can't be worse than I've got at home. I'm in the yard milking and feeding the stock morning and night, and in between I've to help Ma with washing and cooking for the eight of us. I reckon it will be a holiday at your house.'

Tom hadn't given Mary Jane's reasons for wanting to wed him a thought, taking for granted that she fancied him. Now he understood that perhaps she went deeper than he'd believed. As the eldest girl in a family of five boys and three girls, she would have to work hard. None of her brothers were married yet and that meant a mountain of washing and a lot of meals to be served.

'Well, as long as you know what to expect,' he said. 'I can't afford to take a week off but there's a train to Hunstanton on Saturday evenings. I'll telephone from the post office when I go into the market next week and book two nights at a hotel. We'll come back on Tuesday in time for the evening milking. I was thinking that maybe your Sarah would help Ma out while we're away. I'll pay her two shillings a day.'

'Sarah would jump at the chance to earn some money but I'm not sure my ma can spare her. Can't your Carrie do a bit more to help out?'

'She's capable of doing the work, but as soon as Ma turns her back she'll be out the door and away across the fields for hours on end. Ask your ma if Sarah can help; if not I'll have to look for someone else.'

'All right.' Mary Jane reached up and kissed him. 'You're a lovely man, Tom Blake. I never expected a honeymoon at a hotel.'

'You're a pretty girl and I like you.' Tom kissed her back. 'I reckon we'll do all right together. So I'll see the vicar tomorrow and call on your parents on the way home.'

'You can stay for tea and tell Ma that you're taking me away for a honeymoon.' Mary Jane looked pleased with herself. 'I don't know of any other girl that went for a honeymoon round here – except for Roz Thornton.'

'Do you know Miss Thornton?'

'She visits the vicar's wife with things for folk what can't manage on what they earn, and sometimes she gives pretty clothes to the church jumble sale. If I get there first I can find a bargain because I'm good with my needle.'

'She gave our Carrie some stuff. Ma sent her away but Carrie went after her.'

'Ma and me sometimes do a bit of sewing for Lady Thornton. She told Ma she'd had a letter from Mrs Rushden and she says Paris is wonderful. She's buying so many new clothes and she told her ma to give away everything she'd left at the dower house so there'll be some bargains going at the bazaar.'

Tom felt his stomach lurch. The idea of Mary Jane wearing Roz's old clothes made him angry, though he hadn't minded Carrie doing the same thing.

'I don't want you wearing her things. I'll buy some material in the market and you can make something new for yourself.'

Mary Jane gave a little scream of delight and hugged him. 'Our Sarah will be green with envy. She fancied you herself but I told her she'd have to find someone else because you're mine.'

Tom pulled her hands away. 'Don't strangle me. I've got work to do. Tell your ma I'll be there tomorrow at three, after I speak to the vicar.'

Tom heard the shouting as he walked into the kitchen that evening. Carrie was sitting on the sofa holding her baby and crooning a song to herself.

Tom went to the bottom of the stairs and listened. His father was yelling something unintelligible at Ellen, who by the sound of her was trying to quieten him.

'I'd better go up and see to him,' Tom said but Carrie wasn't listening.

As Tom entered the bedroom, he saw his father strike out with his right fist, catching a blow on the side of his wife's head as she tried to wipe the spittle and vomit from his face.

'Now then, Pa,' Tom said and drew his mother out of the way. 'Ma is only trying to help you.'

His father babbled something that sounded like gibberish. Tom caught the stink of vomit and something more. His father had soiled himself again and that meant stripping the bed and him.

'I've been trying to clean him up,' Ellen said. 'It isn't right that you should have this mess to see to when you get in, Tom.'

'I'm used to mucking out the stock. It's no trouble to me, though what you'll do while I'm away I don't know.'

'I'll fetch the clean sheets,' Ellen said. 'If he won't let me help him he'll lie in his own filth until you get back.'

As she left the room Tom's father grabbed his arm and muttered something. The words were jumbled up but Tom thought he was asking where he was going.

'I'm marrying Mary Jane Forrest. I've told you, Pa. We'll be going away from the Saturday night until Tuesday evening. I've arranged for a girl to help Ma in the kitchen and I've taken on a man in the yard because I can't manage everything alone.'

John seemed to become even more agitated and Tom sighed inwardly as he rolled his father to one side and pulled the sheets out from under him. He washed his father, placed the fresh sheets beneath him and then lifted him higher in the bed so that he was comfortable.

John was in visible distress. He kept repeating something over and over but the words didn't make sense.

'Slow down and then maybe I'll understand. Are you worried about the farm while I'm away?' John shook his head. 'We can afford to employ another man. I'm going to buy a few more acres and keep some of the calves this year. I want two more cows and we'll rear our own bullocks.'

John moved his head negatively, a tear sliding down his cheek. 'Don't leave me with . . .'

His first words were slurred but recognizable, though the rest of the sentence degenerated into gibberish.

'Are you asking me not to leave you with Ma?'

His father nodded and spoke rapidly, leaving Tom none the wiser.

'Why don't you want to be alone with Ma – you can't think she would hurt you?'

His father nodded, his words slurred but clear enough. 'Hates me . . . wants me dead.'

'That's nonsense, Pa. I know what you said but I know it isn't true. I know you quarrel a lot but she would never harm you.'

John lay back against the pillows and closed his eyes. His whole demeanour told Tom that he had shut off and gone into himself.

Tom gathered the soiled sheets, taking them downstairs to the kitchen and through into the scullery. There was a fire under the copper and the water was already hot. He pushed the linen into the soapy water and put the lid on, pausing to wash his hands before going into the kitchen. Ellen and Carrie were seated and dinner was on the table.

'I've put yours in the oven to keep warm,' Ellen said. 'We'll have to think of wrapping him in rags, Tom. I might manage to pull them from under him and they can be burned rather than washed.'

'It might work while I'm away.' Tom fetched his dinner and sat down. 'What have you been saying to him, Ma? Why does he think you want him dead?'

'What makes you think he does?'

'His speech is slurred but sometimes I can understand a few words. He says you hate him and want him dead – you don't, do you?'

'Sometimes I do, but I've never told him that. I'm tired, Tom. Worn out with years of nothing but work to look forward to – and your pa would try the patience of a saint.'

'Sorry, Ma. I know how hard you've always worked and it has been worse since Dick . . .' He glanced at Carrie, who was pushing her food around the plate. 'What's wrong with that, Carrie?'

'Squire's back,' she said, a dreamy smile on her lips. 'He didn't see me but I saw him. He was riding near the stream. That's Pa's land, isn't it, Tom?'

'Yes, that's our land, Carrie. I wonder what he's after.'

'Does she mean the old squire's son?' Ellen frowned. 'Is he back from his wedding trip, then?'

'I expect so. I hope he doesn't offer me money for the land again, because I've got my own plans and it doesn't include selling to him.'

'I suppose he's rich now he's got his wife's money.'

'We aren't going to sell and that's it – especially to him.'

'Farming is hard work, Tom. You like horses. You could keep the house and sell the land. You might buy a livery stable with the money.'

'Pa would never agree to sell.'

'You know what the doctor told us. If he has another stroke he could die.'

'He isn't dead yet. Besides, I'll be master here then because Pa has left the land to me. He made his will years ago and it was for Dick and me, but now it will be mine. You'll always have a home here, Ma – but I'm not selling, especially to Thornton.'

'You get more like your pa all the time.' Ellen took a mouthful of pie. She chewed for a moment, then: 'I thought you were different, had more ambition, but you can't see any further than the end of your nose.'

Tom ignored her and ate his supper. Things would be better once he was married. Ellen would have company and help in the house. He might even be able to give her a little holiday somewhere.

'Has Pa eaten anything today?'

'He refused the broth I made for him but he drank some warmed ale. It's all he seems to want.'

'I'll take him some bread and milk up in a minute.' Carrie had left most of her supper and was drifting towards the door. 'Where do you think you're going, miss? You can help Ma with the washing up. I mean it, Carrie.'

His sister stopped in her tracks then came back to the sink and plunged her hands into the soapy water.

Tom got up and started to break bread into a bowl. He heated some milk over the fire and poured it over the bread, adding a few precious spoons of sugar.

'And that's a waste,' Ellen said as he set the bowl on a tray. 'Just watch he doesn't tip the lot over the bed.'

Nine

'I've never seen you look so elegant.' Lady Thornton stood back to admire her daughter's expensive ensemble. 'She is lovelier than ever, Harry. I can see you've been spoiling her.'

'My wife deserves spoiling, and she pays for it,' he said, his gaze going over Roz. 'She does me credit, do you not think so, Mama?'

'She is as fine as any London society lady. Paris must have been a wonderful experience for you both.'

'I shall leave you alone together,' Harry said. 'Ask your mama to stay for dinner this evening, dearest. I am sure she would enjoy the company. We shall be entertaining extensively, Mama, and we shall expect you to visit often.'

He nodded to Lady Thornton and went out. Roz indicated that her mother should sit and took a chair opposite her. Harry had given such a good performance that she could only follow his lead.

'You look well, Mama. Have you seen Philip since he returned?'

'Julia invited me to dinner. She came down to the dower house to make certain I have all I need. Your brother has not visited me. Julia says he is busy. He has thoughts of buying more land.'

'Philip is thoughtless like most men. I dare say Julia will be glad of your company. She may wish to ask your advice about managing the house.'

'I do not think so. She seems very capable and the servants mind her more than they ever did me. Philip may not know it but she has a knack of getting her own way.'

'Yes, I think she does. Have you settled to life at the dower, Mama?'

'It is strange to visit the hall and know it is not my home, but I suppose I must be thankful to have you settled near enough to visit often.' Lady Thornton's eyes narrowed in suspicion. 'Are you happy, Roz? Your letters were full of the delights of Paris but you said little of yourself.'

'What is there to say? You can see for yourself that Harry has been generous. We visited the palace of Versailles, various museums and some beautiful gardens in Paris, but most of our time was spent with friends we made.'

'You made some nice friends? Were they French or English?'

'Sir Raymond Jenson is English and his wife Madeline is French. Harry spent some evenings in the gaming rooms but I preferred to stay at the hotel and read.'

'Indeed? I am not sure I approve. I would not have taken Harry Rushden for a gambler. He always seems such a hard-working man.'

'Harry is wealthy enough to spend what he wishes on gambling. I did not interfere with his pleasure in Paris. Nor shall I in future, Mama.'

'If he gambles his fortune away you may regret not taking an interest before.'

'Harry may do exactly as he pleases,' Roz said and rang the bell. 'We shall have some tea, Mama – and then I shall take you upstairs and show you the gifts I brought for you. I had an evening gown made to fit you. Since Harry invited you to stay for dinner you may wish to wear it this evening.'

Roz took off her pearl earrings and placed them on the dressing table. She was brushing her hair when the adjoining door opened and Harry entered.

'Did you want something, Harry?'

'I seem to have misplaced a box of collar studs I purchased in Paris. They have not been mixed up with your things, Roz?'

'No, I do not believe so. I will look for them tomorrow.' She waited, certain that he had come for more than some collar studs. 'Mama was very pleased with the gifts we brought. You were generous to her, Harry, and she appreciates it.'

'Your mama deserves the respect I would expect to show my wife's mother.' Harry's tone had reverted to its usual coldness. 'I came to tell you that I invited Madeline and Raymond to visit us next week.'

'Next week? We have only just left them in Paris. Surely there are other friends you might prefer to have visit?'

'I know you dislike Raymond, but I won too much from him

in Paris. I must give him the chance to retrieve his losses – besides, they amuse me. You may invite your friends to visit when you choose.'

'I dare say I might invite Julia and Philip – and Mama, of course. There is no one else I particularly wish to see.'

'I enjoy good company and entertaining. I want you to give a dinner party next week. Since you have no particular friends, I shall provide you with a list of people to invite.'

'I shall do my best to please you and your friends, Harry. I am perfectly willing to receive guests whenever you wish.'

'I didn't buy you all those expensive clothes to leave them in the closet. We shall entertain and visit our friends, and we may go to London for a week or two. With any luck we shall be invited to a few weekends in the country. I may hold a shooting party here later in the year.'

'Of course. Papa enjoyed hunting and shooting. We often had house parties in the autumn and winter.'

'Your mama would have a list of his friends, I dare say. I intend to mix with the best, Roz, and you can help me if you try. Your father's name still counts for something despite the scandal.'

'Is that why you married me? Because you had ambitions to move up in society?' She'd thought he loved her but if he cared he would surely have forgiven her by now.

He took a step towards her, anger in his eyes as he towered over her.

'You know damned well why I married you, Roz, but since you turned out to be frigid I might as well take what I can from this sham marriage.'

'You are the one who makes the rules, Harry. I have not locked my door against you. If you wish to come to my bed I shall not turn you away.'

'You'll just lie there like a martyr being condemned to the stake,' he said in a bitter tone. 'I'll not beg for favours, Roz. In Paris there were plenty of ladies willing to oblige me – and I dare say there are one or two in Wisbech who might welcome the chance to have a gentleman caller.'

Roz turned away and sat down at her dressing table, picking up her hairbrush. In Paris he'd stayed out late most nights. She'd known he was gambling recklessly at the tables because Madeline had told her, but it seemed he was lucky at cards and he'd won more than he'd lost. She hadn't known that he'd been with other women and she'd hoped he might think better of his decision and give her another chance to be the wife he claimed to want.

She was aware of him standing there staring at her as she started to brush her hair, then he turned, walked back into his own room and slammed the door.

Roz shivered and her eyes filled with tears. Money, beautiful clothes and a comfortable house were nothing without at least respect and liking. She'd thought her marriage would be so different, believing that she could find happiness in her children. Now all she felt was humiliation and despair.

How could she bear to live this way? Most nights Harry didn't even come into her room to say goodnight. In public he was the considerate husband, laughing and paying her compliments, but as soon as they were alone he withdrew. He called her frigid but he was like ice, refusing to listen to her or accept that she was genuinely sorry for what she'd done and for not being able to love him the way he had loved her. At first she'd wept and begged him to forgive her, but now she held back her tears until after he left her.

'I thought we might change the menus, Mrs Martin,' Roz said the next morning when she visited the kitchens. 'We hardly need seven breakfast dishes. I believe four should be sufficient, unless we have guests.'

'If you're certain, ma'am,' the housekeeper said and looked doubtful. 'Mr Rushden has always liked a varied choice at every meal.'

'Four dishes is sufficient at breakfast, and I've written down a list of dishes for this week. Next week we shall have guests and then we shall need more choices but for two of us it seems a waste. Most of it was untouched this morning.'

'Yes, ma'am. If you say so.'

Roz walked about the kitchen, inspecting various objects and then nodded to the cook.

'Everything is very clean. You are to be congratulated.' She turned to Mrs Martin again. 'I shall require a fire in the small back parlour in the mornings, but you need not light the fire in the drawing room until just before tea.'

Most of the reception rooms were in Roz's opinion overlarge for private use. She had decided on the small back parlour because it looked out on to a pretty little walled garden and she enjoyed the view. The French windows opened out on to a paved area and when opened on a warm day let in the fragrance of roses.

Having written some letters of invitation to Harry's friends she decided to go for a little walk about the grounds and returned with a basket of leaves and flowers in time to wash her hands before going into the dining parlour for lunch. Harry was standing at the sideboard examining the dishes set out for their meal. He turned and frowned as he saw her enter.

'Where have you been? One thing I expect from you, Roz, is punctuality. I'm sorry luncheon is so mean today. You must have a word with Mrs Martin and tell her this just will not do.'

Roz looked and saw there was a selection of roast beef, cold chicken and ham; also mashed potatoes, vegetables and pickles.

'What more could you wish for, Harry? I told Mrs Martin that we did not need so much food. Half of the breakfast dishes were wasted this morning . . .' She saw the cold glitter in his eyes and faltered. 'Why are you annoyed?'

'Must I do everything myself? If you have no idea of what is proper in a gentleman's house I shall tell Mrs Martin to come to me before making changes.'

'You wouldn't humiliate me in my own home? I am the mistress here. I must be allowed to order my household.'

'Then show me you know how to behave. I do not need to economize and I will not allow you to make me look mean. The food that we don't eat is eaten by the servants or given away to the poor. For goodness' sake, Roz, anyone would think we were paupers.'

'I was merely trying to be a thrifty housekeeper.'

'Then don't interfere. Mrs Martin knows what I like. You are here to look pretty and entertain our guests when they call. Please leave the arrangements to those who understand them.'

'Just as you wish.' She controlled her feelings behind a mask of indifference. As Harry finished filling his plate she helped herself to some chicken and a little potato.

'Is that all you're having?' Harry glared at her. 'You will become too thin and lose your looks if you refuse to eat properly.'

'I never eat a great deal at luncheon.'

'No, you prefer to sit brooding like a ghost at the feast. I hope you are going to show a little more animation when our guests visit. Madeline asked me twice in Paris if you were ill.'

'I am perfectly well, Harry.'

'Then eat something. Damn you, Roz. That face is enough to put a man off his food.'

'Then I shall leave you to enjoy your lunch, Harry.' She pushed her chair back and got to her feet but he was at the door before her. He caught hold of her arm, forcing her back to the table. 'Please let me go. I'm not hungry.'

'Sit there and eat something,' he muttered, pushing her into the chair. 'For goodness' sake, Roz. Surely you can hold a conversation and eat your meal?'

'Very well. What would you like to talk about?'

'Tell me what you did this morning.'

'I went for a walk and picked some flowers for the house. Don't frown at me. Before I picked the roses, I asked the gardener which blooms were for use in the house.'

Harry forked a piece of rare beef and put it in his mouth. Roz cut a tiny piece of chicken. It tasted like sawdust and she chewed it for a long time before swallowing.

'At least you used your head for once. It would be a shame to spoil the symmetry of the gardens and we want them to look at their best for our guests. We'll give a dinner and the younger ones can dance in the gallery if they wish, but there will be cards set up in the back parlour for the gentlemen.'

'Couldn't you use one of the other reception rooms? I like that parlour, Harry. It will smell of cigar smoke in the mornings if the gentlemen sit at cards all night.'

'That is why I thought we'd keep to the back parlour and leave the best rooms to you ladies.' Harry finished his food and got up to replenish his plate. 'I suppose we could use the library if you prefer.'

'Would you mind? I've taken one or two of my own things to that parlour because I admire the view.'

'Well, have it if you want. After all, it's your home.'

'Thank you.' Roz forced a smile as a maid came in to ask if she wanted the sweet course brought in. 'Not yet, Iris. I'll ring for you if Mr Rushden wants anything more.'

Harry sipped his wine and looked thoughtful. 'It's better without the maids about when there's just the two of us. I suppose that was another of your suggestions?'

'I hate being hovered over when I'm eating. I thought you liked serving yourself at the hotel?'

'Yes, I do prefer it, but only when we're alone. I want to keep up a certain style when we have guests, Roz.'

'Yes, I think I understand that.'

'You will speak to Mrs Martin, then?'

'Yes, of course. Thank you.'

He hesitated, then: 'I have no wish to humiliate you – but think before you change things in future and ask me if you're not sure.'

'Yes, Harry. Shall I ring for Iris?'

'No, I'll have another glass of wine.' He refilled his glass and tried to pour her some but she put her hand over her glass. 'No? Suit yourself. What are you going to do this afternoon?'

'I thought I might read or do some embroidery.'

'Don't you want to visit friends?'

'Not really.'

'You should ride over to see Julia.'

'Yes, perhaps I should.' Roz stood up. 'Will you excuse me.'

'For goodness' sake, Roz. You're not a child and I'm not your mother.'

Roz walked from the room. Tears pricked her eyes but she refused to let them fall. One minute Harry spoke to her as if she were a fool and countermanded her orders, the next he was accusing her of acting like a child. What did he want from her – or had she committed such a vile sin that he needed to punish her all the time?

'I've been hoping you would ride over,' Julia said and kissed her cheek. 'Philip said I shouldn't intrude because you needed time to settle into your new home, but if you hadn't come I should have ordered the carriage and visited you tomorrow.'

'You look content, Julia. I think you must be happy in your marriage.'

'Yes, of course. I always knew that Philip didn't love me, but he is considerate and does not interfere with the way I do things.

I never expected more and when I have children I shall have all I need.'

'I am so pleased for you,' Roz replied and glanced around the parlour. Julia had rearranged the furniture, bringing in things she liked from other rooms. 'You have made this parlour your own. I think it looks much nicer – more comfortable.'

'I am not sure Mama thinks as you do.' Julia smiled. 'She notices each change. However, she is trying to be diplomatic and pretends to like what I've done. I'm having new drapes made for all the best rooms.'

'I think several of the rooms need refurbishment,' Roz said and sighed. 'Harry has had everything done at the Towers. I have little to do with my time. He says all he asks of me is to entertain our guests and look attractive.'

'He intends to spoil you because he loves you,' Julia said. 'You are fortunate in that way, Roz – but when you have children your time will just evaporate.' She placed her hands on her stomach and then leaned towards Roz, lowering her voice. 'Philip wanted to be sure before he told anyone, but I shall tell you that I believe I am carrying his child.'

'Julia! That is wonderful,' Roz said and moved closer, taking her hands and then kissing her cheek. 'I am very happy for you.'

'Perhaps it will happen for you soon.'

'Yes, perhaps.' Roz turned away and sat down on the little sofa as one of the maids brought in the tea tray. She waited until the girl had gone before adding, 'We are to have visitors staying next week. Some friends Harry met in Paris and others. We are giving a dinner for our neighbours to start things off. I do hope you and Philip will come?'

'Yes, of course. I shall enjoy that, Roz. We shall be having a dinner for friends ourselves soon. I will send an invitation for both of you, and any guests you have staying with you.'

'Thank you. I am sure Harry will be pleased to accept.'

Something in her tone alerted Julia. 'Is anything wrong? You don't seem quite yourself.'

'I am perfectly well. I suppose . . . everything happened so quickly. It isn't much more than a year since Father died and then Philip married you and I married Harry. Nothing is the same.'

'It feels strange coming back here as a guest, I dare say?'

'Oh no, I'm happy to see you as the mistress here. You mustn't think I resent you, Julia, because I don't. I can't explain.'

Julia was silent for a moment, then: 'If you ever need a friend, Roz, I shall always be here for you.'

'Thank you.' Roz hesitated, tempted to confide at least part of her problem. Then, before she could continue, her brother walked in. 'Good afternoon, Philip. How are you?'

'Busy. I've hardly stopped since we returned.' He bent and kissed his wife's cheek. 'What has my sister been saying to you, my love?'

'She came to invite us to dinner next week,' Julia replied. 'Will you have some tea with us, Philip? I can send for a fresh pot if you wish?'

'Thank you, no. I shall leave you to your cosy chatting since you have company. Roz, perhaps we could have a talk one day?'

'Call whenever you please. I am sure Harry will be pleased to see you.' Roz stood up and began to pull on her gloves. 'I ought to be leaving, Julia. I shall see you both next week. If what you have to say is urgent, Philip, you may walk me to the door.'

'It will keep,' he said and sat down, looking at his wife. 'I think perhaps I will have some tea after all.'

Roz walked from the room. The footman sprang to open the door for her and she nodded to him as she passed through. Outside, a cool breeze had sprung up and there was a hint of rain in the air. Perhaps she ought to have brought the carriage rather than riding the five miles from the Towers. If it started to rain heavily she would be soaked by the time she got home.

The rainstorm burst as Roz was leaving Thornton land. She put her head down and kept riding but it was heavy going, the wind driving the rain into her face. When she saw the lean-to at the side of a hay barn, she changed direction and headed for it, even though it was on Tom Blake's land. Dismounting, she led her horse into the shelter and tied the reins to a wooden post.

'It was sudden,' a voice said from behind her. 'You look wet through. Here, take my coat.'

Roz turned and saw the man who had spoken. Her heart did an odd somersault and she found herself smiling, reminded of a summer's day when he'd helped her by finding her brother's horse.

'Mr Blake,' she said. 'I am wet but I can't take your coat. You will turn cold yourself.'

'I can use some of this sacking.' He removed his heavy grey coat and placed it about her shoulders. Its weight made her feel warmer at once. The cloth smelled of horses and hay and something more she couldn't define but associated with him.

'You are generous to give me this,' she said. 'Do use some of those sacks. I feel so guilty taking your coat.'

'I got here before it came on heavily. Come and sit on these hay bales. If I put them either side of us they will keep out the cold.'

Roz hesitated, then took the hand he offered. He had made a place for them to sit on the bales and sat next to her, pulling the bales round them. The hay smelled sweet and dry and Roz felt warmth beginning to spread through her.

'How are you, Mr Blake? And your mother – and Carrie?'

'Ma and Carrie are all right. Pa had a stroke and he's been a right devil since he came through it. I'm getting married this Saturday.'

'Really?' She did not know why the news should come as a shock. 'I must congratulate you. What is the fortunate lady's name?'

'Mary Jane Forrest. She and her ma do sewing for you and Lady Thornton sometimes.'

'Yes, I know Mary Jane well. She is pretty and a happy girl, which must be a good thing in a wife, I think. I wish you both happiness, Mr Blake.'

'Do you think you might call me Tom?'

'Yes, if you wish it.' Roz laughed softly. 'You keep rescuing me, Tom Blake, so perhaps I should treat you as the friend you've been to me.'

'You're beautiful,' Tom said and leaned towards her. For a moment they looked into each other's eyes. Roz felt her heart begin to beat wildly and something moved inside her.

His kiss took her breath away, sending little charges of excitement through her body. Without realizing what she was doing, she ran her hands into his dark hair and kissed him back. The hunger in the kiss shook them both and they drew back, staring at each other in shock.

'Oh . . .' Roz put a finger to her lips. 'You kissed me . . .'

'I shouldn't have done that – but I'm not sorry. I've been wanting to kiss you since the day you got caught on the briars.'

'You scolded me for taking the roses that belong to the poor people.'

'I shouldn't have done that.' Tom reached out to touch her face. 'I have to marry because Ma can't manage alone and Carrie is more trouble than she's worth, but I haven't stopped thinking of you. I dream of you all the time – of loving you.'

'You shouldn't . . .' Roz began, then leaned into him and kissed him. This time he put his arms around her and held her close. She was trembling when he let her go. 'I married for the wrong reasons too. I wasn't in love with Harry. I'm so unhappy, Tom.' It had come out so suddenly; all she'd wanted to say to Julia and couldn't. The tears slid down her cheeks and he wiped them away with his fingers. 'I'm sorry. I shouldn't have said that – it was wrong of me.'

'It's being here in the rain.' Tom brushed her bottom lip with his thumb. 'You're Roz and I'm Tom while we're here. When you get on your horse and leave I'll be a farmer you know slightly and you'll be Mrs Rushden who lives at the Towers. Nothing will have changed.'

'But it has already. I feel wanted, loved.' Roz moved closer, her lips seeking his once more. 'Love me, Tom. Just this once. Let me live in your arms and then we'll part. We'll never do this again.'

'Are you sure?' His look was disbelieving, his eyes searching her face. 'It's what I want but . . .'

'Don't question, just love me,' Roz whispered against his lips. She was reckless, lost to all caution. Here, marooned by the rain, nothing else seemed real. 'I'll never ask you for anything more. Please . . .'

'I'm the one who should be saying that,' he murmured and drew her back into the hay bales. His hands caressed her face, his lips moving against her throat and her hair. 'I've dreamed of this so many times. I know it's a dream. I shall wake up soon and find you gone.'

'If it is a dream let's make it one to last a lifetime.'

Roz trembled as his hands moved over her body. She lay back, gazing up at him, expecting the feelings of revulsion to start, to feel herself freezing, rejecting him, but it didn't happen. She was alive and warm, her flesh leaping at this man's touch. She didn't understand why or what had happened, just that she was on fire with need and wanting, the wetness between her thighs testimony to her willingness for what happened next.

Roz arched her back, a long, shuddering sigh leaving her lips as Tom moved inside her. It was such a sweet feeling, her breath coming faster and faster as she moved in time with his thrusting, reaching out to him and welcoming him deeper and deeper inside her. She had never known there could be such pleasure, never understood that she could be so abandoned or eager for a man's touch.

When he came inside her, Roz felt the tears trickle down her cheeks. She tasted their salt; it mingled with the taste of him on her lips and she ran her tongue over them.

'You taste so good,' she murmured and opened her eyes to look up at him.

'Tears? Did I hurt you?'

'You made me feel wonderful.' Roz reached up to stroke his cheek, feeling the faint roughness where he was beginning to need a shave and touching the tiny cleft in his chin. 'How did you learn to do that?'

'I've no idea. It has never been that good for me before.' He bent and kissed the bridge of her nose. 'No regrets, then?'

'None. It was lovely. Something I shall remember when I'm sad.'

'I won't marry Mary Jane. We'll run away together. Ma can have the farm and I'll find work . . .'

'Hush, Tom.' Roz touched a finger to his lips. 'You know it can't be that way, my love. This was just a dream we shared. When we leave here after the rain it will be as if it never happened. You can't desert your family or Mary Jane and I . . .' She leaned up and brought him down to her. 'Just hold me. Let's keep the dream alive for as long as we can.'

'I want you so much. Why did you have to be a lady and me a farm labourer?'

'It isn't that keeping us apart and you know it. If we were both free – but we're not and we never can be, Tom. Marry Mary Jane and be happy. You can't break her heart and I can't leave my husband.'

'You don't love him.' Tom grabbed her hair and held her face close to his. 'You love me. Say it, Roz. Say you love me.'

Tears were trickling down her cheek. She gazed into his eyes and knew that it was the truth.

'Yes, I love you. I think perhaps I've loved you since we first met that day I was caught in the briar patch but I didn't have the sense to see it.'

'One day I'll have you again,' Tom said and bent his head to kiss her. 'One day you will be mine, Roz – and then I'll never let you go.'

Ten

'Where have you been?' Harry walked in as Roz was rubbing her hair with a towel. He looked at the gown lying on the floor where she'd dropped it; the material seemed to be drier than he'd expected. 'It stopped raining an hour ago.'

'I took shelter in a lean-to that was full of hay and I didn't realize the rain had stopped,' Roz said without looking at him. 'I'm sorry if you were worried, Harry. I didn't think you would notice.'

'What is that supposed to mean?' He glared at her as she slipped out of her wet petticoat, standing naked before him until she pulled on a silk dressing robe. 'You're my wife. Of course I worry if you're caught in a storm.'

'Then I ask for your pardon, Harry. Next time I go visiting and the sky looks dark I'll take the carriage.'

'How was Julia? You seem in a better mood than you were earlier.'

'Yes, I am.' Roz smiled at him in the mirror. 'Julia told me that she may be carrying Philip's child. Don't you think this quarrel between us is foolish? I know I was nervous on our wedding night but it won't happen again. I'm sure you want an heir – don't you?'

'Perhaps. Something is different – what has changed you, Roz? Why are you looking at me that way?'

'It's foolish to go on quarrelling. I can't force you to come to my bed, Harry – but I shall not be frigid if you do.'

'I'll think about it. You'd best hurry and get dressed. We have guests for dinner this evening. Raymond and Madeline came earlier than I expected.'

'Very well.' Roz turned away and walked into her dressing room.

Harry stared after her, suspicion in his eyes. Something had changed Roz. She was like the girl he'd wanted to marry him, before their wedding night and the subsequent quarrels.

★   ★   ★

'How are you, Madeline?' Roz kissed the Frenchwoman on the cheek. 'That dress is so beautiful – is it the very latest style? I love the colour and the way it sweeps up dramatically to the bustle at the back.'

Madeline was stunningly beautiful with her blonde hair and blue eyes, and she had a rare sensuality that turned heads.

'Yes, it is the latest thing.'

In Paris Roz had been quiet, reserved, and she knew the Frenchwoman had dismissed her as a nobody. Roz was aware that Madeline had flirted shamelessly with Harry and they'd possibly had an affair, but she hadn't minded. She still didn't mind but she had no intention of being eased to one side in her own home.

'I thought it must be – but you are always so elegant.'

'You are better now? In Paris perhaps you were unwell?'

'I may have been a little queasy; the food at the hotel was very rich and not particularly well cooked. Home cooking is so much better if one has a good chef – do you not think so?' Her gaze flicked to Sir Raymond who was an older, distinguished-looking man; the perfect foil for his wife's outstanding beauty. 'I am so pleased you were able to come sooner than expected, sir.'

He moved forward, bowing over her hand. His eyes travelled over her with new interest. In Paris he had ignored her but now he was noticing her.

'I am delighted to meet you again, Mrs Rushden. I was uncertain as to whether I would enjoy a stay in the country, but now I'm certain it will be much more interesting than I'd thought.'

Roz pretended not to understand him. 'Harry has had the house renovated to a high standard. The plumbing is modern and less noisy than at the hotel – and the gardens have been redesigned.'

'I wasn't thinking of the renovations,' he murmured as he kissed her hand. Roz laughed. She had rediscovered the art of flirting and saw to her satisfaction that both Harry and Madeline looked less than pleased at her performance. 'You must show me the gardens tomorrow morning.'

'I should be delighted,' Roz said and took his arm. 'My housekeeper is looking desperate. Perhaps we should go into dinner?'

'Harry is a lucky dog,' he said close to her ear. 'I didn't notice in Paris but here you have blossomed.'

'An English rose does best in English soil, perhaps?'

Roz laughed as he whispered something in her ear, then drew a chair for her at the table. They were dining in the smaller parlour; the atmosphere was intimate and Roz suddenly found herself the centre of attention.

Harry was staring at her with new interest. Roz felt the laughter bubble inside her but she held it back, giving Harry an enigmatic look across the table. In Paris he had responded to Madeline's flirting but she did not particularly care. At this moment she was bursting with happiness and nothing Harry could do or say mattered. For the moment she was nursing her secret, holding the memory of those precious hours with Tom in the hay barn inside her.

Roz had forgotten all the things she enjoyed, her natural sense of self-worth repressed and buried beneath a mountain of shame. But she felt no shame in what had happened that afternoon. Tom's uncomplicated loving had set her free of all the doubts and humiliation. Paul had raped her, making her feel dirty and worthless. Harry said she was frigid and without feeling – but Tom made her feel as if she were special.

'Do you like archery, Sir Raymond? If the weather is fine tomorrow we might set up a target in the grounds.'

'I've never been much good with arrows. I'm more of a huntsman myself. I like to follow the hounds, but Madeline enjoys the sport. You should make a match of it and we'll cheer you on.'

'Yes, perhaps.' Roz smiled inwardly. The only person she wanted to match her skill against was Tom. She wished that she might ride out again in the morning and meet him, but they'd agreed that it must not happen again. What had happened in the hay barn was wrong – but that didn't stop the happiness spiralling through her. She wouldn't go to meet him deliberately but they would meet again and it would happen again, when the time was right. The certainty of it made her want to laugh or dance for joy.

'What are you thinking about, Roz?' Madeline asked. 'Do you have a secret? There is such a look in your eyes.'

'A secret?' Roz lifted her wineglass and sipped it. 'Now what makes you think that, Madeline? I have no secrets from my husband – any more than he has secrets from me.'

Did she imagine the guilty glance that passed between them? She had suspected something in Paris. It might be the real reason Harry had invited them to visit so soon.

'Roz, did you find those collar studs?' Harry asked as he entered her bedchamber that night. She was standing in her nightgown, her hair brushed and hanging loose about her shoulders. 'You looked so beautiful tonight . . .' He moved towards her. 'Did you mean it when you said we should try again?'

'Yes, of course. I've never been unwilling. I was just nervous that night.'

'I was so hurt,' Harry said and there was a husky note in his voice. 'I've been such a pig to you – but I had to strike back to hurt you, as you hurt me. I'm ashamed of what I said. Can you forgive me?'

'Of course, Harry. It was so foolish of me to shut you out like that. I didn't mean to but . . . it won't happen again, I promise.'

'I still love you, Roz.' He took a step towards her. 'You led me on in the carriage and then . . . but I shouldn't have lashed out at you. It's Richmond who should be punished, not you.'

'Yes, he should, but there's nothing you can do, Harry. We are married for better or worse and we ought to try to make the best of things. I respect you for what you've made of your life and I want to have your children. Please let me at least try to make you happy.'

'Roz . . .' His voice broke as he took her into his arms and held her close. Roz clung to the thought of Tom's loving in her mind, remembering the scent of him and the way he'd made her feel. She slid her hands into Harry's hair and lifted her face for his kiss. He groaned and swept her into his arms, carrying her to the bed.

This time, Roz knew better than to lie like a dead thing as he touched her. She stroked his face and then ran her hands down his back, her eyes never leaving his. He tore off his nightshirt and she removed her own. For a moment he stared at her body hungrily, then he began to kiss her breasts. Roz ran her hands over his back, parting her legs for him as he sought out the moistness of her inner citadel. She closed her eyes as he came to her and remembered the sweetness of Tom's touch. Harry wasn't the same; she didn't feel the same joy and freedom she'd known with Tom, but she felt something and she let Harry sense her response. When he reached a swift climax she gasped and dug her nails into his shoulders, which seemed to please him. She turned her head to smile at him as he rolled away from her and lay on his back.

'It's all right now, isn't it?'

'Yes.' He put out a hand to touch her hair. 'I've been an idiot, Roz. You're my wife. It's all right now. We can't change what's done and I was wrong to deny you. We both want children and we can at least find some comfort in each other.'

He left the bed and retrieved his nightshirt, going through to the other room without looking at her. Roz closed her eyes. It was all right, she could still feel Tom's touch and Tom's kisses. It was as if Harry had never been with her. She'd done what she had to do to breach the gulf between them. Harry wasn't fooled. He knew she didn't love him but his hurt pride was healed, his anger against her gone. They would have a marriage of sorts, even though he might still find his pleasure in other women.

Had she not known about Madeline she might have felt guilty, but Harry had broken his vows first. Instead of trying to understand her hurt he'd blamed her for deceiving him, forgetting that she'd tried to tell him when he'd proposed.

Roz banished her husband and his mistress from her mind and tried to picture Tom in his bedchamber. Was he asleep or was he thinking of her?

Tom heard his mother's cry and threw back the patchwork quilt, jumping out of bed. He hadn't been able to sleep because Roz's perfume seemed to cling to his skin and he couldn't stop thinking of her. Was she lying alone or in her husband's bed? That wasn't his business. She was unhappy in her marriage but she'd refused to run off with him. He couldn't blame her. He had little to offer a woman like Roz.

Putting his feet to an icy cold floor, he went through the hall to the room where his father slept. As expected, he discovered his mother trying to change the bedclothes.

'Here, let me do it, Ma.'

'I'll have to manage him while you're away.'

'Sarah Forrest is coming to help with the chores. Get Granny Hubbard to give you a hand with Pa. For goodness' sake, we'll only be away for a couple of days.'

John Blake was swearing and muttering as Tom rolled him to one side and pulled out the folded sheet beneath him, tossing it to the floor and replacing it with another. It saved the mess going through to the bottom sheet and the mattress, which would have made things worse. Once his father was dry and settled, Tom left him to sleep and went down to the kitchen. Ellen had taken the sheets into the scullery. Tom stoked up the range fire and was putting the kettle on when she came through.

'I can't break my promise to Mary Jane, Ma. It will be hard enough for her once we get home.'

'I know. I don't expect you to, Tom. You do too much already, but he makes such a fuss when I try to change him.'

'He still thinks you want him dead,' Tom said with a sigh. 'I'm making tea. Do you want some?'

'I might as well. I can't sleep,' Ellen said. 'Carrie was gone most of the afternoon and you know it rained, but she was as dry as a bone when she got back. Where do you think she goes to?'

'She probably found shelter in a barn or something.'

'I swear I'll kill her if she does it again.'

'Squire is dead,' Tom said and looked at his mother's face. 'What do you mean?'

'I hope it's not true but sometimes I think she lied to us, Tom. She's so pleased with herself and the babe. Seems to me she knew exactly what she wanted – and how to get it.'

'Mebbe she did. Does it matter now?'

'Dick is dead because of what she told us that day, and your pa's been worse since she had the babe. Poor little mite. When she feels like it she nurses and croons over her, then she's away across the fields and there's no one to look after the child but me. I love her, Tom, but it's too much for me.'

'You will have Mary Jane to help you soon.'

'Yes, that's the one bright thing in all of this.' He got up to make the tea and found his mother watching as he brought the large brown pot to the table. 'You are all right with it, aren't you – the wedding?'

'Of course I am, Ma. Why wouldn't I be?'

'I've nagged you into it,' Ellen said as he set the pot down and fetched a jug of milk from the pantry.

'I want to get on in life, Ma. I was trying to save every penny but that's a false economy. I can't do everything myself, any more than you can. A man in the yard and Mary Jane in the house, and things will be easier all round.'

'Your lass was up to see me today. Her ma wanted to confirm the numbers for the meal after the wedding. She asked to have a look round so I took her upstairs. She looked in on your pa and spoke to him, but you know what he is.'

'I hope he didn't shout at her?'

'He just shut his eyes and pretended he was asleep.'

'Mary Jane knows what to expect. I warned her before the banns were called.'

'Well, she asked if she could bring some things here today. Seems she's got a chest of stuff she's been saving for a year or two.'

'Before we started courting.'

'Aye. I think she had her eye on Dick once but that's water under the bridge now.'

'I'm not head over heels, Ma. Mary Jane's pretty and she knows what I want from a wife.'

'Yes, I thought that was it. I'm sorry, Tom. If Dick had been alive you might have taken your time and found someone you could truly love.'

'I doubt it would've made much difference. I've had my dreams, Ma – but I know that's all they were. Mary Jane will make me a good wife.'

'Are you prepared to be a good husband?'

'What's brought this on?' Tom finished his tea and put the mug in the deep stone sink. 'I'm off to bed. It will soon be morning and I've a lot to do tomorrow if I'm to be married on Saturday.'

'Get off to bed then,' Ellen said and then hesitated. 'She was never for you, Tom. Not in a million years.'

Tom made no answer. His mother didn't know Roz. She had no idea that he'd been with her in the hay barn during a rainstorm. She would never guess what they had been to each other – or that Tom's body yearned for her in a way it never would for Mary Jane.

'The gardens are lovely, I'll give you that,' Sir Raymond said as they finished the tour and began to walk towards the house once more. 'But a woman of taste like you must long to change things in the house?'

Roz turned her gaze on him. Just what was he up to? Harry had given the architect and the decorator carte blanche and Roz wished he'd left the furnishings to her, because there were just too many fussy details that spoiled the look.

'Everything is very new,' she replied. 'In time things will become more comfortable.'

Sir Raymond turned to her. 'You should never have married a man like Rushden. He has no taste or sensitivity.' He took her hand, his finger stroking the palm. 'You would find me more skilled in the arts of love, Roz.'

Roz drew her hand away, repressing the shudder that ran through her at his touch. 'Sir Raymond! You ought not to say such things to me.'

'You're not such a little prude. I saw that look in your eyes last night. You looked like a woman who had been to meet her lover and was well satisfied.'

'How dare you?' Roz moved away, half angry, half fearful. He caught her arm and swung her back to face him. 'Please let me go, sir.'

'Won't you call me Raymond? There's no reason why we shouldn't amuse each other. Madeline and your husband began their affair in Paris. Surely you knew that?'

'Why did you come here if that is the case? Don't you care what she does?'

'Madeline has her lovers and I have my pleasures. We don't believe in petty jealousy. I always know when she has a new lover – and I saw that look in your eyes last night. I doubt your husband knew what to make of it, but if I alert him to the truth he will soon catch on.'

'Are you trying to blackmail me?'

'Blackmail is an ugly word. You could be nice to me while

we're here. We shan't stay more than a couple of weeks and I'm not demanding; once a day would be sufficient.'

'Once would be more than enough for me,' Roz flashed at him. 'If you wish to tell Harry lies do so. He will not believe you – and there is no reason for him to be jealous. I do not have a lover and I have no intention of obliging you.'

She broke away and walked into the house. She was seething inside as she went into her favourite parlour and found Madeline going through her sewing box.

'What are you doing?'

'I need a thread to sew on a button,' Madeline said but there was a guilty look in her eyes. 'Your embroidery is very neat, Roz. I am hopeless at anything more than plain sewing and I don't care for it at all.'

'Perhaps you prefer other pastimes?'

'Yes, perhaps.' Madeline smiled. 'Your husband took me riding this morning. Yesterday, we arrived in a rainstorm, as you know – but of course you didn't know. You were out riding. Harry was worried because the rain was so heavy. Did you take shelter somewhere?'

'For a while, yes. Why do you ask?'

'We passed a hay barn this morning. Harry said it belongs to a neighbour of your brother's. The land lies between your brother's estate and Harry's – he said both he and Sir Philip want to buy it but the owner is refusing to sell.'

'I know nothing about Harry's business or Philip's.'

'I thought perhaps you might have sheltered in the hay barn?' Madeline smiled and got up, wandering over to the window. 'There was a man with a cart near the barn. I think he was fetching hay. He turned to stare at us – at me really, but then he seemed to lose interest and turned his back on us.'

'You are a beautiful woman. Is it surprising that a man stares at you?'

'It was the way he looked – the eagerness, as if he expected to see the woman he loved. When he realized I was a stranger he lost interest.'

'I have no idea what you mean,' Roz lied, because she knew exactly what Madeline was getting at. Something about her the previous evening had told both Sir Raymond and his wife that she had come from a lover. Madeline was fishing. She could know nothing for sure but she was watching Roz's reaction. 'The barn belongs to Mr Blake. His family and mine have nothing to do with each other. It's an old quarrel best forgotten.'

'Ah, I see.' Madeline inclined her head. 'Was that the bell for luncheon? Riding always gives me an appetite – and sex makes me ravenous.'

Harry came to say goodnight that evening. He kissed Roz and smiled but then made an excuse about being tired and left her to sleep alone. She thought that perhaps he'd come from Madeline because she could smell a perfume about him that wasn't hers.

As she lay in bed Roz was remembering that the next day was Tom's wedding to Mary Jane Forrest. She would have liked to go the church and see them wed but Harry would be annoyed if she deserted their guests to go riding alone. In a week or two, when Madeline and her odious husband had gone, Roz might take a gift for Mary Jane. Perhaps some lace or a paisley shawl. She wasn't sure if Tom would want his wife to do sewing for other people, but she could ask. A part of her was jealous of the girl who would be Tom's wife, but she knew it was what he needed. If things had been different . . . but that was impossible. It was because she cared for Tom that she hoped his marriage would be good for him.

Roz smiled as she drifted into sleep. She was probably just making an excuse to go to Tom's house in the hope of seeing him. It might be better to send someone with the gift and stay away. Yet what harm could it do to pass the time of day?

She was married to Harry and he was being considerate and courteous – everything she'd expected from her marriage. Roz must do nothing to make him suspect her of having a lover.

She slept and her dream was pleasant. She woke feeling refreshed. During the morning the sound of church bells from the direction of the village made her stop and look out of the window towards the church spire. It was just visible because it was built on a rise and the surrounding land was so flat.

So Tom was married to his Mary Jane. She tried to imagine them with their friends around them, the dancing and laughter. For a moment Roz was overcome with a sense of regret. She wished that she had been marrying Tom Blake that morning, even though she knew it wasn't possible. Neither his family nor hers would have permitted it; the rift was too wide, made deeper by the blood spilled on both sides.

'You do love me, Tom?' Mary Jane looked at him as they went out to the pony and trap that was waiting to take them to the railway station in Wisbech.

'You know I care for you, Mary, lass. Why do you ask now?'

'You've hardly spoken a word since we took our vows in church. You never said you liked my dress or a word about how I looked.'

'You looked pretty as always, Mary Jane – but that dress wasn't made from the material I brought you from the market.'

'It was a dress Lady Thornton sent me as a wedding present. The material was so good, Tom, and I turned up the hem and let out the waist and it fitted me a treat. I thought it made me look like a lady.'

'Yes, it did,' Tom agreed and frowned. 'I'd rather you looked like yourself, Mary Jane. You've no need to pretend to be Roz Thornton by wearing her old dresses. I prefer you to be you.'

'Lady Thornton said her daughter never wore it because she didn't like it. I think it had been worn once, but it was like new and it made me feel beautiful. I made a dress with your material and I'll wear that at the hotel. Please don't be cross with me.'

'I'm not cross.' Tom leaned towards her, giving her a brief kiss on the mouth before handing her up into the trap. He climbed in beside her and took her hand. 'How could I be cross with you on our wedding day?'

'I want us to be happy, Tom. Ma and Pa are at each other's throats half the time. I don't want us to be like that, always arguing.'

'Your ma and pa care about each other; they make up their quarrels. My parents can be bitter over things, Mary Jane. I wouldn't want that for us. If I say things you don't like, you should tell me and not brood.'

'I'll be all right if you love me,' Mary Jane said. 'There was someone else I fancied once, Tom – but the only one I want now is you.'

'Ma thought you were after our Dick. Maybe he would've asked you if things had been different – but that's water under the bridge. You're my wife and I mean to do right by you.'

Tom watched the countryside pass by as the trap was driven at a smart pace towards the railway station. He'd made himself a vow as he was shaving that morning. There would be no more dreams about Roz, no more clandestine meetings at the hay barn.

Maybe it was imagination but he'd smelled Roz's perfume clinging to Mary Jane's dress and it had haunted him as he took his wedding vows. Even as he spoke the words and kissed Mary Jane, he had seen Roz standing there at his side and he'd known he loved her. Mary Jane was a good lass and she'd be a good wife to him, but he couldn't give her what belonged to someone else.

Eleven

'I don't know how you can bear to have that woman staying in your home,' Julia said as she kissed Roz goodbye after dinner at Rushden Towers the following week. 'The way she looks at your husband is disgraceful. Forgive me for saying it, but it is the truth.'

'Yes, I know. She threw herself at Harry when we met them in Paris. I don't really mind, Julia. She and Raymond will be leaving in a few days and I think Harry will not invite them again in a hurry.'

'What makes you say that?' Julia smoothed on her gloves and glanced back to where Philip was standing with Harry and Madeline.

'Harry won Raymond's money in Paris and thought he ought to give him a chance to recuperate, but I think he lost heavily to him the other evening. He didn't exactly say but he seemed to imply that he thought . . . well, he was annoyed over it.'

'It is best not to say these things in company, unless they can be proved. I hope that Philip has the sense to stay away from them. He cannot afford to gamble if he wishes to improve the estate.'

'Perhaps you should not have invited them to dine next week?'

'Philip invited Sir Raymond. I could hardly refuse to entertain them, though I do not particularly like either of them. Ah, Philip is coming at last. I must go, Roz. Please visit me when you can.'

'Yes, of course. I shall as soon as I'm free.'

Roz watched as her sister-in-law went out to the carriage. She saw a look pass between Madeline and Philip and wondered if Julia had also noticed that a subtle flirtation had been going on between them during the evening. It seemed that Madeline had turned her attention to Philip. Perhaps she had not yet realized that Julia held the purse strings.

Rebuking herself for being spiteful, Roz went back to her guest. 'Did you enjoy your evening, Madeline?'

'Yes, very much. Your brother is an interesting man, Roz – even though his wife tries to keep him on a leash.'

'Philip is grateful to her for enabling him to improve the estate. Money was tight after my father died.'

'Philip told me the story,' Madeline said. 'Dick Blake killed your father because he blamed him for raping his idiot sister.'

'Carrie isn't an idiot,' Roz snapped, 'just a little dreamy and slow at times.'

'You defend her? Do I sense that you are sympathetic to the whole family, Roz?'

'Dick Blake was wrong to murder my father, but he paid for his mistake with his life. The rest of his family are no more to blame than I am for what happened to Carrie.'

'Still pretending to be holier than thou?' Madeline smirked. 'I liked your brother, Roz. At least he is honest enough to admit what he wants.'

'Please don't hurt Julia,' Roz said. 'I should have thought one lover at a time was sufficient – even for you, Madeline.'

Madeline's green eyes narrowed.

'Don't forget that I know about you and the farmer's son. If I were to drop a word into Harry's ear, it would wipe that superior look from your face.'

'You know nothing, because there is nothing to know,' Roz replied. 'I think Harry has seen through both you and your husband. He wouldn't believe your lies.'

'He might not like what I am but he loves what I do to him,' Madeline said, a smile of triumph on her full red lips. 'Don't underestimate me, Roz. I can break the string or jerk it and bring him running whenever I like.'

'Then do your worst. Excuse me, I must say goodnight to my brother.' She walked to catch Philip before he got into the carriage. 'Goodnight, Philip.'

'I still want that talk,' Philip said. 'I'll call tomorrow morning – you will be at home?'

'Yes, of course. Do not keep Julia waiting.'

She returned to the hall to find Harry standing with Sir Raymond. He glanced at Roz but said nothing. Her rebuff of his advances in the garden had made him treat her with scornful disdain, barely speaking more than a word to her these past several days.

'I'm going up now, Harry,' she said. 'Come when you're ready.'

'I shan't be late,' he promised and kissed her cheek. 'Madeline has already gone up and Philip was the last to leave.'

Roz passed the two men and walked up the stairs. Her maid was waiting to unhook her gown at the back. As soon as that was done, Roz dismissed her.

'I can manage now,' she said. 'Go to bed, May. I'm sure you're tired.'

'No, ma'am. I don't mind sitting up for you but I shouldn't want to work for that other one.'

'Do you mean Lady Jenson?'

'Yes, Mrs Rushden. I took some hot water up for her earlier and she threw a hairbrush at me because it wasn't the right temperature.'

'I'm sorry she was so appallingly rude to you, May. I apologize on her behalf.'

'You're a proper lady, ma'am. She and that husband of hers are . . . well, it ain't for me to say.'

'It isn't necessary, May. I know more than you may imagine. She and Sir Raymond will be leaving soon and I very much hope they will not be invited again.'

'Yes, ma'am. So do us all. I should count the silver before they leave if I were you.'

'Now that is too much,' Roz said but smiled inwardly. It was ridiculous to be so pleased that her servants had such a low opinion of Madeline and Sir Raymond. 'Run along now, May.'

Feeling a little restless after the girl left her, Roz brushed her long hair then stood up and went to the window to look out. Less than five miles separated her from the house where Tom Blake lived. She splayed her fingers on the window, as if she could somehow breach the cavern between them and bring him closer.

'Roz . . . is something wrong?'

She turned and saw Harry watching her. He was wearing a striped velvet dressing robe and his feet were bare. She knew why he had come and his reason for seeking her out. Madeline had been a little too obvious in flirting with Philip that evening.

'No, nothing is wrong,' she said and smiled at him. 'Do you want to stay with me tonight, Harry? I mean, stay all night?'

'I've been a fool,' he said huskily as he moved towards her.

'Nothing has happened since Paris except a few kisses, though it wasn't for lack of trying on her part. I got involved with them in Paris and it was difficult to say no when he asked if they could come and stay. They are leaving tomorrow.'

'Sooner than they planned?'

'He has seen a house he likes in Wisbech. They are going to lease it for the winter – at least that is what he told me.'

'I wish they had chosen London instead.'

'Don't worry, Roz. The madness has passed. I think he cheated at cards the other night. I lost ten thousand pounds to him.'

'Harry!' Roz was shocked. 'That is so much money – as much as Julia brought to Philip when they married. If they get their claws in him . . .'

'I shall warn him,' Harry promised. 'I can weather it, though it means I shan't be able to top your brother's offer for Blake's farm.'

'Why would you wish to?' Roz gazed up at him as he untied the belt of his robe.

'Just because it's good land and there's access to the stream in the dry weather. Your father wanted that land, Roz, and now Philip is after it. Blake won't sell to him, of course, but I thought he might to me. I sold him some oats the other year when they were short.'

'I doubt if the Blakes would sell to anyone. They are a proud family.'

'What do you know of them?'

'I met Ellen Blake when I took some things for Carrie – and I know Tom Blake's wife. Mary Jane does sewing for Mama and me sometimes.'

Harry nodded. He was naked beneath his robe and Roz smiled as she saw he was fully aroused. She went to his arms, lifting her face for his kiss.

'I don't care what happened between you and Madeline,' she said. 'I hurt you in Paris and you wanted to hurt me back. Promise me it is all over now and we'll forget any of it happened.'

'You're so lovely,' Harry breathed and kissed her, sweeping her up in his arms. 'From now on it's just you and me. I promise.'

'Make love to me, Harry,' she whispered. 'We can be happy together if we try.'

Roz responded to his touch and found she felt so much better this time. She wasn't in love with him but perhaps they could like and respect each other again.

Mary Jane straightened and put a hand to the small of her back. She had just finished milking the herd of ten cows single-handed, because Tom was busy helping a neighbour to thresh his corn. The neighbour had helped him thresh their crop three days earlier and now he was repaying the favour. Sighing, she took her bucket, which was three-quarters full, and tipped it into the churn. She'd already put some by for the kitchen and she'd skimmed some of the milk for making butter in the churn.

At home Mary Jane had worked all hours but she'd been able to chat with her mother, brothers, sisters and her father. Here, she was expected to milk alone and the butter churning took ages. The memory of her trip to the seaside had already faded into a distant memory, though it was only three weeks since they'd come back to the farm.

'You've finished the milking, then,' Ellen said as she carried the jugs to the kitchen. 'You're a good girl, Mary, lass. Sit down and have a mug of tea before you start on the butter. I've collected the eggs and we've far more than we need. I'll be asking Tom to take them to market in the morning and if there's enough butter we'll send a crock or two. The egg money has always been mine but I'll share it with you, lass. You can have half to spend as you like.'

'Thanks, Ellen,' Mary Jane said and sat down at the scrubbed pine table to drink her tea and eat a piece of her mother-in-law's spiced cake. 'Would you mind if I went to see Ma and the children when I've finished in the dairy? I'll do any other chores when I come back this evening.'

'Yes, I don't see why you shouldn't,' Ellen said. She heard the baby cry and stood up. 'I'd better see to the poor little mite. Carrie went off this morning and I've not seen her for hours.'

'Where do you think she goes?' Mary Jane said. 'I never see her when I take Tom a drink in the fields.'

'I try to make her do her share of the work, but she starts a job and when I turn my back she's gone. It's easier to do things myself than ask, especially now that you're here, lass. Tom was lucky when he got you, Mary Jane.'

'There's more to marriage than work,' Mary Jane said but Ellen was headed up the stairs.

She finished her tea and went out into the yard. Tom had made love to her every night while they were at the seaside but since they came home he'd hardly touched her. He kissed her goodnight and then turned over and went to sleep. She knew he was working very hard; there were root crops to take out of the ground as well as the threshing, but it wasn't natural for a man to be so uninterested in sex. They'd only been married just over three weeks. She'd lived in a small cottage with her parents and she knew her father was still regular in his attentions to her mother. She'd heard them at least twice or three times a week – so what was wrong with Tom?

Maybe when the threshing was over he wouldn't be so tired at nights. Mary Jane wasn't going to put up with this; she hadn't married him just to work for his mother like a slave.

Tom spent some time wandering round the market that morning. He'd been working hard the past few weeks and it was good to get away for a few hours. The money for the eggs was in his pocket, as well as a few pounds for a pig he'd sold. He'd done a deal for his corn and barley, and he'd bought in extra oats for the winter. They'd grown more mangles this year which, when they were harvested, would be extra feed for the stock through the cold months.

His business over, he was looking for a small trinket of some kind for Mary Jane. Tom was aware that he hadn't been fair to her recently but it wasn't easy to put away his thoughts of Roz. He'd managed it while they were at the hotel in Hunstanton, but since then he'd found it more difficult to make love to his wife.

Finding a stall selling pretty scarves, Tom purchased one for his wife and then turned and saw Roz at the other side of the market. She was alone and seemed to be looking at a stall displaying beadwork purses and fans made of ivory and lace. At that moment she looked up and their eyes met, locked together for what seemed like eternity but was possibly only a few seconds before she nodded and smiled.

Tom stared at her hungrily. He was about to go to her when he saw that she was looking elsewhere. His eyes sought what she had seen and discovered she was looking at her brother talking to a young, very elegant and beautiful woman with blonde hair and blue eyes. Neither of them had eyes for anyone but each other. As Tom watched, they linked arms and walked towards the hotel, disappearing inside.

Roz was looking at him now. He could tell that she was anxious or disturbed but when he took a step towards her she shook her head. A moment later he saw her husband join her and turned away as she smiled at Harry Rushden.

Jealousy ate at his insides. For a moment as their eyes met Tom had thought she felt as he did, but the smile she gave to Rushden was intimate and welcoming.

He was a damned fool to care, but he did. The longing for her was like a sickness in his blood.

He turned away and strode back through the market to the livery where he'd left his horse and cart. It was time he got back to the farm and his work. Roz was not for him. She never had been. The day she let him love her was just something that happened because of a rainstorm; it was a dream. He was kidding himself otherwise.

Mary Jane draped the filmy pink scarf around her throat and preened in front of the spotted mirror in her bedroom. Tom's loving had been passionate the night he gave her the scarf. A month had passed and since then he'd been busy on the farm again, making love to her only twice in that time, but she was fairly certain that she'd fallen for a child and that pleased her. Perhaps when she told him she was pregnant Tom would take more time off to be with her. He seemed fond of Carrie's little girl so he was bound to love his own child when it was born.

She had finished her chores for the morning and she was going to visit her family. It was nearly three weeks since the last time and Ellen had told her to go.

'You work harder than Carrie ever did,' Ellen said when she came in for tea and cake mid morning. 'As soon as you've finished in the dairy, you get off to see your ma, lass.'

'Thanks, Ellen. I'll be back in time for the milking this evening.'

'Tom isn't so busy as he was now the threshing is done and

they've got most of the ploughing done as well. You stop a bit longer and make a day of it, lass.'

Mary Jane called out to her mother-in-law as she left the kitchen, but she was upstairs seeing to the baby or John Blake and didn't hear. As Mary Jane crossed the yard she saw Carrie ahead of her. She was about to call out to her, then decided against it. Just out of curiosity, she would follow Tom's sister and see where she went this afternoon.

Philip dismounted from his horse and tied it to a post outside the cottage. He looked over his shoulder but there was no sign of Madeline. She had promised she would get away if she could but he knew she couldn't always make it. The drive out from Wisbech was further than she liked and she had been nagging him to find somewhere closer where they could meet. He was unwilling to go to a hotel because he was well known in the small market town and it would cause gossip that might come to Julia's ears.

Philip was grateful to his wife for all she'd brought him in the marriage contract. He knew that without her money he would have gone under before this and he had no intention of ruining his marriage. He'd stopped meeting Carrie as soon as he married, but Madeline had tempted him. She'd made it plain from the beginning that she was available and Philip just hadn't been able to resist.

He turned with her name on his lips as the door opened but the smile died as he saw who had entered. He was suddenly angry and nervous, because if Madeline saw him with the Blake girl she would put two and two together. No one but Roz knew and she'd promised him she wouldn't say anything for Julia's sake.

'What do you want?' he asked and glared at Carrie. 'I told you it was over. You're not supposed to come here.'

'I come whenever I like,' Carrie said and smiled. 'You promised me a shilling for the babe but you broke your promise.'

Philip thrust his hand in his pocket and drew out a guinea, shoving it at her. 'Take this and go. I don't want you here. I have nothing more to say to you.'

Carrie's eyes grew dark with distress. 'You said you loved me and you gave me a baby. I did as you told me and said it was your pa – but it wasn't. He smiled at me and gave me a shilling but he didn't give me a baby. You were the one that loved me. You brought me here and told me this was our secret place.'

'It was then but it isn't now. Go away, Carrie. I don't want you here ever again. Take the money and stay away – or I might be angry.'

Carrie looked at him, a mutinous line to her mouth. 'I'm not daft in the head. Everyone thinks I am but I know what goes on. I saw you with her . . . the woman who lives in Wisbech. You brought her here.'

'Damn you!' Philip moved towards her, his expression threatening. 'Go away now or I shan't be responsible for my actions.'

'Kiss me; do it again, the way you did before. I like babies. Make another baby for me, Philip.'

'I'm the squire to you,' Philip muttered. 'I don't want to touch you – and don't think you can blackmail me. I'll deny it and I'll make you sorry.'

Carrie sidled up to him, unbuttoning her dress to show him her full breasts. 'Touch me and suck me like the baby does, Philip. I want to do it again . . . the way we did before.'

'No, damn you. Are you too stupid to know when a man doesn't want you?'

'I'm not stupid . . .' Carrie flew at him, her nails going for his face.

Philip grabbed her by the wrists and shoved her away from him, hard. She fell and struck her head on the wooden arm of a heavy chair. A little gasp left her lips and then she lay still.

'Get up, you silly bitch,' Philip said and touched her with the toe of his boot. She didn't move so he kicked her but she still made no sound. Suddenly anxious, he dropped to his knees on the floor and bent over her. Carrie's eyes had closed and the colour had gone from her face. He shook her and her head flopped to one side. A sense of panic sweeping over him, he felt her neck and discovered that it had broken. 'No. God, what have I done?' Vomit rose in his throat as he realized what a single act of temper had done. He'd killed her. Surely it wasn't possible. He felt for a pulse but there was none.

How could it have happened? Philip hadn't meant to kill her but he had; he was a murderer. Fear set in as he realized he'd murdered Carrie and he felt cold all over. If anyone discovered what he'd done he would hang for murder.

Fighting down the panic, Philip tried to think about what to do for the best. Hearing sounds from outside, he pushed Carrie's body under the table. It was covered with a long chenille cloth that hid her completely. A moment later Madeline entered the room. She smiled and came towards him, her perfume so over-powering that Philip found it difficult to breathe.

What was he going to do? He couldn't make love to Madeline now. Not when Carrie's body lay under the table. He had to think about what he needed to do to cover up the murder. The body wasn't safe here because Madeline knew about the cottage. He had no illusions. She wouldn't hide a thing like that for him, unless he paid her and he didn't have enough money to keep her quiet. She was a greedy, grasping woman and he'd been a fool to become involved with her.

'I thought you weren't coming. I was just about to leave.'

'After I've come all this way to see you?' Madeline pouted. 'You might at least kiss me – be a little pleased to see me, Philip.'

'Of course I'm pleased to see you, but we can't stay here.'

'I don't understand. I thought this place belonged to you?'

'No, it isn't mine,' he lied. 'Father sold it some months before he died but no one told me until recently. Apparently the owner is due to arrive at any moment – so we can't come here again. I'll find somewhere near Wisbech, as you wanted.'

'The owner isn't here now.' Madeline pressed herself against him. 'Show me how pleased you are to see me, darling – or I might not meet you again.'

If he didn't get out of here he would be sick. The fear of discovery was so strong that he couldn't think properly.

'Perhaps that is best.' Philip took her arm and thrust her ahead of him, through the small hallway and out of the front door. He took a deep breath. At least he could breathe out here, but the panic wasn't far away. He had to get rid of Madeline so that he could hide Carrie's body.

'What does that mean? Are you dropping me?' Madeline looked at him, her eyes green and malevolent like an angry cat. 'No man does that, Philip Thornton. You'll regret treating me like this.' She turned away, using a boulder to mount her horse without his help. For a moment she sat there, glaring at him. 'You'll be sorry for this, believe me.'

Philip stood and watched as she rode away. Then he turned and went back into the cottage. His chest hurt and he felt suffocated by fear. Madeline would never look at him again but at the moment he didn't care. Oh, God, he wished he hadn't come near this place. He wished he'd never met Madeline. If he hadn't been afraid she would turn up and find him with Carrie he would never have hit her. He'd liked Carrie. She was worth two of the bitch that had just ridden away.

What should he do about Carrie's body? He couldn't move her in broad daylight. He would have to come back at night after Julia was in bed. He would carry her on to her brother's land and leave her – perhaps near the hay barn. Tom Blake was sure to look for her when she didn't return but with luck he would leave it until the morning.

Mary Jane was thoughtful as she walked back from her mother's house that evening. She had solved the mystery of where Carrie went to when she disappeared for hours. She'd followed Tom's sister to an old cottage on Thornton land and seen her go in. A horse had been tied up outside but Mary Jane didn't know who owned it. She'd hurried on after she'd seen Carrie go inside the cottage because she'd wanted to get home and have tea with her family. There were some questions she needed to ask her mother about what happened when a woman was pregnant.

Carrie was probably meeting a man. Mary Jane wondered whether she should tell Ellen or Tom what she'd seen. They might think she was spying and say it wasn't her business, and maybe they were right. Yet if Carrie was seeing a man it might result in yet another baby and that would be one too many. It was going to be hard enough when Mary Jane gave birth to her own baby. Carrie hardly ever did anything for her daughter, except feed her and it was left to either Ellen or Mary Jane to change her and soothe her when she cried. Carrie's daughter would be a toddler by the time Mary Jane gave birth and more difficult than she was now. If Carrie had another baby it would make too much work.

It was time Ellen took a firmer hand with her daughter. Maybe she'd wait until her mother-in-law was in a mellow mood to tell her what she'd seen. Perhaps she ought to have waited to discover who owned the horse she'd seen tied up outside the cottage, but she'd been satisfied to know where Carrie went. At least if she was late another day, Mary Jane could tell Tom where to find her. That might be the best. Say nothing for now and let him discover what his sister was up to for himself.

Twelve

'Carrie didn't sleep in her bed last night.' Ellen looked at Tom anxiously. 'That girl will be the death of me. She has stayed out for hours before, even missed her supper — but the babe was crying half the night. I gave her a bottle of warm cow's milk and she quietened, but she's fretful this morning and she was sick. She still needs her mother's milk.'

'Do you want me to look for her?' Tom asked. 'I haven't much on this morning other than the milking and mucking out the sheds. If Mary Jane helps with the milking as usual I'll go as soon as I've done.'

'You couldn't go before you clean out the sheds? I'm sorry to ask it, Tom, but I've got a strange feeling. She always comes home at night. I think something has happened to her.'

'All right, Mary Jane can get on with the milking and I'll search for Carrie. I'll give her a good telling off when I find her. She's been allowed too much freedom, Ma.'

'Yes, I know. It's just that I've had so much to do with your pa. I'm washing sheets three times a day, Tom. If it weren't for Mary Jane, I don't know what I'd do.'

'She's a good girl,' Tom acknowledged. He pushed his chair back after draining his tea. 'I'll eat later. If Carrie is hurt and lying out in the fields she could catch her death of cold.'

'That's what worries me,' Ellen admitted. 'Wrap up warm, Tom. It's freezing out.'

'There was a frost last night.' Tom met his mother's worried look. 'I know what you're thinking, Ma, but our Carrie isn't daft enough to stay out in the fields all night. She'd find somewhere to keep warm.'

'If she could,' his mother agreed, 'but I feel something bad has happened to her, Tom. I felt it last night. I should've told you then, but I kept thinking she would creep in late and go to bed, as she has before this.'

'I'll find her,' Tom promised, pulled his old felt hat down low over his brow, and went out.

Mary Jane entered the kitchen a few minutes later. 'I've been seeing to the baby,' she said. 'She was crying because she was wet, but she's settled now.'

'You'll make a wonderful mother,' Ellen told her. 'Eat your breakfast, lass. You'll have to start the milking alone. Tom had to go somewhere.'

'He said he would give me a hand,' Mary Jane said and sat down. 'It won't be long before he'll have to help me a bit. I shan't be able to do it all in a month or two.'

'What do you mean?' Ellen looked at her sharply. 'Are you saying you're having a baby?'

'Yes, I think so. I asked Ma yesterday and she said the signs were all there. Do you think Tom will be pleased?'

'Yes, I dare say,' Ellen said and sighed. 'We may have to take another girl on for a while but it isn't your fault. We should have expected it to happen sooner or later.'

'You wish it had been later.' Mary Jane gave her a sulky look. 'I'm Tom's wife, not a slave.'

'Don't take it like that, lass. You know how I'm pushed – listen, he's started again and I've only just come down from seeing to him. Sometimes I wish the good Lord would take him out my way.'

'Ellen!' Mary Jane looked at her in shock. 'You shouldn't say things like that – Ma says we're punished for bad thoughts as much as bad deeds.' She crossed herself quickly.

Ellen turned away and went upstairs. She had a terrible feeling that she was about to be punished for a great many bad thoughts.

Carrie was getting to be a lot of trouble. Tom had always loved his sister despite her dreaming and her strange ways. He'd felt it was his duty to look after her but just recently he'd been too caught up with his own dreams to give her more than a passing thought. His mother had complained about Carrie wandering off for long periods. Tom ought to have made it his business to find out where she went and make her see that her baby was her responsibility and not Ellen's.

Mary Jane had worked so hard since they were wed and he knew it wasn't fair on her. He'd asked her to be his wife, not to work like a slave. Even with the extra man Tom had taken on he'd had more than enough to do himself. It would be best to buy the land he wanted and take on a lad to do some of the work his wife was currently doing. Money might be tight for a while but in another year the new stock would make all the difference to their income. Clearly they couldn't rely on Carrie to do much, but if Ellen were not so rushed she could keep an eye on the girl and stop her wandering off.

Tom knew how much Carrie loved the wild meadow in summer so he went down to the stream and walked along the bank to the beginning of Thornton land. He'd been half afraid he might find her body caught in the reeds and felt better as he walked on to the village. Seeing the vicar's wife in her garden, he asked if she'd seen his sister.

'Not for several days, Tom. She sometimes comes to see me and stops for a glass of my cordial but I haven't seen her recently.'

'She didn't come home last night. Ma was worried and I promised I'd find her. If anyone mentions seeing her, would you send word?'

'Yes, of course. I'll tell the vicar. If you don't find her let us know and we'll rouse the village. Everyone likes Carrie, Tom. We should be sorry if anything happened to her.'

'I expect she's just dreaming and doesn't even realize we're worried about her.'

Tom took a shortcut through the lane that crossed between his and Thornton's land. Carrie wouldn't have crossed over, would she? He glanced across the flat fields at a windmill and some barns in the distance. He knew there was a cottage on the edge of Thornton's land that had once been used by a farm manager but had been empty for a while, since before the old squire died. Shaking his head, he walked towards the hay barn. For a moment his stomach clenched as he recalled the day he'd sheltered from the rain with Roz. Then, as he saw something lying on the ground, his heart lurched and he ran towards what he could now see was a body.

Carrie's body. She seemed to be lying in an odd position with her head on one side. She was dead. A wave of grief and pain swathed through him as he knelt by her side and touched her cheek. He could see at once that there was no hope and she felt like ice. He didn't need to be told that she'd been dead for hours.

Tears trickled down his cheeks as he ran his hands over her face, stroking her hair back from her cheek. Poor little lost Carrie. What had happened to her? Tom looked round for the cause of her accident – if it had been an accident? What had made her fall and how had she come to be spread out this way – almost as if someone had placed her there and arranged her limbs.

He sat back on his heels, his brow furrowed. Her death wasn't natural. It looked to him as if her neck had snapped but how? There was nothing to trip her, nothing for her to strike her head against.

What ought he to do? His mother was waiting for news. She grumbled about Carrie but she would be devastated by her death, just as Tom was himself. He looked about him but knew there was no one to help. Everyone would be seeing to the cows or the morning chores. He supposed he ought to fetch a constable and let him see how she was lying because there was something wrong – something suspicious about it – but he couldn't go and leave her here now he'd found her. She was dead. Nothing was going to change that so he might as well take her home to her mother.

Tom wiped the tears from his cheek. He got to his feet, bent down and lifted Carrie into her arms. He was choking with grief and regret, blaming himself for not watching out for her more. He would take Carrie home and fetch the doctor, then he'd go into Wisbech and report that his sister had had an accident of some sort. The last thing he wanted was people asking questions and upsetting everyone. But he wouldn't forget what he'd seen and he'd find out what had happened somehow. If he discovered that Carrie's death wasn't an accident he would thrash the man who'd murdered her.

It had to be a man, perhaps the father of her child if, as he'd begun to suspect, Carrie had lied to them about the old squire raping her.

Ellen ran to meet Tom as he walked into the yard carrying his sister's body. She saw the way Carrie's head was flopping and screamed at him.

'Where did you find her?'

'She was lying near the hay barn, Ma. She must have fallen or something. I don't know how it could have happened. There's blood in the back of her hair but when I lifted her there was none on the grass.'

'What are you saying?' Ellen's face was grey with shock and fear. 'You mean she was put there? Was she murdered? Tom, who killed her? Some devil has hurt our Carrie.'

'I'll fetch the doctor and tell him Carrie's had an accident. We've got enough to cope with as it is without having the law out here nosing about.'

'I think she may have lied about the old squire,' Ellen said. 'I reckon she's been seeing someone else and it's him that done this to her.'

'Well, it's our fault for letting her wander off,' Tom countered. 'If I find out who did this, I'll make him pay. I promise you he won't get away with this, Ma.'

Mary Jane had come out of the dairy. She followed them into the kitchen, watching as Tom placed his sister's body gently on the old sofa.

'What's wrong with her?'

'She's dead,' Ellen said, tears were running down her cheeks. 'Our Carrie's dead, lass. Tom found her up by the hay barn.'

'She wasn't there when I walked back from my mother's last night. I went right past it and I'd have seen her.'

'Tom thinks she was put there.'

'You mean . . . she was murdered?' Mary Jane's face went white. 'No . . . she was all right when I saw her earlier . . .'

'I thought you said she wasn't near the hay barn?' Tom's gaze fixed on her face, his tone harsh. 'When did you see her?'

'I saw her when I left here yesterday. I wondered where she was going so I followed her . . . she went into the empty cottage on the Thornton estate.' Mary Jane swallowed hard. 'Don't look at me like that, Tom. I didn't know he was going to . . .'

'Who?' Tom moved towards her, his expression thunderous. 'What are you trying to say? Was she with someone – a man?'

'There was a horse tied to the post outside.' Mary Jane swallowed hard. 'I don't know whose it was, Tom. I just saw her go into the cottage and I left. I wanted to see my ma.'

'Why the hell didn't you tell us last night?' He took her by the shoulders and shook her. 'I might have found her alive.'

'Let go. You're hurting me.'

'Stop that, Tom. It isn't Mary Jane's fault.'

Tom let her go abruptly and she stumbled forward but righted herself by grabbing the back of a chair, looking at him sullenly.

'How was I to know she was in danger?'

'You couldn't have known but it's a pity you didn't tell us, lass.' Ellen looked at Tom. 'Where are you going?'

'To fetch the doctor and then to Wisbech. After that I'm going to Thornton's cottage. If that's where she was killed I might find evidence there . . .'

'Dick died because he went off in a temper the time Carrie was attacked. Think what you're doing, Tom.'

Tom glared at his mother. 'You don't want him punished?'

'Aye, I do — but do it the right way. Let the doctor give his opinion and then go to the law. If he killed her he should hang but I don't want you hung for murder. We can't manage the farm without you.'

Tom muttered beneath his breath and went out, leaving Mary Jane and Ellen staring at each other in silence.

'He won't do anything daft, will he?'

'Tom has more sense than his brother,' Ellen said. 'Sit down, lass. You look all in.'

'I feel shaky,' Mary Ellen said. 'If you don't mind I'll go upstairs and change the sheets on Carrie's bed. You'll want her laid out properly once the doctor has been.'

'Why don't you have a lie down yourself afterwards? You're as white as a sheet, lass.'

'I feel a bit odd,' Mary Jane said and then gave a little shriek and clutched at her belly. 'It hurts, Ellen. It's sharp like my courses only worse.' Her eyes widened in horror. 'I'm bleeding. I can feel it running down my leg.'

'Go up and lie on your bed.' Ellen looked at her sadly. 'It sounds like a miscarriage. I've had three in my time. The shock of seeing Carrie like that — and Tom shouting the way he did. He didn't know, lass. He'd have been more careful if he had.'

'Tom doesn't care,' Mary Jane said. 'He married me because

he needed a strong girl to work in the yard. He won't care that I've lost the baby.'

'You don't know that yet. Lie down and it might be all right. The doctor can take a look at you when he's done with Carrie.'

Mary Jane left the kitchen without looking at her. She'd been so happy tending Carrie's baby and thinking of her own child but now it was all spoiled. She wished she'd never met Tom that morning in the meadow. If he hadn't taken her to the dance she would've asked someone else – someone who wanted her for herself and not as a scullery maid.

'I'm sorry, Mary Jane,' Tom said as he entered the bedchamber they shared and found her curled up in bed. She'd been crying and her eyes were red. 'I shouldn't have shouted at you like that, lass. I was upset over Carrie but it wasn't your fault. According to the doctor, she was already dead by the time I came in for my supper last night. He can't be exact but he thinks probably yesterday afternoon.'

'*He* must have killed her when she went there,' Mary Jane said but didn't look at him. 'I've lost the baby, Tom. The doctor took him away. We would've had a son if . . .' She choked on a sob. 'Our little boy but he wasn't finished . . . he was only a little bit of a baby.'

Tom sat on the edge of the bed and reached for her hand. 'Please don't cry, Mary Jane. I'm more sorry than I know how to say. I've been neglecting you recently. If I'd noticed I would've got a lad to help with the milking. Forgive me for not realizing you weren't right.' A wave of guilt went over him because if he'd spent less time thinking of Roz he'd have noticed she was carrying his child.

'Ma said I should've told you sooner, but I wasn't sure. Besides, I thought I could work for a bit yet. Ma always works until the last few weeks.'

'You're not your ma and you had a shock – and then I shook you. If I'd known . . .' He put a hand to his eyes. 'I feel awful, Mary, lass. As if I killed him . . .'

'It wasn't your fault. The doctor said it could've happened even if I'd sat around and done nothing. He says it's like that sometimes. The babe – he wasn't right or something.' She sat up, wiping her cheeks with her fingers. 'What did he say about Carrie?'

'He thinks she might have hit her head on something and the force of the blow broke her neck. It would've been instant. He says she didn't suffer – but he thinks someone must have knocked her down.'

'I'd know that horse again if I saw it, Tom. It had a white bit on its left back leg.'

'A lot of horses have white bits on their hocks,' Tom said. 'The doctor says he's going to have the body examined by the coroner and then perhaps we'll know if it was murder or an accident.'

'Will the constable come and ask us questions?'

'Yes, I expect so. They may blame me for bringing her home instead of fetching someone to her – but I couldn't leave her there.'

'No, of course you couldn't, Tom.' Mary Jane reached for his hand and held it. 'Will you go to the cottage?'

'I went as soon as the doctor had been but there was nothing to see. The cottage is still furnished and it has been used recently, because the dust covers are off and someone had a fire there, but not as recent as yesterday.'

'Do you think that's where Carrie used to go? She often came home dry when it'd been raining.'

'We shall never be certain. I ought to have followed her like you did, Mary Jane. We wouldn't even have known she met someone at Thornton's cottage if it wasn't for you. At least I have something to go on.'

'You won't do what Dick did? I don't want you to die too.'

'I was angry enough to do it when I found her, but I've calmed down now. I don't know who was at the cottage, Mary, lass. If I ever discover the truth I might thrash him, but it would be best left to the law.'

'There's no proof, is there? You looked in the cottage but didn't see anything.'

'It didn't look as if there was a fight and I couldn't see any blood, but she didn't bleed much. A few drops could easily have been wiped up when he moved her – if that's what happened. We can't be sure it happened there. Someone might've attacked her on her way home.'

'Yes, perhaps a stranger. She could've have been killed in the struggle and left where she lay.'

'It didn't look that way. Her legs had been covered so that she was decent, and her head was turned to one side. She looked odd, unnatural, as if she'd been put there – but respectfully.'

'Perhaps whoever killed her liked her. He might not have meant to do it, Tom. An accident . . .'

'Yes, perhaps. Carrie was a nuisance at times. She wouldn't take no for an answer. If she was bothering him and he thought . . .' Tom shook his head. 'We can't know. Besides, I don't want you to lie here and worry about it, Mary Jane. You have to get well and strong again.'

'So that I can help your ma with the chores?'

'I know that's how it seems, lass, but it wasn't what I meant. I'm sorry if I've not treated you fair. I was going to get a lad in to help with the milking. I'll do it now rather than later. Once you feel like it you can look after Carrie's baby – unless that would upset you?'

'No, of course it wouldn't. I love Milly. She's beautiful and now there's no baby . . .' Mary Jane caught her breath. 'I'll soon be on my feet again. I can help with the baby and the cooking, but not the heavier chores for the moment.'

'Don't worry about them. We've done most of the fieldwork until spring. It's just hedging and maintenance, and a new shed for the extra stock I'll be buying, but they'll mostly be bullocks, a few cows – and some pigs.'

'I don't mind the milking when I'm strong enough. It's the butter churning that tires me.'

'We'll just make enough for ourselves,' Tom said. 'Once I've got things running smoothly I'll have more men and a girl to help in the house. It won't be hard work for ever, Mary Jane. I've got plans for the future. When there's more money we'll be taking a holiday at the sea every year, and not just Hunstanton either.'

Mary Jane smiled. 'I thought you didn't care about me, Tom. I don't mind the work if I know you love me.'

'I'm not much good with words,' he said and leaned down to kiss her on the mouth. 'I'm truly sorry for all this and I'll make it up to you when I can.'

'If I can help Ellen more in the house and not bother with so much in the yard, she will have things a bit easier. Your father is a tyrant, Tom. He pinches her when she tries to help him and throws things over her. He isn't as bad with me or you, but I'm sure he could use the commode. He makes out he's worse than he is because I've seen him sitting on the edge of the bed when he doesn't know I'm around.'

'She didn't tell me how bad he was getting,' Tom said and frowned. 'I'll fetch the doctor to him. If he's able to get out of bed, it would save the both of you fetching and carrying for him.'

Roz dismounted and gave the reins to the groom, lifting the skirt of her riding habit as she walked into the house. Julia was sitting in her favourite parlour, some sewing on her lap. She put it aside and stood up to greet Roz as she entered.

'I was just wishing you would visit me. I didn't hear the carriage?'

'I rode over. Are you making baby clothes?'

'Yes. I was smocking this gown. Doctor Hughes confirmed my hopes when he visited this morning. I am carrying Philip's child. I'm so lucky . . .' Julia's smile faded. 'Have you heard the terrible news, Roz? Carrie Blake was found with her neck broken yesterday morning.'

'No, I hadn't heard.' Roz sank down into the chair opposite. 'That is terrible. Did she have an accident?'

'I was told that she has been taken away to have a post mortem – I think that's what Doctor Hughes called it, but I may have it wrong. Special medical people are examining the body to find out how she died, apparently.'

'Surely they don't think it could be murder?'

'Murder?' Julia looked upset. 'Yes, I suppose that's what he must've meant. I didn't realize until you said – but they wouldn't go to all that trouble if they didn't think it was suspicious.'

'Where was she found?'

'Near the Blakes' hay barn, I think. Yes, I'm sure that's what I was told. Doctor Hughes told me he had been called to the farm – but I asked him because my housekeeper had heard rumours.' Julia frowned. 'I know Dick Blake killed your father but you let his brother win that archery prize for her, didn't you? Philip said you had done it deliberately.'

'Yes. I gave Carrie some clothes I didn't wear. I saw her daughter. She called her Milly.'

'Oh, I didn't realize you knew her. Was she really an idiot?'

'No, just dreamy and slow I would say.' Roz looked down at her hands. 'She was proud of her baby and herself.'

'That sounds a little odd – if she was raped. If it happened to me I don't think I could bear to look at the child.'

'Carrie wanted her baby. I'm not sure she was raped. I think she knew what she was doing. She didn't understand the trouble she caused.' She couldn't tell Julia the whole truth now. It would hurt her too much.

Julia looked thoughtful. 'Why would anyone want to kill a girl like that do you suppose?'

'I've no idea,' Roz said. Surely Philip wouldn't kill the girl. He would have forgotten all about Carrie in pursuit of his new mistress. Roz was fairly certain her brother had been seeing Madeline but of course she had no proof. 'Perhaps they'll discover that it was just an accident.'

'Yes, perhaps they will,' Julia agreed. 'They may not be able to prove anything. Doctor Hughes told me it is not an exact science, just informed guesswork that sometimes helps to decide how someone died.'

'We may never know the truth,' Roz said. 'May I see your work?' She took the garment from Julia and exclaimed over the stitching. 'Very pretty. I'm no good at smocking but this is lovely, Julia.'

The talk turned to babies and Julia invited her to see the nursery, which had been made ready for the baby. There were piles of new blankets, clothes and trinkets.

'I think it's bad luck to get all this stuff too soon,' Julia said. 'Philip insisted and sent for most of it from an expensive shop in Cambridge. It is sweet of him, but we can't be sure I shall have a son.'

'It doesn't matter, you can keep the blue things for another time and use just white. I prefer white for small babies anyway.'

'Yes, I do too.' Julia smiled. 'You will stop for luncheon, Roz?'

'Yes, thank you. Where is Philip?'

'I think he went to see someone on business. He says he wants to sell a piece of land and a cottage.'

'I thought he wanted to buy more land?'

'Yes, he does – but this land isn't much good, apparently. He wants John Blake's land, but I can't see the family accepting an offer from us – can you?'

'I hope he has the decency to wait for a while,' Roz said. 'They won't wish to deal with anything like that for a few months at least.'

'No, of course not. It is very sad, even if she wasn't quite right in the head.'

Roz didn't answer. Carrie knew enough to make trouble for Philip if she wanted – but perhaps she was worrying for nothing.

Her death might have been an accident – or perhaps she'd had an affair with another man and he'd killed her because she was a nuisance. Or was Roz simply trying to hide from a truth she feared?

'Can you arrange the sale quietly?' Philip asked his lawyer. 'I would rather not let people know I'm selling. It isn't that I'm short of money, you understand. I want to buy better land and the cottage and that bit near the lane is right on the edge of my estate. I shan't miss it, because it's only good for sheep or a plot to keep chickens and pigs on. What I want is that wild meadow and the stream.'

'That belongs to Tom Blake and I know he won't sell.'

'John Blake wouldn't sell to me, but he might sell to you. He's ill and he might feel he could use the money to make his last years more comfortable. You need not say where the offer comes from.'

'I know he won't sell whatever you offer,' lawyer Moss told him. 'Mr Harold Rushden has made a generous offer to the family. He increased the offer twice – more than the land is worth in my opinion, but all offers were refused.'

'Damn the stubborn fool,' Philip muttered. 'Just sell that cottage for me. There was an offer last year but I refused it.'

'I can contact the person who offered, but he may have purchased elsewhere. Did you say there's an acre with it?'

'Yes, thereabouts. It would do for a young man wanting to marry. There's enough land to make it worthwhile, and I'll reduce the price if I have to.'

'I'll do what I can for you, sir.'

'Thank you.'

Philip walked out into the street. It was a frosty winter's day and the small town was busy because it was market day. He walked past the stalls in the direction of the hotel because his mouth tasted like ashes and he needed a drink.

As yet, he seemed to have gotten away with Carrie's murder. Philip had waited until dark before fetching Carrie. His heart thudding with fear, he'd thrown her over the saddle and led his horse up to the hay barn. Philip had arranged the girl's body on the ground to look as if her neck had broken as she'd fallen, but he'd pulled her skirt down to cover her bare legs and buttoned up her bodice. Somehow he'd wanted her to look decent, give her a little dignity. Perhaps he ought not to have done that; he'd thought afterwards that it looked artificial. How would her body look if she'd fallen? Was anyone suspicious?

He couldn't change things now and there was no point in worrying himself sick over what he'd done. In truth it had been an accident because he hadn't meant to push her so hard that she fell against the chair with such force. The magistrates wouldn't believe him because he'd tried to cover up the death. Perhaps if he'd fetched someone and explained what had happened – but it would all have come out. Julia would turn from him in disgust if she guessed he was the father of Carrie's child. Their marriage contract was complicated and Philip wasn't sure how he would stand if she decided to leave him.

No one knew he'd had anything to do with Carrie. Roz knew that her child was his but Philip had warned her what he would do if she told her stories to anyone and she'd kept her mouth shut. She couldn't know that he'd seen Carrie since his marriage. Even Madeline hadn't guessed the body was under the table.

Philip breathed deeply. He was in the clear. No one was going to connect him to Carrie's death. Her brother had found her and taken her home. As far as anyone else knew, Tom Blake might have struck her because she was so much trouble to her family.

Philip saw Madeline and Sir Raymond enter the hotel and turned away. He didn't want to see her because it would bring back the memory that haunted him no matter how much he tried to put it out of his mind.

There was a pub in the next street. He would have a couple of drinks there before he went home.

Thirteen

'The evidence was inconclusive,' Tom said as he entered the kitchen where his mother and Mary Jane were baking. They had Milly's cot in the room and she was sleeping peacefully next to the fire. He went to look at her and smiled sadly before turning back to the two women. 'It has been recorded as an open verdict. We can bury Carrie as soon as we like. I asked the vicar and he said this Saturday. Is that all right, Ma?'

'Yes, whatever you think best.' Ellen paused in the act of thumping her pastry. 'I know someone killed her and so do you, Tom – but we can't grieve for ever over what can't be helped. At least they didn't blame you.'

'I was reprimanded for not summoning the constable when I found her but since I was working with others all day and here with you all night, they decided I couldn't have killed her.'

'No one in their right mind would think it was you, Tom,' Mary Jane said. 'It might have been one of those gypsy lads. Pa says they were camped in the copse on his land when it happened. He told the constable when he went into market and they wrote it down. The gypsies cleared off a day or so later without him having to tell them so it might have been one of them.'

'Yes, mebbe,' Tom said and held his hands to the fire. 'Once the funeral is over we can think about Christmas. I thought you might both like to go shopping in Wisbech?'

'I should like that,' Mary Jane said instantly. 'I want to buy things for Milly. She's growing fast and she needs some more clothes.'

'And something for yourself – Ma too.' Tom looked at his mother, who hadn't spoken. 'If you're worrying about Pa, I'll ask Granny Hubbard to watch him for a few hours.'

'He'll not stand for it. He threw something at her the last time she came.'

'Well, leave him on his own then. He can get up and sit on the commode if he wants. The old devil has you two at the end of his string and he knows it. Leave him alone for once and he'll come round to being more amenable.'

'I might. It's a long time since I went anywhere. I'm not sure I've got anything decent to wear, except my black dress that I keep for church – and I haven't been there since your pa was taken bad.'

'We could refurbish one of your old dresses and then buy some material to make some new things,' Mary Jane said. 'Tom is right, Ellen. We can leave him some food and drink on a tray and ask Granny Hubbard to pop in for a while. If he gets into trouble she'll see to him.'

'I'll think about it,' Ellen said and put her jam tarts into the range oven. 'Sit down and drink some tea, Tom.'

'I need to fetch some hay for the stock but I'll have a drink before I go out again.' He went to the sink and washed his hands, then glanced back at his mother. 'Don't think I've forgotten Carrie, Ma. If I find the man responsible, he'll pay for what he's done. I shan't kill him but I'll give him a good thrashing.'

'Why do you not visit me more often?' Lady Thornton complained as Roz was about to leave. 'It is an age since you were here, and I know you've seen Julia at least twice.'

'I'm sorry. Harry doesn't like me to be out too long in this weather. Anyway, you visit us all the time. Julia doesn't like to travel because she's carrying the baby.'

'I can understand you visiting her, but you might spare a few minutes for me.'

'Dine with us tomorrow. We are having a few friends in the evening and you could stay the night. That will give us plenty of time to talk before you return home.'

'My home was the hall. I have never thought of this house as home.'

'Perhaps you would be more content if you did, Mama.'

'Your father died before his time. Had that wicked man not murdered him I should have still been mistress at the hall.'

'I am sorry Father was murdered, but it is a long time ago now, Mama. Visit Julia more often. She likes to see you.'

'I heard that Blake girl was murdered. She was a bad lot and I blame her family. Had she not been allowed to roam all over the place none of this would have happened.'

'I'm sorry you are so unhappy here. I must go now or Harry will worry.'

Leaving her mother to mourn the comedown in her circumstances, Roz went out to the courtyard and mounted her horse. Harry would not be worrying about her because he had gone to Cambridge on business on the train and would not return until the evening. She had wanted to escape because after weeks of bitter weather it was a little milder, the sun shining despite it being mid December.

Roz was not certain why she chose to ride past the hay barn. She was trespassing on Tom Blake's land for the first time since the day Carrie's body had been discovered there. Before that, she'd ridden this way once or twice, but she'd never been lucky enough to see Tom.

As she got nearer the barn, she saw a man loading hay with a pitchfork on to a cart. He turned as she approached and looked at her; sticking his fork into the stack, he came to her as she dismounted.

'Tom,' she said. 'I wrote to your mother when I heard the dreadful news, but I was afraid to come to the cottage in case I distressed her.'

'Ma wouldn't blame you; why should she?'

Roz gave a little shiver as she glanced around her. 'This was our place. I wonder what Carrie was doing here – who she was meeting?'

'What makes you think she'd been meeting anyone?' Tom looked at her oddly, as if trying to read her mind.

'Someone killed her, Tom. Unless it was a chance meeting, she must have come here to meet him. Besides, my father wasn't the father of her child; she told me it wasn't the old squire.'

'The magistrate decided there was insufficient evidence to say whether it was murder or just a fall.' Tom's gaze narrowed. 'Did she tell you who the father was?'

Roz hesitated, then shook her head and turned away. 'I shouldn't be here. I ought to go.'

Tom took hold of her arm, swinging her back to face him. 'You know something, Roz. Tell me the truth – did Carrie tell you who fathered her child?'

'I can't,' Roz said, her throat tight with emotion. 'There's been too much hurt and pain already. It won't bring her back, Tom.'

His fingers tightened on her upper arms and he gave her a little shake. 'You must tell me what you know. She sometimes visited your brother's cottage – the one at the edge of your land. On the day she died she went there to meet someone. Mary Jane saw a horse with a white mark on its back hock tied up outside when Carrie went in. Was that Philip's horse, Roz? Did she tell you that he was the father of her child?'

'Don't ask me to tell you, Tom. Julia is expecting her first child. Even if Carrie did lie about my father – if someone else gave her a child – it doesn't mean that he killed her. Besides, I think Philip has been seeing someone else; a woman he met at my house. Why would he be meeting Carrie if he was having an affair with another woman?'

'You're protecting him, Roz. You know that your brother is Milly's father.'

'Even if that were true it wouldn't make him a murderer.'

'No, but it makes it more likely. If they used to meet at the cottage she might have gone there to make trouble. He might have killed her to stop her spoiling his love affair with this other woman.'

'You're surmising, Tom. You have no proof.' He was gripping both her arms, forcing her to face him. 'Please let me go. I shan't come here again. It's all spoiled . . .'

'What's spoiled?' Tom stared into her face and saw the tears she was barely suppressing. 'Roz, I'm sorry. This mess isn't your fault.'

'I thought of this as our place – the place where I was happy for a few hours.'

'Roz . . .' Tom groaned and drew her against him. He hesitated and then kissed her fiercely, hungrily, holding her pressed into his body. Roz clung to him. She loved him and all the rest was a sham. 'Damn it! I'm such a fool. I can't get you out of my head. I wish I'd never seen you.' He flung away from her, an expression of anguish in his eyes. 'If I'd been thinking of my sister I should've noticed what she was doing and made sure Ma kept her at home. It's my fault she's dead.'

'Don't say such things. Carrie would have found a way to

escape your mother whatever you did. I wish we'd gone away that night. Everything is a mess here. Let's go now. Let's run away together and forget all the horrible things.'

'You're saying that to make me forget about Philip. It's no use, Roz. We might have had a chance once but it's too late. We're both married. Mary Jane has just lost my child and she's grieving. I couldn't desert her and Ma. Go back to your husband, Mrs Rushden. You were never for me and I've always known it.'

'Please don't say that,' Roz begged, tears on her cheeks. 'I love you, Tom. I've tried to make a life with Harry, but it's you I love.'

'There's too much between us, Roz. Your father's murder, Dick's death – and Carrie. Don't worry, I'm not going to storm into your brother's house and accuse him in front of his wife. One day I'll find the proof that Philip killed Carrie in that cottage and dumped her body here and when I do . . .'

'You must go to the law. Don't kill him, Tom. Please don't ruin your own life. You loved me once even if you've decided to shut me out now, but I still love you. Please don't break my heart. If you hang for Philip's murder I shan't be able to live with the pain.'

'I'll thrash him but I shan't murder him,' Tom said, his lips white with temper. 'Go home, Roz, before I do or say something I'll regret.'

He gave her his hand, throwing her up into the saddle, then stood for a moment looking up at her.

'Goodbye, Tom.'

'Forget me, Roz. Try to shut me out of your mind, as I intend to shut you out of mine.' He slapped her horse on its rump, making it start forward.

Fighting to control the startled beast, Roz knew she was crying as she rode away. Her thoughts were confused, some of them too awful to contemplate. If Philip had killed Carrie he ought to be punished, but he wouldn't be the only one to suffer.

Julia was living in a little cocoon of content. Even if she suspected her husband of having an affair with Madeline she had shut it out because she was having a child and that made her happy. Roz's mother, too, would suffer if there was more scandal. Some of their friends had cut them after Roz's father was murdered; any further scandal might lead to them being ostracized altogether.

Roz didn't even want to think about Harry's reaction. He was generous with his money and most of the time he was polite and courteous to her, but she knew that he'd never forgiven her for not telling him the truth before they were wed. Their marriage was at best uneasy. If Harry ever guessed that she'd been with Tom Blake – but that secret was safe. She would never tell him; there was no point in hurting him. Her wild plea to Tom to run away had tumbled out because of her raised emotions, but even before he'd denied her she'd known it wouldn't happen.

He was right; however much it hurt she must put that day in the hay barn out of her mind and forget him, as he intended to forget her.

Tom scowled as he drove the cart back to the farm. He wasn't sure what had made him so harsh with Roz. Perhaps it was her refusal to betray her brother when she knew the truth. He cursed himself for a fool. Carrie had aroused his suspicions once or twice and he'd sensed that she had lied to them. Someone had put her up to lying that day and Tom believed it was the man who had given her the child. Philip Thornton had seduced Carrie and then, when she told him she was with child, he'd told her to keep his secret and blame his father.

It was Dick's tragedy that had kept Tom from going after Philip and thrashing him. Mary Jane's evidence had convinced him that it was most likely to be Philip who had killed Carrie, but there had to be a reason for him to do it after all this time. What had his sister done or said that made Philip Thornton desperate enough to kill her?

Tom dismounted from his cart and started forking the hay into the manger for the cows. His thoughts were gradually locking into place. He hadn't been certain that Philip was the one until he saw the look in Roz's eyes and knew that she suspected her brother of being Carrie's murderer.

'Damn . . .' Tom had been angry with her, partly because he was angry and partly because he'd known that he wanted to do exactly as she'd asked – just go and leave everything, run away somewhere he could forget all the grief and hurt. Except that he knew it wasn't possible. 'Trouble follows wherever you go . . .'

'What did you say?'

Tom turned to look at Mary Jane. He hadn't noticed her there, standing just behind him. She was carrying a jug of milk and had come from the dairy. She looked pretty with her soft hair blowing over her face and her cheeks pink from the wind. 'I was merely talking to myself.'

'They say that's the first sign.' Mary Jane gave him a mischievous look. It was some time since she'd flirted with him and Tom realized that she was beginning to feel better. 'I've heard there's a dance on in the church hall this Saturday. It's the Christmas dance, Tom, and everyone goes. Will you take me? It's been a long time since we went anywhere.'

He hesitated for a moment, then nodded. 'We might buy you a pretty dress ready made from the shop in Wisbech tomorrow. You'd like a new dress for the dance, wouldn't you?'

'Oh Tom, if I hadn't got the milk jug I'd hug you,' Mary Jane cried. 'You spoil me. You're the best husband a girl ever had.'

Tom remembered the way he'd kissed Roz half an hour earlier, the passion he'd felt and the longing to make love to her. Shame washed over him and he turned away from Mary Jane's bright smile.

'Go on up to the house and put the kettle on. I've just got to finish feeding the stock and then I'll be up for my tea.'

Mary Jane went off smiling to herself. She was so easy to please and he was a brute to wish that he was free to leave her and his parents. They couldn't manage without him. It was one of the reasons he hadn't gone rushing off to confront Philip Thornton. He might want to punish the man who had killed his sister, but if Tom were dead or in prison his family would be left to struggle alone.

Tom had arranged to buy another ten acres of pasture the other side of the stream. It was right on the edge of Harry Rushden's land and Tom was surprised that he hadn't bought it up before now. The owner had come to him personally and asked if he wanted to buy. He'd waited while Tom got the money together when he could almost certainly have asked more from Rushden. He hadn't known why until he was about to sign the papers.

'There's a condition to the sale,' the lawyer had told Tom when he went into his office after his other business in Wisbech was done. 'When you sell, you're not to let it go to Harold Rushden or Sir Philip Thornton.'

Tom paused with the pen in his hand. 'I wouldn't sell to either of them – but why is Baxter set against them?'

'He told me he had fallen out with them both at various times; that's why he sold to you for less than he could have got otherwise.'

'I wondered about that. He's no need to worry. They've both been after my land but I told them to go to hell.'

'Sign there then,' the lawyer told him. 'You've got yourself a bargain, Mr Blake. Mr Baxter has more land he may be selling in another year or so. If you wanted to improve your holding I could probably arrange a loan for you, sir.'

'A loan?' Tom hesitated. 'I'm not sure about borrowing from the bank. If I've got some spare cash I'll probably buy what I can afford at the time. I'd like more land but I'll wait until I can pay.'

'I thought that would be your answer, but it might be possible to raise money from a private source – all legal and with sufficient time to repay. It's up to you, of course, but you might like to give it some thought. If you want to be a successful businessman you sometimes have to take risks.'

'Thank you. I'll give the idea some thought.'

Tom was deep in thought as he finished his chores. With any luck he'd have more money coming in next year than ever before. He could choose to make life easier for his mother and Mary Jane or he could press on and buy more and more land. Until he met Roz Tom had been willing to settle for a life tied to his father's land, working for his keep and a few pounds he got for selling the pigs he reared. After Dick's death the farm had been left to him to manage and he'd begun to realize there were ways of improving their income that didn't rely solely on working longer hours. He might be a rich man one day if he set his mind to it, but it still wouldn't be enough. He was just a farmer and Roz was gentry. Even if neither of them were married the gap was too wide.

A part of Tom knew that money was nothing without a good home life and all the things that went it, like love and children. He'd seen respect in the lawyer's eyes when he'd bought that ten acres and spoken of buying more when he could afford it. Perhaps respect in the community was the next best thing – and that meant he couldn't rush off in a temper and thrash Philip Thornton to an inch of his life without proof of his guilt. He would just have to wait until the right moment.

'Attend the Christmas dance at the church hall?' Roz looked at her husband in surprise. 'Why would you want to go there, Harry? We are holding a party for our friends here on Christmas Eve – and the long gallery is big enough for a few couples to dance if you wish it.'

'Are you a snob, Roz?' Harry looked at her across the breakfast table. 'Most of the farmers take their wives and families to the Christmas dance; it is a local tradition.'

'My mother would never let Philip and I go – though we wanted to when we were younger.'

'You're a married woman now. I wasn't intending to ask your mother to come with us.'

'She would be horrified.' Roz laughed. There was no reason why she should not go. She couldn't even be sure that Tom Blake would be there. 'Yes, if you wish it, we shall go. I had no idea you liked dancing so much, Harry.'

'I doubt very much that I'll dance,' he said and pushed his chair back. 'I just like to mingle with the other farming families once in a while – and sometimes business is better done in a sociable atmosphere.'

'Ah, I see.' Now she understood. 'Why didn't you say it was business in the first place? About Christmas, Harry. Mama is dining with Julia and Philip on the day itself. I asked her to come and stay for a few days afterwards – is that all right?'

'You know I never interfere with your arrangements as far as Mama is concerned.' Harry went to the door and glanced back. 'I met Madeline and Raymond in Wisbech a few days ago. She asked me why I was avoiding them and I invited them to the Christmas Eve party. I suspect he may have cheated at cards the last night they were here, but I can't cut them completely.'

'As long as they do not intend to stay over Christmas?'

'Apparently your brother has asked them for Christmas Day,' Harry said and frowned. 'I tried to warn your brother about Raymond but he was very abrupt and practically told me to mind my own business. He's a fool if he gets too involved because he could lose all he gained through marrying Julia. You should warn him – or her.'

'I saw Julia a day or so ago but I'll talk to Philip next week if you think that would help. Julia is so wrapped up in the child that I would rather not distress her.'

'I should imagine it would distress her more if Philip lost the estate.'

Roz stared at the door as it closed behind him. She could hardly bear the thought of speaking to her brother; after her meeting with Tom Blake the previous day she was almost certain that Philip had killed Carrie.

The idea that her brother had killed the mother of his child made Roz sick to her stomach. If he'd killed her at the cottage he must have moved Carrie's body to where it had been found. Even the thought of what he'd done was so horrifying that she wanted to vomit. It would serve her brother right if he did lose everything at the card table – and yet the consequences for Julia and Roz's mother were not to be contemplated.

Roz rang the bell for the maid to clear the breakfast dishes, then she ran upstairs to change. She would ride over to the hall and see if her brother was about.

'Julia is resting,' Philip told her as she was shown into the study. Some thick ledgers lay on the desk before him. He closed the one nearest to him with a snap as his sister entered. 'You may go up to her if you wish, but don't tire her.'

'Actually I came to see you, Philip.'

'Why?' He got to his feet and stood in front of the window, gazing out at the gardens. 'You don't think that I had anything to do with that wretched girl's death, do you?'

'Now why I should I think that, Philip? You told me you wanted to talk. Is there some reason why I might suspect you?'

'No, damn you. You believed her lies before . . .'

'I didn't tell anyone, did I? It would have hurt Julia – and mother, because Julia would never have married you if she'd known. Does she know about you and Madeline? I saw you together in Wisbech.'

'Shut your stupid mouth or I might shut it for you.'

'Is that why you killed Carrie – to stop her talking? Had she seen you meeting Madeline? Carrie wasn't daft. If she thought you had another lover she might have told someone about her baby's father.'

'I warned you.' Philip shouted and suddenly lunged at her, striking her across the face. Roz recoiled, a hand to her cheek. 'If you breathe a word of your lies to anyone, I'll make you wish you'd never been born.'

Suddenly it was all clear to Roz and she knew just what had happened.

'You were meeting Madeline at the cottage. Carrie turned up and you had to get rid of her – is that how it was?' Roz saw the colour leave his face and sensed she was right. 'I'm not the only one who knows Carrie was there that afternoon, Philip. Someone saw her enter the cottage and your horse was outside. You think you've got away with it but one of these days someone will discover the truth about you.'

'Damn you, be quiet!' Philip grabbed Roz by the throat. Roz kicked his shins and jerked back just as someone knocked at the door. He swore and let her go. 'Bitch! I should've taught you a lesson a long time ago.'

Roz turned away, a hand to her throat as one of the servants entered.

'Madam is asking for you, sir. She feels unwell and thinks she may need the doctor.'

'I'm coming. Get out,' Philip snapped, glaring at his sister as the door closed behind the unfortunate maid. 'One word of this to anyone and I'll make you sorry.'

'More threats, Philip? You can go to the devil for all I care.'

Roz left the room and ran through the hall, ignoring the curious looks of the servants. Nothing went unnoticed in a house like this, even if you were discreet. Her brother was a brute and any doubt she'd had of his guilt had gone. If the maid had not come at that moment, he might have killed her.

Harry entered her bedroom as she was dressing for dinner that evening. He seemed pleased about something and moved towards her eagerly then stopped, his eyes narrowing.

'Is that a bruise on your cheek?'

'Does it show too much? I've tried to cover it, Harry – but

if it looks awful perhaps you should go to the dance on your own this evening.'

'There's a mark on your neck too. Who did that to you, Roz?'

'I can cover my neck with lace and my pearls, but I can't do much about this.' Roz touched her cheek. 'I had an argument with Philip this morning . . .'

'Your brother hit you?' Harry's mouth thinned. 'Damn him. I'll give him a thrashing.'

'No, please, Harry.' Roz reached out to him. 'Julia isn't well. If you quarrel with Philip it may upset her.'

'Be damned to Julia. You don't expect me to stand by and do nothing after this? I'm a man not a weakling, Roz. I protect what is mine.'

'Yes, Harry. I'm sure you could thrash Philip — and to be honest, he deserves it. He is violent and this is not the first time he has hurt me, but Julia is vulnerable and I should hate it if she lost the child. I dare say he will apologize when he calms down.'

'He'll grovel or I'll give him a taste of his own medicine, Roz. You know I'm not a violent man, but you're my wife. I've no wish to harm Julia but if he hit you for warning him about gambling he's out of control.'

'It wasn't just about Sir Raymond . . .' Roz said and then wished she hadn't. 'Philip was the father of Carrie Blake's child, not my father. Something I said made him imagine I was accusing him of . . .'

'Her murder?' Harry frowned. 'I know there was insufficient evidence but there was an open verdict. People are talking about murder. You don't think it was Philip?'

'No, of course not,' Roz said quickly, too quickly. 'The magistrate said there was insufficient evidence. No one knows if it was murder — and there's no evidence against Philip. She might have been seeing someone else. I know there were gypsies in the area at the time because I saw them when I was out riding.'

'Why would a gypsy want to kill a girl like Carrie Blake? She was harmless, if a bit slow. Only an evil bugger would murder a girl like that — and if Philip did that he deserves more than a thrashing.'

'I shouldn't have told you.' Roz caught at his arm. 'Please don't do anything foolish, Harry.'

'He's not getting away with what he did to you, Roz,' Harry said quietly. 'I'll wait until after Christmas because I know you want to see Julia and your mother – but after that I'll have it out with him. If he killed that girl he must give himself up, Roz.'

'Think of the scandal, Harry. Mother would never hold up her head again.'

'More fool her then. We don't know anything for sure, Roz – but I shan't let this rest. If Philip attacked his own sister he's more than capable of killing that girl.'

'Yes, I know.' Roz shuddered and closed her eyes for a moment. 'Do you still want to go this evening?'

Harry took a moment to answer. 'I think I should, but if you would rather not you can stay home and have an early night.'

'No, I'll come with you. If anyone asks about the bruise I'll say I fell when out riding. You promise you won't do anything foolish?'

'I've told you I'll bide my time,' Harry said and smiled at her. 'If you'd told me he'd hit you before I would have sorted him out. He won't do it again, Roz.'

Fourteen

Tom caught his breath as he saw her come in with Harry Rushden. When Mary Jane asked him if he would bring her to the dance he hadn't given a thought as to who else might be here. He certainly hadn't expected to see Roz this evening. She was wearing what was for her a simple evening gown in grey silk with lace ruffles at the neck but she made every other woman in the room look dowdy. His throat tightened and he experienced a fierce desire to go to her and take her in his arms.

'Why are you looking so cross, Tom?'

Mary Jane's petulant tone made him look at her. 'I'm not cross. Do you want to dance? I think they've just announced a barn dance.'

'Yes, please.' She took his hand as they joined the other dancers on the floor for the progressive. 'Did you see Roz Thornton? I wonder what she paid for that dress?'

'More than I pay for a year's feed for the stock I should think,' Tom said harshly. 'Don't envy her, Mary Jane. She doesn't look particularly happy.'

'I'd rather have you than her husband,' she said and pressed herself close as the music started. 'And I like my dress better than hers, even if hers cost more.'

'Just as well, because you're not likely to get a dress like that — not yet, anyway.'

'You'll be rich one day,' she said, smiling up at him. 'You're going places, Tom Blake. I knew that when I set my cap at you that day in the meadow.'

'You're a bold one, lass.' Tom laughed, because it was nearly Christmas and he had a pretty wife who pleased him in bed and he ought to thank his lucky stars rather than hanker after a woman he couldn't have.

'We'll sit this one out,' Harry said as he steered Roz to one of the empty seats at the far end of the large room. The wives of the wealthier farmers had gathered together, most of them watching the younger people dancing. Like him, their husbands had come to see and be seen, and to talk business. The married women were satisfied with a glass of cordial and the chance to gossip. 'Would you like a drink, Roz?'

'Not sweet sherry,' she said. 'I wouldn't mind wine – or just a fruit cordial if that's all they have.'

'It probably will be at an affair of this kind,' Harry said. 'Sit next to Bristow's wife. Her father was a parson and she's a nice enough woman.'

'Yes, I think we've met at church,' Roz said and sat down next to the elderly lady. 'Good evening, Mrs Bristow. It is crowded this evening, isn't it?'

'Mrs Rushden,' the lady said and glanced at her cheek. Roz knew she'd noticed the bruise despite her efforts to hide it. 'These things are a little noisy. It's the children running around, but it's meant to be a family affair.'

'Yes, I know. I always wanted to come when I was a little girl but my mother wouldn't allow it.'

'Your father came on his own – and with your brother at times. How is his wife? I heard the doctor had been to see her today.'

'Yes. I haven't heard anything so I suppose it was nothing serious.'

'I am glad about that,' Mrs Bristow said. 'She is a lovely lady and comes to church regularly. She was supposed to help with the Christmas bazaar but cried off last week because she felt she ought to rest.'

'Julia wouldn't do anything that might harm the baby.'

'She is very excited about starting a family.' Mrs Bristow's eyes seemed to hold a question.

Roz knew that she was wondering if there was any similar news from the Rushden house but she just smiled and then looked at Harry as he brought her lemonade.

'Are you all right for the moment if I speak to a few people, Roz?'

'Yes, perfectly,' Roz said. 'Do whatever you wish, Harry. I'm happy to watch the dancing.'

He departed and Roz saw that he made for a group of farmers and businessmen who had gathered together and were laughing quite loudly in one corner of the room. Her gaze moved round the room. She smiled as she saw some children dancing with each other. Then she saw Tom Blake dancing; it was a progressive and he was partnering a young woman Roz didn't know by sight. A little further through the line of dancers Mary Jane was dancing with another young man. She was laughing up at him and Roz recognized him as one of her brother's grooms.

Roz sipped her lemonade. The room was very warm and her head had begun to ache. Her cheek was tender and she wished that she had taken Harry up on his offer and let him come alone.

Finishing her drink, she decided that she would go outside into the garden. The door was a short distance from where she was sitting. She could take a breath of air and return before Harry noticed she was missing.

'I think I need a little air,' she told Mrs Bristow. 'I shan't be long.'

'Are you all right, my dear? Should I fetch your husband?'

'No, no, I'm fine,' Roz said. 'Just a little warm.'

She wove her way through the crowd, smiling as a young girl charged into her and then blushed as she apologized.

Outside, the light from the windows made it easy to find her way to a wooden bench. Roz sat down, breathing deeply. It was so foolish of her to feel hurt because there was no reason she should. Tom had every right to bring his wife to the dance and to look happy. She had no right to resent that or to feel regret. Harry cared for her, loved her: he had wanted to thrash Philip for hurting her.

Tears pricked her eyes but she refused to cry. What a selfish person she was to feel sorry for herself when she had so much. She heard a burst of loud music and laughter as the door to the hall opened and then closed. Roz didn't look round, hoping that whoever had come out wouldn't see her.

'You'll get cold if you sit out here long.' Roz turned as she heard Tom's voice. He sat down on the wooden bench beside her. 'I saw you come out and followed when the dance ended.'

'I just wanted a little air. The room felt warm and my head started to ache.'

'Are you unwell? Shall I call your husband?'

'No, please do not. Harry came for a reason. He wants to talk to people. I shall come back inside in a few minutes. You should go in or your wife will look for you.'

'Mary Jane is dancing with Jack Dawson. She won't notice I'm not there for a while.'

Roz turned to look at him. Tom was silent for a moment, then he reached out to touch her cheek. 'Did your husband do this to you?'

'Harry isn't a violent man. Philip hit me and then tried to strangle me.' Roz caught her breath as she saw the anger in his eyes. 'Harry wanted to thrash him for me. I begged him not to.'

'Why did he attack you?'

'Because he thought I was accusing him of something.'

'Were you?'

'Yes and no.' Roz shook her head. 'I think you are right to believe your sister was murdered, Tom – but I have no proof. Nothing has changed from the other day.'

'Hasn't it? Philip lost his head for a reason, Roz. I'll be speaking to him myself one of these days. He needs to be taught a lesson.'

'Not on my account. I told you how I feel the other day. If they arrested you for Philip's murder I don't think I could bear it.'

'I love you, Roz. I know I told you to forget me but it's no use, I can't get you out of my head.'

'What you said was right – we have to,' she said, tears on her cheeks now as she stood up. 'I want to run away with you, Tom – but we both know it's too late.'

'Roz . . . hush,' he said and leaned towards her, brushing his lips over hers. From behind them the sound of loud music told them someone had opened the door to the hall. Roz drew back sharply.

'I have to go back,' she said and took a step forward, then gave a little gasp as the world around her suddenly went black and she fainted. Tom was there to catch her as she fell.

Roz moaned and opened her eyes, looking up into Harry's anxious face as he bent over her.

'Where am I?'

'Mr Blake said you fainted. He carried you in here – it's the ladies' rest room.'

Roz felt the coarse horse hair sofa beneath her and realized that several anxious eyes were watching her: Mary Jane, Harry, Mrs Bristow and Tom Blake amongst them.

'I went out for a little air,' she said. 'I think Mr Blake saved me from a fall. It was fortunate that you were there, sir. Thank you.'

'Glad to be of help,' Tom said stiffly. He took hold of his wife's arm. 'Come on, Mary Jane, we'll leave Mr and Mrs Rushden alone. They don't want us gawking at them.'

Mrs Bristow moved towards Roz and offered her a small bottle of lavender water. 'Put a little of this on the back of your hand and sniff it,' she said. 'I always carry it and it helps with the nausea in your condition, my dear.'

'My condition?' Roz looked at her. 'You think . . . perhaps. I hadn't thought about it, but that might be why . . .' Harry was frowning as she sat up. 'Mrs Bristow is suggesting that I might be pregnant.'

'I may be wrong, but I did think it might be the case earlier,' the elderly lady said and accepted her lavender water back, nodding as Roz inhaled the scent from the back of her hand. 'Well, if you've recovered now, I'll leave you together.'

The other curious watchers had departed with Tom and his wife. Harry sat down beside Roz on the sofa. He reached for her hand, a tender and yet anxious expression in his eyes.

'Did you have any idea? You didn't tell me, Roz.'

'Because I hadn't thought about it. I suppose I should have noticed – I haven't had my courses for . . . it must be seven weeks.'

'I'll fetch the doctor to you in the morning.' Harry kissed her hand. 'You shouldn't have come this evening.'

'Please don't blame yourself, Harry. I was enjoying watching the dancing and then I felt a little unwell so I went out for some air. It was fortunate that Mr Blake also wanted some air. He saved me from a fall.'

'Yes, I must thank him properly,' Harry said. 'I've been trying to buy some land from him for weeks but he wasn't interested. Baxter told me he bought some of his land; it was something I was after but now I've got another proposition for Blake. I'll speak to him on Monday, after we've got you sorted. I think you should have the doctor from Wisbech over. He's better than our local man.'

'Doctor Hughes is very good,' Roz said and smiled at him.

'I'm feeling better now. It was so foolish of me to faint like that – forgive me?'

'I should be the one asking for forgiveness – and that brother of yours. If he's harmed you, I shall thrash him whatever the consequences.'

'I'm sure he hasn't. Would you mind if I went home now, Harry? You can stay longer if you wish. The carriage can return for you in an hour or two.'

'I'll come home with you. There's nothing more I need to do tonight.' His eyes glowed with pride. 'A child, Roz. Until now I didn't know how much it would mean – but I'm thrilled.'

'I'm so pleased.' She took his hand and he helped her to her feet. 'Don't worry. I'm not faint now. I can walk to the carriage.'

'Take my arm and lean on me if you feel faint,' Harry said. 'There'll be no more riding about the countryside on a horse until you're over the baby, Roz. If you want to visit your mama you can take the carriage – or send it to fetch her. You must take care of yourself now.'

'I'm not an invalid. I'm just having a baby – and we're not sure of that yet.' Roz smiled because his concern was touching. 'Thank you so much for caring, Harry. I know I haven't always deserved your love.'

'That's over and done,' he replied. 'This is my child, Roz, and the rest is forgotten.'

'Yes,' she said, but as she took his arm and walked from the room, she was wondering. If she was seven or eight weeks pregnant, it could be Tom Blake's child . . .

'Why did you go outside?' Mary Jane asked. They were alone in their bedchamber and she was dressed in a white cotton nightdress sprigged with blue flowers. 'Was it to meet her?'

Tom didn't look at her as he took off his breeches and then pulled on his nightshirt. 'Don't talk daft, woman. Why should I want to meet Mrs Rushden?'

'I don't know – unless she's the one you want.' Mary Jane's face was sullen. 'I know there was someone else – someone you wanted more than me. You took me because you couldn't have her.'

'That's ridiculous. When do I have time to be meeting another woman?'

'I don't know. I know you don't love me the way you ought. You married me because I was willing and you needed someone to help your ma.'

'Is this just because I was there when Roz fainted?' Tom sat on the edge of the bed. 'You're being silly, Mary Jane. Come to bed and let's get some sleep. It will soon be morning and I've got work to do.'

'All you think about is work.' She got into bed reluctantly and lay stiffly beside him as he slid between the sheets.

Tom snuffed out the candle and turned towards her. 'Make up your mind, lass. One minute you're accusing me of wanting another woman, the next you're saying all I think of is work – which is it?'

'Why did you go outside, then?'

'To pee if you must know,' he said. 'There was a queue for the lavatory so I went out – and I saw her swaying. I just managed to catch her and that's all there was to it. Now will you let me get some sleep?'

'Go to sleep then,' Mary Jane said and turned on her side.

Tom heard her sniffles. He knew she wanted him to take her into his arms and love her but he couldn't. All he could think of was the bruise on Roz's cheek and the smell of her perfume as he'd carried her into the restroom. Tom had called for help and her husband had come in before Roz recovered her senses. He'd had to stand back and watch as Rushden took over, and that hurt like hell.

Mrs Bristow had smiled and told him not to worry. She'd hinted that Roz was possibly carrying her husband's child. Tom knew that he had no right to resent the likely explanation for her fainting, but he couldn't help the tide of anger rising inside him. He knew he'd been quiet all evening and wasn't surprised that Mary Jane had picked up something.

He put his arm around her and kissed the back of her neck. 'Go to sleep, love. I'm tired. It will be all right tomorrow.'

Mary Jane turned over and flung her arm about his neck. 'I love you, Tom. I'm sorry I lost our baby. She's having a baby, isn't she? That's why she fainted.'

'I don't know,' Tom said. 'If she is it's her business not ours. Now let me go to sleep.'

Mary Jane moved to her side of the bed. Tom knew she was

hurt but he just couldn't rouse himself to do what she wanted. He loved Roz so much it was like a physical pain in his guts. It didn't matter how many times he told himself to be sensible: he still wanted her and something told him he always would.

Her brother was a brute and one of these days Tom would pay him back for Carrie – and for what he'd done to Roz.

Philip stared at his wife as she lay curled up in bed, her eyes closed. The doctor had told him it was touch and go whether she held on to their child.

'She isn't built for child bearing, sir,' Doctor Hughes had said when he visited. 'If I were you I should cancel Christmas in this house. Your wife needs rest and care or she will lose the child.'

'But we have people coming for the day.'

'Then you will have to entertain them yourself or put them off,' the doctor replied. 'Unless you wish to lose both the child and your wife? I'm advising you that any excitement or distress might cause her to miscarry and she could die.'

Philip felt nothing but annoyance as he now looked at Julia. Why couldn't she do a simple thing like carry a child full term without all this fuss?

'I hope you are going to get up and come downstairs on Christmas Day?'

Julia raised her head to look at him. 'I'm not sure I should, Philip. The doctor told me I must stay in bed for a few weeks until I'm stronger.'

'Hughes is an old woman. You look perfectly well to me. If you force me to cancel our arrangements I shall not stay here to play nursemaid. I can get a decent dinner in the hotel in Wisbech and I'll invite Madeline and Raymond there.'

'No, please, you mustn't,' Julia said, a tear sliding from the corner of her eye. 'Have them here and I'll come down for a while.'

'I don't wish to force you, Julia, but I'm sick of seeing you lie there like a dead thing.'

'Please don't say things like that,' Julia begged. 'I want to see Roz. Why hasn't she visited? Have you quarrelled with her?'

'What makes you think that?' Philip's eyes narrowed. 'If anyone has been telling tales they'll be sorry.'

'So you have quarrelled with her,' Julia said. 'Please leave me alone to rest, Philip. You have what you want, now let me sleep – and send one of the servants to ask Roz to call on me.'

Philip walked out. He had no intention of sending for his sister. The last thing he needed was Roz telling tales to his wife. He was already in debt to Sir Raymond and unless he could win back some of his losses he would have to borrow money from the bank again. Julia was in no fit state to go begging to her aunt. If he could manage until the child was born, Lady Mary might feel more like giving them a few thousand guineas to get him out of a scrape.

'I can cancel the Christmas Eve party,' Harry offered over breakfast that morning. 'If you don't feel up to it, Roz, we'll simply put it off for this year. Your mama can come and stay, naturally, for as long as you wish – but I don't want you to tire yourself.'

'I feel wonderful,' Roz said and laughed at his concerned expression. 'Honestly, Harry, I've never felt better. The doctor told me that the sickness and fainting is often a temporary thing. He says I am carrying the child well, much better than poor Julia. He advised her to keep to her bed. I am to carry on as normal because I'm perfectly healthy.'

'I'm glad but you must still take care. I shouldn't want to lose you.' Harry touched her hand across the table. 'If you wish to visit Julia, please take the carriage.'

'I should like to visit her, but only if you have the time to come with me. I don't feel like facing Philip alone.'

'Yes, of course I'll come,' Harry said. 'My business can wait until after Christmas. If Philip is there I shall give him an ultimatum. Should he abuse you again I'll thrash him to an inch of his life.'

'He wouldn't dare to harm me with you there. I've made up my mind not to go there alone again. I do not wish to see him ever again but Julia is my friend. I am concerned for her – and I should tell her our news, Harry.'

'Do you have a present to give her? We can take the Christmas things over so that you do not have to visit again.'

'I have gifts for Julia and the baby but nothing for Philip.'

'Quite right. He doesn't deserve anything.' Harry frowned.

'Unless the idiot pulls himself together he is going to ruin them all and lose the estate.'

'Have you heard something?' Harry nodded. 'If he does lose everything it serves him right – but what about Julia and Mama?'

'I have a decent house on the estate which has become empty recently. I was going to lease it again but your mama could have it – and I suppose Julia could live with her if the worst happened, but we must hope it won't. Depending on the size of the debt I might settle it for Philip – on the understanding that he becomes my tenant and the hall is my property.'

'He would never agree. I know Philip. He will borrow from the bank until they foreclose and he loses everything.'

'Well, that is his privilege. We shall have to wait and see, Roz – but don't worry about your mother and Julia. I wouldn't see them starve.'

'No, I know,' Roz said, her throat tight. 'You are so generous, Harry. I don't know what I've done to deserve you.'

'You married me and now you're having our child.' Harry got up, came round the table to kiss her cheek and whisper in her ear. 'I love you, Roz. I'll tell them to get the carriage ready in half an hour. I have a letter to write so take your time getting ready.'

Roz watched him walk from the room. Harry was kind and generous. At times he could seem distant, but at the moment he couldn't do enough for her.

She told herself that her afternoon with Tom Blake was no worse than Harry's affair with Madeline. She had forgiven him – but he would never forgive her if he guessed that the child she was carrying might not be his.

Of course the baby was Harry's. It had to be. Anything else was unthinkable, and yet the timing was so close that Roz knew she *could* be carrying Tom's child.

'Roz . . . thank you so much for coming,' Julia said as she entered and placed her armful of gifts on the dressing table. 'Did Philip send for you? I've wanted to see you so much.'

'I came as soon as I could once I learned you weren't well. I'm so sorry to see you like this, dearest. You were so very happy.'

'I am trying to save my baby. The doctor says that if I rest for a few weeks it should be all right, but I mustn't be upset or I may lose it.'

'Then you must keep to your bed, Julia. I know Harry would insist on my resting if I were to become unwell . . .' She smiled as Julia stared at her. 'Yes, I wanted you to know. I shall tell Mama on Boxing Day so please do not mention this to anyone – but I'm having a child too.'

'That is lovely,' Julia cried and sat forward as Roz bent to kiss her. 'They will be cousins and friends one day. We shall have so much in common, so much to share.'

'Yes, I feel that too,' Roz said and sat on the edge of the bed. 'I just wish you were not so unwell.'

Julia reached for her hand. 'I do feel better now that you are here.' She hesitated, then: 'You wanted to tell me something before I married Philip. He doesn't love me, Roz, but I've always known that – and I truly don't mind if he has an affair, but I feel there is something more. He is trying to hide it but his temper is awful and he frightens me sometimes.'

'Philip shouldn't lose his temper with you.' Roz held her hand. 'Harry could have a word with him if you wish, try to find out what is upsetting him?'

'He mustn't know I asked. He would be furious with me.'

'He is a beast to be unkind to you. If it were not for you – but I mustn't say. He makes me angry at times but he is your husband.'

'And your brother.'

'Sometimes I wish he wasn't.'

'I shouldn't have married him. Paul told me to wait and find someone else. He thought your husband would suit me – but I knew Mr Rushden had eyes only for you. You are very fortunate, Roz.'

'Yes. I have become very fond of you, Julia. I hate Philip for hurting you.'

'No, don't hate him. I love him no matter what he does. Love is like that, isn't it?'

'Perhaps. Harry might be able to help if Philip has money problems.'

'You don't think Philip has run through the money already?' Julia looked stunned. 'I know he's made improvements to the house and was talking of buying land – but he couldn't have gambled it away, could he?'

'I know he has been playing for high stakes. Harry thought – well, I must not say, but Philip should be careful of Sir Raymond and his wife.'

Julia was silent for a moment. 'Philip is having them here on Christmas Day. He says I should get up while they are here. I promised I would . . .'

'You shouldn't let him bully you.' Roz squeezed her hand. 'Let Philip go to the devil in his own way, Julia. If you need help, send for us. Harry wouldn't stand by and see you in trouble.'

'Oh Roz, I do love you,' Julia said and held her hand to her cheek. 'I couldn't bear it if we weren't friends any more. Philip is reckless and careless. I don't know why he couldn't be more like you.'

'I'm a long way from perfect, but I care about the people who are close to me, Julia. If Philip becomes unbearable come to us and we'll look after you when the baby comes.'

'Philip would be furious if I did that.' Julia sat back against the pillows. 'Why do things have to be so horrible, Roz? All I wanted was a home and a family.'

'I know. I'm sorry, dearest. I wish I could force some sense into Philip's head.'

'Your presents are on the settee under the window.' Julia brushed the tears from her cheek. 'I'm not going to be miserable. Next year I'll have a baby to love and care for – and so will you.'

'Yes, I shall. It doesn't matter about Philip, Julia. We'll have each other and the children.'

'And you have Harry.'

'Yes, I have Harry.'

Roz stood up and went to the window. 'It has started to snow. I think Harry and I should leave before it comes down too hard. I'll come and see you when I can after Christmas.'

Roz was fighting the urge to weep. She had much more than Julia to look forward to; why then was she so desperately unhappy?

Fifteen

Attending church on Christmas morning with her husband and mother, Roz noticed that Tom Blake's wife and mother were in the congregation, though he was absent and so was Philip.

'I know Julia isn't well enough to attend,' Lady Thornton whispered to her as they took their places, 'but Philip ought to have made the effort. It's too bad of him, Roz. He should set an example.'

'Philip seems not to care what people think of him.'

Lady Thornton gave her a hard stare but Roz refused to enlarge on her statement. As the service began a few seconds later the conversation was forgotten and it was not until they left the church that Roz knew anything was wrong. She exchanged a few words with neighbours and was about to enter her husband's carriage when one of Philip's grooms came forward.

'May I speak to you, Mrs Rushden?'

'Yes, of course. Is something the matter?'

'The master sent me. He said to tell you that the mistress is ill and wishes to see you.'

'Julia is ill?' Roz stared at him in concern. 'Is the doctor with her?'

'He was sent for after her fall, Mrs Rushden.'

'Julia had a fall?'

'She fell downstairs this morning. She was in terrible pain and the master sent for the doctor straight off.'

'Is something wrong, Roz?' Harry had stopped to speak to a friend. 'What does this fellow want?'

'Julia has had an accident. We must go there immediately, Harry. She has fallen down the stairs. The doctor told her she ought not to get up but Philip wanted her to go down because they had guests.'

'Damned fool,' Harry muttered. 'I suppose you want to visit her, Roz?'

'Yes, I must. I'm afraid she may lose the child. It is all Philip's fault.'

'Roz!' Lady Thornton looked at her angrily. 'You should not blame your brother. Whatever has happened it was clearly an accident.'

'I'm not saying Philip pushed her but he should not have made her get up when the doctor said she must rest.'

'You are too ready to blame your brother.'

Roz bit back a hasty retort. Lady Thornton would not listen to criticism from Roz. Goodness knows what she would think if Roz implied that not only was Julia's accident entirely Philip's fault, he was also a murderer.

Following her mother into the carriage, Roz was silent as they were driven to the hall. Her brother deserved to be punished for his lack of consideration for others but Roz could never do anything that would hurt Julia more than she'd already been hurt.

There was a hush over the house as Roz and the others walked in a few minutes later. The housekeeper came hurrying towards them, her face grave.

'How is my daughter-in-law?' Lady Thornton asked. 'How did she come to fall down the stairs – the silly girl.'

'She turned dizzy, ma'am.'

'I shall go up and see her at once.'

'The doctor is with her, madam.' She hesitated and then looked at Roz. 'The mistress was calling for you, Mrs Rushden. The doctor said you were to go up as soon as you arrived.'

Roz glanced at her mother. 'Perhaps you should wait for a while, Mama? The doctor will not wish for two of us at once.'

'Very well.' Lady Thornton looked annoyed. 'I should like a cup of tea.'

'Yes, my lady. The guests left soon after the accident happened and the master went out as soon as the doctor arrived.'

'Philip left Julia alone?'

Roz was shocked. Philip was callous but this was beyond anything. Seeing confirmation in the housekeeper's eyes, Roz went hurriedly from the room. Had Philip walked in at that moment she would have struck him.

Approaching Julia's bedchamber she heard the sobbing cries and her heart caught. It sounded as if her worst fears were coming true.

As she entered the bedchamber she saw the doctor and a midwife bending over Julia as she screamed and writhed. Then the midwife drew something away from her and looked down at the child's body. It was very tiny and looked blue. She shook her head and turned away, wrapping the lifeless body in some clean linen.

'No!' Julia wailed. 'My baby. Give me my baby.'

'She is dead. It's best you don't see her.'

'Please, I want to see her.'

'Let her see the child,' Roz said and took the bundle from the midwife. Opening it, she was shocked to see how tiny the child was and yet she was perfect in every way other than her colour. 'Here she is, Julia.'

Roz placed the bundle in Julia's arms and sat beside her on the edge of the bed.

'She is lovely,' Julia sobbed. 'I thought there was something wrong with her.'

'She was born too soon; otherwise she was perfectly normal,' the doctor told her. He had finished his work and turned away to wash his hands. 'In time you may have another child, Lady Julia, but next time perhaps you will take my advice and stay in bed.'

'It wasn't Julia's idea to get up,' Roz said, defending her. 'She was asked to go down. Philip should have known better.'

'Where is he?' Julia asked, tears slipping down her cheeks. 'He should be here to see her.' She kissed the child's face. 'My poor little girl.'

'I am so sorry, dearest. You must rest now and Philip will come soon. I should have been here sooner had I known but we were not told until we left church.'

'I'm so glad you were here. I didn't mean to kill my baby, Roz. I just missed my step and turned dizzy.'

'Philip should never have asked you to get up.' Roz stroked her hair. 'Please don't blame yourself, Julia. It wasn't your fault.'

'I should have stayed in bed, as you told me.' Julia gave the child back to Roz, who returned her to the midwife, who took her out of the room. 'She should have a name. I'll call her Rosemary.'

'Yes, she was like a little rosebud,' Roz agreed and held her hand. 'Try to rest now, Julia. You need to sleep.'

'I shall give you something to help,' the doctor said. 'In the morning you will feel better.'

Julia moved her head negatively on the pillow. Her fingers closed about Roz's hand. 'Stay with me, please? I know it's Christmas Day and I've ruined your celebrations, but please – just until I fall asleep.'

'Yes, of course,' Roz said. 'Harry and Mama are here. Do you want to see Mama?'

'No. I don't want to see anyone but you, Roz.'

'Then I shall send them home and stay with you for a few days,' Roz told her. 'Take the sleeping draught, Julia. I shall sit here with you while you rest.'

'Thank you.' Julia smiled and took the small glass offered her, swallowing the liquid obediently. She lay back with a sigh and closed her eyes.

'I should be glad if you would stay with her for a day or so,' the doctor told Roz. 'She is strong and her body will recover but she needs rest and care.'

'I intend to stay. Would you ask my husband to step up when you go down, sir?'

'Yes, of course. It is nice to see you looking so well, Mrs Rushden. You mustn't tire yourself. Allow the servants to look after Lady Julia. All she needs from you is friendship and a little kindness.'

'Do not be anxious, sir. I shall not put my child at risk.'

Julia was sleeping when Harry entered. Roz put a finger to her lips and he nodded.

'Will you take Mama home and look after her, please? Julia doesn't want her fussing over her yet.'

'You are asking me to leave you alone here?'

'The house is full of servants, Harry. Besides, Philip has gone off somewhere. If he comes back and quarrels with me I shall summon the servants.'

'I'll leave one of the grooms here with orders to protect you,' Harry said. 'As soon as your mother is settled I'll come back.'

'I'm going to stay for a day or so.'

'I'm not sure that is a good idea.'

'Julia needs me.'

'In that case I'll find Philip and warn him to stay away. If he lays a finger on you I'll kill him.'

'Be careful, Harry. My brother is violent.'

'All the more reason that I should see him before he gets a chance to see you or Julia.'

'Thank you.'

Roz smiled at him and he went out. She found a comfortable chair by the window where she could look out and still watch over Julia.

Tears trickled down her cheeks. It was so sad that Julia should lose the child she had longed for. A miscarriage was always an unhappy occurrence but Julia had wanted her baby so badly.

'Damn you, Philip. If it wasn't for Julia I'd . . .'

What could she do? She was certain that her brother had been the father of Carrie Blake's child – and that he had killed her and taken her body to where it was found – but she had no proof.

'If there were any justice it would be you suffering not Julia,' she murmured. 'I hope either Harry or Tom do thrash you.'

Tom couldn't believe it when he saw Philip Thornton near the hay barn. He had dismounted and tied up his horse and was staring at the spot where Carrie's body had lain. Incensed, Tom strode towards him, red-hot anger working through him.

'What do you want?' he demanded. 'This is my land and you're trespassing.'

'Damned upstart,' Philip muttered but his voice was slurred. 'Who the hell do you think you're talking to?'

'Do you really want to know?' Tom glared at him. 'Well, I'll tell you. I think you are a filthy rotten swine. You gave Carrie her baby and told her to blame it on your father – and then you killed her. You killed her somewhere else and dumped her body here. If I could prove it I should see you hang.'

'Bloody farmer,' Philip muttered and swung out with his right fist. 'Got above yourself. Deserve to be taught who the master is here.'

Tom dodged the blow easily, holding on to his temper by a thread. 'Go home, Thornton. You're too drunk to pick a quarrel with me.'

'I'll teach you . . .' Philip raised his arm and tried to hit him with his riding crop but Tom caught his wrist. 'Bloody cheap little bitch. She deserved what she got.'

'You devil.' Tom forgot caution. His fist connected with Philip's chin three times in quick succession. Philip went down under the flurry of blows and Tom kicked him in the ribs twice. 'I ought to kill you but you're not worth it. You're scum, Philip Thornton. You weren't fit to lick her boots. Come near me again and I shall kill you.'

Turning away, Tom left him lying on the ground. His knuckles were sore and bleeding and he was breathing hard.

It was early in the evening when Harry entered Julia's bedchamber again. Roz was drinking a cup of tea the housekeeper had brought up for her.

'How is she?'

'She woke for a moment or two and then went back to sleep. She knew I was here and smiled.'

'You promise not to tire yourself?'

'I shall do nothing to endanger my health. I don't want to lose our child, Harry.'

'Your mother is staying with me until you come home and then she will stay with Julia.'

'That rather depends on Philip. Have you seen him?'

'No. I had a ride round the estate but there was no sign of him. He may have taken himself off to Wisbech to stay with his friends.'

'I hope you are right. I don't want him to come back and upset Julia.'

'It is a pity she married him. Your brother is rotten to the core.'

'Yes, he is. I pray that he stays away for a few days to give Julia a chance to recover.'

Harry gave her an odd look. 'I'll second that. Anyway, I've told my groom to sit outside your room all night and wake the household if he tries to get to you or Julia.'

'I'm sure we shall be safe enough.'

'I'm pretty certain he's in Wisbech with his friends. You needn't lose sleep over it, Roz.'

She stood up and went to kiss him. 'I'm sorry I haven't been with you today. Your present is in my room on the dressing table.'

'We'll celebrate when you feel Julia is well enough to leave.'

'You're so good to me.'

Harry moved away from her, looking slightly uncomfortable. 'I'll see you tomorrow, Roz. Please get some rest yourself.'

'Julia's maid is going to take my place so that I can sleep later. I'm being well looked after.'

'Yes, I am sure you are. This was your home. I'll get back to your mother before she starts to fret . . .' At the door he turned back to look at her. 'Do not worry, Roz, I am sure this will all turn out well in the end.'

'I wish I could think it. Julia wanted that baby, and even if she could have another . . .' She shook her head. 'Damn Philip. I hate him, Harry. I wish he would die.'

'Do you really mean that?'

'I'm not asking you to kill him – but I should be happy if he had an accident and broke his neck.'

'Well, the way he's been drinking recently . . .' Harry smiled wryly. 'No one would mind too much – except your mother. She seems to think he is everything he ought to be.'

'Only because she doesn't like to face the truth. In her heart she knows what he is.'

'Yes, I dare say she does.' He inclined his head and went out.

Roz looked at the bed. Julia was still sleeping. She was the one person who might miss Philip, because she loved him despite all he had done to her.

'What is wrong with your hand?'

'Nothing,' Tom said and frowned as he glanced at the knuckles. 'I grazed my hand when I was mending something.'

'Let me look,' she insisted and grabbed his hand as he would have turned away. 'Grazed it? It looks as if you've been in a fight.'

'Look at my face, Ma. Do I look as if I've been fighting?'

'No . . .' Ellen shook her head. 'Dick used to come home with bruises all over him – but that hand looks more like a fight than a graze.'

'Well, it isn't and if it were it's finished. Stop fussing, Ma. Where is Mary Jane?'

'She went out earlier. I thought she must've gone to visit her mother.' Ellen looked at the mantle clock. 'It's getting late, Tom. Do you think perhaps you should go and look for her?'

'Damn,' Tom said and plunged his hand into a bowl of cold water. 'Don't tell me she's started running off the way Carrie did, Ma?'

'Not as often but she has been out for a couple of hours or so once or twice recently.'

'You should've told me. I'll have a word with her – leaving you with all the work to do on Christmas Day.'

'She helped me prepare the food earlier then said she was . . .' Ellen broke off as the kitchen door opened and Mary Jane walked in. Her hair was windblown and her cheeks were red from the cold but her eyes were bright. 'We were just starting to worry, lass.'

'Sorry I'm late, Ma.' Mary Jane went to the sink to wash her hands. 'Is dinner ready yet? I'm starving. I've not eaten since breakfast.'

'Did your mother not give you anything?'

'Oh, I had a piece of cake. But I wanted to wait for your dinner because you're a better cook than Ma.'

'Well, help me get the goose up then, lass,' Ellen said. 'Sit down at the table, Tom – unless you want a dressing on that hand first.'

'It's all right,' Tom said. 'Let's have our dinner and then I'll give you your presents.'

Roz wondered how Tom Blake and his family were spending Christmas Day. She knew that the work never stopped for small farmers. There was always the milking to do and the animals to care for, but at the end of the day they must surely have time to celebrate.

It was ridiculous to let herself think about him. She could never be with him, never share the same bed – or make love to him whenever she wanted.

Her thoughts were suspended as the door opened and Julia's maid Alice entered.

'You should rest now, Mrs Rushden. You've sat here all day.'

'Yes, I need to sleep for a while,' Roz agreed. 'If Julia wakes and asks for me you must wake me.'

'Yes. I'll call you if you're needed.'

Roz got to her feet. 'Has my brother come home yet?'

'No, Mrs Rushden.' Alice hesitated, then: 'He often stays out for a whole night – sometimes more.'

'It is not well done of him,' Roz said. 'Remember I'm not far away and ready to come if she needs me.'

Leaving the room, Roz went to the chamber that had been hers as a girl. Julia had left things much as they always were because she'd said Roz was always welcome to visit.

It seemed strange going to bed in this house. Roz thought about her husband, sighing as she realized that she was quite happy to know that she could be sure of sleeping alone tonight. That wasn't fair to Harry but Tom had been too much in her thoughts.

Harry would never forgive her if he knew about Tom Blake. She could only pray he never had cause to suspect anything was wrong. If the child had his eyes and hair it would be fine – but what if the babe looked like Tom?

Roz wished she knew who the father was so that she could settle it in her own mind, but she really had no idea.

'Forgive me,' she whispered to her unborn babe. 'I shall love you, whoever you are.'

Locking her bedroom door, Roz undressed and then went to bed. She blew out the candle but it was a while before she slept.

It wasn't so very strange that Philip should stay out all night since he'd done it before, but she couldn't help wondering why he hadn't wanted to know how his wife and child had fared. His selfishness was beyond words.

It was the middle of the next morning when the housekeeper entered Julia's bedchamber and glanced anxiously at the bed.

'How is the mistress?'

'She was awake earlier and she had the tea and bread and butter you sent up, but she didn't want the broth. I think a nice piece of cold chicken later might tempt her appetite.'

'There's plenty of roast meat, including capon and duck,' the housekeeper replied. 'None of it got eaten yesterday. Shall I send up a sandwich or leave it on the plate with a little relish?'

'I think that would be best – and I'll have the same.' Roz saw that the other woman hesitated. 'Was there something else?'

'The Reverend Jenkins is downstairs. He wants to talk to you.'

'To me? I'll come down now. Julia is sleeping so she won't miss me for a while.'

'I think there's something wrong, ma'am, but I don't know what.'

'Thank you, Mrs Monks. I'll come immediately.'

Roz had a cold tingling at the nape of her neck as she went downstairs. Why had the vicar come to visit and what had the housekeeper sensed?

She walked into the small parlour and saw the vicar standing looking out of the window. He was obviously alert and waiting for her, because he turned as soon as she entered.

'Ah, Mrs Rushden. Forgive me for calling this way at such a time but I thought it might be best if the news came from me rather than a stranger. You must prepare yourself for a shock.'

'A shock? Has something happened to Philip? He didn't come home last night but I was told it has happened before.'

'No, Mrs Rushden, it isn't your brother.' The Reverend Jenkins looked anxious. 'Mr Rushden – your husband, has been murdered.'

'Harry . . . murdered?'

Roz felt her knees go weak. She gave a little sigh and grabbed at a fragile whatnot for support, sending it and a china figure flying. The vicar sprang to her aid, helping her to the nearest chair.

'Forgive me. I did not know how else to tell you. I was informed that Sir Philip was not here and I knew that your sister-in-law was ill . . .'

Roz shook her head, putting out her hand to stop him. She was stunned, disbelieving. She couldn't have heard him right. Harry couldn't be dead.

'It is not your fault, sir. I can hardly believe – my husband murdered. Harry is dead? How do you know it was murder?'

'He was shot more than once. It happened near that little cottage at the edge of your brother's estate.'

'Why on earth would Harry be there? It doesn't make sense. When he left me he said that he was going home to look after my mother.'

'Was your husband riding a horse, Mrs Rushden?'

'Yes, I am certain he was – why?'

'There were signs that a horse had been near the body but it was not there and the constable seemed to believe the motive would have been robbery.'

'The constable? Did he find Harry?'

'I discovered your husband early this morning. I had been sitting up with a dying parishioner all night and was returning home when I saw him lying there. I summoned help and your husband's body has been taken to a safe place for further investigation. The constable called to see me because he wondered where you were and I was able to tell him that you had been staying here. I asked if he would allow me to break the news. He will call to see you later, either today or perhaps tomorrow.'

Roz's head was whirling.

'I don't understand why anyone would want to murder Harry.'

'He had no enemies?'

'None that I knew of. He was in business but I believe most people liked him.'

'Then I dare say the constable was right and it was a violent assault with intent to rob.'

'Yes.' Roz put a hand to her face. 'Poor Harry. We should have been at home celebrating Christmas but I insisted on staying with Julia.'

'You could not have known what would happen. As you say, he ought to have been on his way home.'

Roz felt tears trickle down her cheeks. She wasn't in love with Harry but she cared for him. To think of him being murdered was so terrible that she could hardly bear it. Standing up, she managed to thank the vicar and make some excuse. She needed to be alone to think.

Alone in her room, Roz sank down on the edge of the bed and covered her face with her hands. Harry was dead – murdered. Why? What had happened and why was he near the old cottage?

Silent, hurtful tears ran down her cheeks. Only last night Harry had been here promising to take care of Roz's mother and saying they would keep Christmas for when Julia recovered.

Roz went cold all over. Had Harry gone after Philip, intending to give him a thrashing? They might have quarrelled and . . . her thoughts came to an abrupt halt. She was sure that Philip had killed Carrie Blake – but was he so evil that he would have killed Harry? Harry's murder was hard enough to bear. If his murderer turned out to be Philip . . . it was too terrible to contemplate.

Roz would say nothing of her suspicions or fears to the constable when he visited her. She had no proof and it was up to the authorities to discover who had done this wicked thing.

'I'm so very sorry, Harry,' she whispered. 'I'm sorry you're dead. Sorry that I never loved you as you deserved. I'm sorry for everything.'

Roz's throat was tight with emotion as the tears flowed. Harry had been so proud of the fact that she was to have a child – and she did not know whether it was his or Tom Blake's. For a moment the unworthy thought that she was now free came to her but she dismissed it instantly. Harry was not even buried and he had been good to her in his way. Besides, Tom was married and the whole idea of a relationship between them was impossible.

Roz got up and washed her face. She was not sure what happened in a situation like this, but eventually the authorities would release Harry's body and she must arrange for his funeral when that time came. Until then, she would stay here with Julia. She could not face returning to Harry's house alone just yet.

Julia was sitting up against a pile of pillows and it was obvious she had been crying.

'Roz, dearest,' she said and held out her hand. 'Mama just told me. I am so very sorry. It must be terrible for you – and such a strain keeping it from me.'

'Mama should not have told you. I begged her not to just yet.'

'She was upset and I asked why.' Julia took her hand. 'I am so very sorry, dearest. Have they told you anything? Do they know who might be responsible?'

'The constable asked me if Harry had any enemies but I was unable to help him. I knew he had business associates but as far as I am aware everyone liked him.'

'I am sure Harry was well liked. He was a kind, generous man – and he loved you. You will miss him, Roz.'

'Yes, I do miss him already. You must know that it was not a love affair. I married him for a home of my own, Julia – but I did care and I would not have had this happen for the world.'

'Of course you would not. Do you know why he was near that cottage?'

'No – unless . . .' Roz shook her head. 'He might have been looking for Philip that night. Harry thought he should be here with you.'

'I wondered if that might be the case. It isn't like Philip to stay away so long, Roz. You don't think that . . .' Her words tailed off, her eyes dark with distress. 'Philip wouldn't . . . would he?'

'No, I'm sure he wouldn't,' Roz said. 'I dare say he is feeling out of sorts and ashamed to come home after what happened on Christmas Day. If Philip hadn't insisted that you go down-stairs . . . but there's no use pointing the finger. What happened, happened.'

'I know . . .' Julia caught back a sob. 'I love him, Roz. I know he is selfish and careless but I do love him.'

'Yes, and I love you, which means that even if I thought Philip might have done something terrible I should not give the constable any assistance in coming to that conclusion.'

'Oh, Roz . . .' Julia wiped her cheek as the tears rolled silently down her face. 'We aren't very lucky, are we?'

'We still have each other.'

'Yes.' Julia hesitated. 'Have they told you when the funeral will be?'

'Harry's body has been taken to a chapel of rest and I may visit there. I can arrange things as soon as I wish.'

'Does that mean you have to go home?'

'I suppose I ought,' Roz said. 'Mama is torn between staying here with you and coming with me. I told her she ought to be with you. I shall be perfectly all right.'

'Could you not stay here – have the funeral from here?'

'I think that might offend his family. Harry's cousin visited me earlier this morning and offered to make the arrangements. I was grateful and left everything to him. I must have the reception at Harry's home but afterwards – well, I am not certain. I may be homeless.'

'Surely Harry would not leave the house to someone else?'

'He has a cousin but as yet no son. I would not expect more than my jointure. I dare say there may be a house for me somewhere.'

'If you cannot stay there you must come to us, Roz.'

'If it were just you, Julia, I should be happy to live here – but not with Philip.'

'I understand.'

'I think perhaps I shall send for the carriage and return to Harry's house this afternoon.'

'You are so strong. If I were more like you perhaps Philip would respect me.'

'Philip is a fool and should I see him I shall tell him so.'

'Please do not,' Julia said and smiled. 'If I am well enough in a day or so I shall come and stay with you, Roz.'

'Please, do as the doctor advises,' Roz begged. 'I want you to be well again.'

Sixteen

It was bitterly cold in the church and people spoke of snow before morning. Harry Rushden had been respected and there was hardly a space to be seen as villagers, farmers and country gentry crowded in to hear and join in the service. Roz had Julia on one side of her, Harry's cousin Keith Rushden and her mother to the other. When the vicar intoned his eulogy, Julia took Roz's hand and held it. Hymns and prayers followed and then the family went outside to witness the internment.

Roz scattered earth and then threw a posy of Christmas roses on to Harry's coffin. Turning away, she saw Tom Blake standing at a respectful distance. For a moment their eyes met, then he bowed his head to her. Roz gave no sign that she had noticed. She was feeling numbed, unable to think clearly as she walked from the churchyard and allowed Harry's cousin to help her into the carriage.

'It is the custom to read the will after the funeral,' Keith Rushden said. 'However, if you wish we can wait for a few days. There is no hurry, Roz.'

'I am able to bear it,' she said. 'You have been very kind. I am grateful to you for all your help.'

'Harry adored you,' he said. 'He told me he never thought he would get you. I don't know why you married him, but he would expect me to take care of business for you.'

'Thank you.'

The reception was tedious. Roz listened to condolences, made the appropriate replies and thanked everyone for coming. She was glad when the last of her neighbours left. Now there was only her mother, Julia and Harry's cousin – and the lawyer, who had come from Wisbech for the occasion.

They retired to the small parlour for the reading. Julia sat by Roz's side and Keith stood by the window, his back turned as he listened to the lawyer's words.

'Mr Harold Rushden was a man of substantial means,' he said.

'He added a codicil to his will quite recently. Mrs Rushden is to receive the settlement as drawn up in her marriage contract, which is the sum of five thousand pounds plus three thousand a year for life. She is also to have the tenancy of any available house of her choosing on the estate. The residue of the estate is left to Mr Rushden's son, if he should have one. If he should fail in this respect, a daughter is to receive ten thousand pounds when she reaches the age of one and twenty. Mrs Rushden is to live in the house until such time as her child is born. If the child is a son she will be his guardian with the help and guidance of Mr Keith Rushden; if a daughter, the remainder of the estate then passes to Mr Keith Rushden.'

He paused for a moment to allow his words to sink in. Julia reached for Roz's hand and held it tightly.

'The codicil added recently is in respect of a house in London that Mr Rushden has just purchased. This will pass to his wife with a capital sum of a further five thousand pounds for its upkeep. There are various small bequests to servants but that is the main body of the will.'

'Well,' Lady Thornton said, her mouth twisted sourly. 'The London house makes things a little fairer for my daughter, sir, but she ought to have had something more. Mr Rushden assured me that she would be wealthy if she married him and this is shabby. I dare say he had more than two hundred thousand pounds.'

'Mama!' Roz said sharply. 'I am quite satisfied with Harry's decision. I should not expect to inherit the estate – and it passes to my son if I have one.'

'I'm sorry, Roz,' Keith said and looked at her apologetically. 'I agree that Harry could have left you more.'

'I may have a son,' Roz said and stood up. She offered her hand to the lawyer. 'I am quite content with my portion, sir. I did not marry for wealth and I shall abide by the terms of Harry's will.'

'My cousin asked me to look after you if something should happen to you. You will never want for anything – whether I inherit or not.' Keith moved towards her, offering his hand, which she took. 'You must know I admire you, Roz. It will be my privilege to help you in any way I can.'

'You are everything that is generous, just as Harry was,' Roz replied with dignity. 'This has been a long day. If you will all excuse me, I shall go to my room. Mr Rushden, you are welcome to call another day. Julia, perhaps you will come with me? Mama, please see that Mr Rushden and the lawyer have all they need.'

Roz left the room before her mother could protest. Julia came after her and took her arm. Roz smiled as she saw the question in her eyes.

'I expected something of the sort,' she said. 'Harry was rich and we had not been married long.'

'Perhaps you will have a son.'

'Yes, perhaps.' Roz drew her inside the bedroom and they sat on the edge of the bed together. 'I wanted to talk to you alone. You have heard nothing of Philip?'

'Nothing. Should I report him as missing, Roz? Your mama is worried but we thought it best to wait until today was over.'

'I wondered if he might be staying with Madeline and her husband.'

'Surely if he knew that your husband had died he would have come home, Roz?'

'Would he? We have not been on the best of terms recently.'

'I am afraid that he has done something foolish.'

'Yes, I am beginning to think he may have done.' Roz sighed. 'I think you should write to Sir Raymond and ask if Philip is staying with him – or would you like me to do it for you?'

'Would you? I hardly know them and I do not like either of them very much.'

'Yes, of course I will. It would be much better if I wrote. You would not wish Philip to think you were spying on him.'

'You understand me so well. What will you do now, Roz? I heard what the lawyer said – but it makes things awkward for you. Until the child is born you do not know whether this is to be your home.'

'I shall remain here for a while. I need to think about the future, Julia. If the estate is my son's I may have to continue to live here at least part of the time for his sake. He should know his home and learn about the estate, but I might prefer to live elsewhere.'

'In London?'

'I think perhaps a house in the country or a small town might suit me better, but I can make no plans as yet.'

'I should miss you if you went away.'

'I should never desert you. We are friends, Julia – but you are right, it is an awkward situation. I do not think I truly wish to live in this house. However, we must see what the future brings.'

'Yes, of course. Forgive me. It is too soon.'

'Had Harry died of an illness it would have been easier but I feel . . . as if a shadow hangs over me. The constable says they have found no evidence other than that Harry's pockets had been emptied and his horse was missing.'

'It is shocking to have such a burden,' Julia said. 'I keep thinking . . . no, I cannot believe it. It's just that he has been away so long. Philip would never do such a wicked thing, would he? He had no reason – did he? Please tell me if there is something I should know.'

Roz hesitated, but what good could come from telling Julia the truth now?

'Do not torture yourself, Julia. I am sure there will be an explanation for his absence in time.'

'Yes, of course. I am going to leave you to rest now, Roz. Otherwise your mama will come looking for us and I do not think you need that at the moment.'

'Thank you for protecting me,' Roz said. 'She wishes to move in here but I do not think I could bear that, which is very unkind of me.'

'Mama is difficult at times but I do not mind her fussing.' Julia laughed softly. 'Lie down and rest. We do not want you to become ill and lose your child.'

'Oh, Julia,' Roz said. 'I wish I could turn back the clock.'

'We can none of us do that,' Julia said and went out.

Roz lay back against the pillows. She felt exhausted and needed to rest. All the images of the past few days kept going through her mind. Not least the look in Keith Rushden's eyes as he'd promised to look after her. She did not know what was in his mind but she was not interested in his attentions.

Tom Blake had come to the funeral. There had been a wealth of meaning in his look. Roz felt a familiar sense of loss wash over her. Tom had a wife and responsibilities. He could never leave his family or his land and she could not step into his world even if he could.

'What's the matter with you?' Ellen asked as Tom entered the kitchen. 'And where have you been dressed up like that?'

'I went to Harry Rushden's funeral.'

'Why?' His mother's gaze narrowed. 'He was killed the day you had that fight – you didn't have anything to do with his murder?'

'That's a disgusting thing to say. Why would I want to murder Rushden?'

Ellen sighed. 'Because you want his wife?'

'Afraid I'll run off with the widow and leave you here to take care of Pa alone?'

'I saw the way you looked at the Thornton girl when you brought her here the day she fell from her horse.'

'You have a vivid imagination. Even if I wanted her I wouldn't murder her husband.'

'I didn't say that – but you did have a fight that day, Tom. Don't lie to me because I know it.'

'I thrashed Philip Thornton if you must know. I blame him for Carrie's child – and perhaps her death.'

Ellen sat down, her face draining of colour. 'You know he's gone missing too? What have you done, Tom?'

'I just told you. I gave him a thrashing but he was alive when I left him. I didn't murder either of them.' Hearing a shout from upstairs, Tom glared at his mother. 'Pa needs attention. Where's Mary Jane?'

'She went to visit her mother.'

'You should tell her she's needed here. You can't take care of Carrie's baby, Pa, and do all the cooking and cleaning.'

'She says she's sick of looking after a dirty old man and working all hours for nothing. She told me you don't love her and she thinks you married her just because she was strong and could help in the yard as well as the house.'

'If Mary Jane has a grievance she should talk to me. I'll take these things off and then I'll see to Pa.'

'You wouldn't lie to me, Tom? You're not in any trouble?'

'I'm not daft enough to do what Dick did so stop worrying.

I wouldn't have thrashed him if I hadn't found him near the hay barn. He was staring at the spot where I found Carrie.'

'I'm glad you thrashed him but I don't want to lose you, Tom. I couldn't manage this place alone.'

'Well, I'm not likely to go anywhere,' Tom said, then stopped and looked at her. 'If Pa were dead I might sell up and move away. Go into some other trade.'

'You wouldn't?'

'I'd make sure you were all right, Ma. I shan't throw you out but sometimes I think there must be more to life than this.'

'Oh, Tom,' his mother whispered as he left the room. 'I should never have pushed you to get married. I thought it for the best but now . . .'

'We ought to tell someone what we saw,' Mary Jane said, looking at the young man leaning against the bales of hay beside her. 'It ain't right keeping quiet over something like that, Jack.'

Jack Dawson frowned. 'What's Tom going ter think if he knows you were with me when you told them you'd gone to yer ma's? He'll think the worst and he'll be right.'

'I don't care.' She pouted at him. 'I would never have agreed to meet you if he'd paid me any attention. I wish I'd never married him.'

'Well, you did and you're stuck with it. Anyway, it would cause a lot of trouble if we told anyone about the squire and Mr Rushden. We had no right to be in that cottage, Mary Jane. They might arrest us for breaking and entering.'

'The door wasn't locked. I can't sleep for thinking of it, Jack.'

'Well, I'm not going to the constable and that's flat. Go yourself if you want but don't involve me. If you say I was with you, I'll deny it.'

'I thought you liked me.' Mary Jane looked sulky. She pressed herself against him. 'You liked what we did that day – couldn't get enough of it. Why don't we run off together?'

'Don't be daft. Where would we go? I've only got what I earn and you've got nothing.'

'I could take the housekeeping Tom gives us.'

'How long would that last?'

'You don't love me at all.'

'I do, though.' Jack swung her into his arms and kissed her. 'If we had enough money to start a little shop or a pub I'd take you away, Mary, lass – but what chance have we got to make a living?'

'Supposing we got some money – a lot of money?'

'What are you planning to do?' Jack grinned. 'Rob the bank in Wisbech?'

'We'll make the squire give us five hundred pounds.'

'You mean blackmail him?' Jack stared at her, half in awe, half in shock. 'He would kill us as soon as look at us – the way he killed Harry Rushden.'

'Not if I ask him and tell him that someone else knows. I reckon I could persuade him to give me some money. Is five hundred pounds enough, Jack?'

'More than enough to set us up selling newspapers and sweets and suchlike. I've alus fancied a little shop of me own, Mary, lass. If you could get us the money I would run off with you then.' He frowned. 'But he's missing, ain't he? He's probably run off because he thinks they'll arrest him for the murder of his brother-in-law.'

'I know where he is,' Mary Jane said. 'I went back to the cottage the other day because I dropped a hair ribbon when we ran away that night. I saw him going in after I'd left. He kept looking back over his shoulder but he didn't see me.'

'We'll go there now. You go in on your own, Mary, and I'll be outside. If he attacks you, I'll come in and stop him.'

'All right.' She threw him a bold look. 'I'll make him give us the money, Jack. Then we'll be rich, won't we?'

'It's not riches,' Jack said. 'But it would be a new life for us.'

Roz was sitting at her writing table looking at the letters of condolence she had received since Harry was murdered. Everyone was kind and all the letters ought to be answered. She picked up her pen and dipped the nib into the ink, then heard a sound behind her and turned to look. Seeing that someone had entered through the French windows she rose to her feet, a startled cry on her lips.

'Philip . . . what are you doing here?'

'I came to see you, Roz. Don't tell me you're not pleased to see me – or did you think I was dead?'

'Julia has been worried about you. You should be ashamed of yourself. Leaving her like that when you knew she had lost the child.'

'Useless bitch. I was a fool to marry her for so little. I should have looked for an heiress with more money.'

'That is evil, Philip. I don't know what has happened to you.'

'You called me a murderer to my face.' He moved towards her, a look of menace in his eyes. 'You told Rushden that you would be happy if I had an accident and broke my neck. Don't deny it, because he told me.'

'Did you expect me to love you after what you've done? You caused Julia's fall and you killed Carrie Blake. You'll hang one of these days.'

'The little slut kept following me about, pestering me to give her money or another baby. I slapped her down and she fell and hit her head. I didn't intend to kill her, just to get her out of the way.'

'So that you could continue your affair with Madeline Jenson, I suppose.'

'She's another scheming bitch – her and her husband both. They cheated me out of all I had. The estate, land, money; it has all gone.'

'Philip . . .' Roz was stunned. 'You gambled everything away? What about Julia's money? How is she supposed to live now?'

'How should I know?' Philip moved towards her. 'I need money to get away, Roz. You must be rolling in it now. Give me five thousand and I'll never darken your door again.'

'Five thousand pounds is far more than I have in the house. Harry didn't keep much here and I'm not rolling in it as you so crudely put it. I have my jointure, which is a mere fraction of Harry's wealth. Had you done your duty as a brother the marriage contract might have favoured me more but all you wanted was to get me off your hands.'

'Damn you,' he grunted and grabbed her arm. 'Give me some money or I'll make you sorry. It gets easier once you've killed. I was terrified when I killed Carrie but it was a pleasure killing Rushden. He thought he was going to teach me a lesson – but I was ready for him.'

'You killed Harry . . .' the strength seemed to drain out of her and she leaned against a cabinet to stop herself falling. 'Oh my God. Philip . . . how could you?' She was trembling as she looked at him.

'He went for me. I had to defend myself. What does it matter? I'm past caring.'

'Harry shouldn't have attacked you but you were wrong to kill him, Philip. What are you going to do now? How can you live with two deaths on your conscience? Supposing you were seen . . .' Roz hesitated; he looked scared, sick and she realized he was desperate. She ought to scream, bring the servants running and have him arrested for his terrible crimes, but Julia had enough to distress her without having her husband hung for murder. 'I have five hundred pounds available but that is all. If I give it to you, I want your promise that you will go away and never come back.'

'Five hundred bloody pounds,' Philip muttered, his lips white with temper. 'How far is that going to get me?'

'I have no idea. You may have to work for a living . . .' Roz gasped as he struck out at her, knocking her against the desk. 'I'm having a child, Philip. Do you want to kill my baby as well?'

'I couldn't care less what happens to the brat. Give me the money. And you can give me the diamond brooch you're wearing too.'

'This was Grandmother's. It isn't worth much.'

'Give it to me or I'll make you wish you'd never been born.'

'Very well.' Roz reluctantly unpinned the little crescent and handed it to him. Then she opened the top drawer of her desk and took out a small purse of gold coins. 'Take them and go. I never want to see you again, Philip. Do you understand me? I have no brother and next time I'll scream for help.'

'Bitch.' He leaned closer, shoving his fist in her face. 'I ought to make sure you keep your mouth shut.'

'You have no need. The reason I haven't been to the law is because I care for Julia. I would see you hang and feel nothing but she still loves you.'

'Well, she won't be seeing me again.' Philip thrust the money into his pocket. 'You were a fool to take Rushden. You could have done better.'

Roz sat down as he walked away from her. Now it was over

she was trembling, icy cold. How could her brother be so evil? What had happened to make him that way? She tried to make sense of things but couldn't.

Julia must never know the whole truth. In time she would learn to make a new life for herself – but where? And what of Mama? If the estate went to pay a gambling debt both she and Julia would be homeless, though she recalled Julia telling her she had a small income Philip hadn't been able to touch.

Roz closed her eyes. It was all such a terrible mess. They could both come and live here but if her child was a daughter they would have to move when Keith Rushden took over the estate.

'I'm so sorry, Harry,' she whispered. 'It's my fault. Why did I let you go believing I wanted Philip dead that night?'

'Here he comes now,' Jack whispered. 'He's going into the cottage. Are you sure you want to do this, Mary Jane?'

'I'm not afraid of squire,' she said and grinned at him. 'He's always had an eye for a pretty girl. Besides, five hundred pounds isn't much to him. He'll give me what I want and I'll promise never to tell or ask for more.'

'I'm not sure this is a good idea, Mary, lass. If anything happened to you . . .'

'It won't,' she said and kissed him on the mouth. 'This is for us, Jack. Think of it: our own shop and no working on the land or milking smelly cows – and you'll be your own boss.'

'I'd like that,' he admitted. 'Go on then but be sure to scream good and loud if he attacks you and I'll be right there.'

'He won't,' she said, looking confident. 'I can handle the squire, don't you worry.'

'Go on then, afore I change my mind.'

They had been lying in the grass out of sight of the cottage. Mary Jane giggled and got to her feet. She walked away from him, looking back once or twice to wave.

Jack watched as she entered the cottage, leaving the door open. She was a brave lass. He wasn't sure he would have had the guts to do what Mary Jane was about to do. The squire was a dangerous man and she was vulnerable. He looked at the door anxiously, beginning to regret that he'd agreed to this mad scheme. It was unlikely that Philip Thornton would simply pay up. Jack was a fool. He should never have let Mary Jane go in there alone.

He was getting to his feet and thinking about whether he should go in after her when he heard the scream. Mary Jane had a good pair of lungs on her, he thought as he took the iron bar he'd brought along as protection and charged towards the cottage. There was no way he was going to let that devil murder her as he had Harry Rushden.

'It's late,' Ellen said as Tom came in after finishing the milking that evening. 'Mary Jane has never stayed out to this hour before – except that once on Christmas Day.'

'I want my supper, Ma. She'll come back when she's ready.'

'She's your wife, Tom. You may wish she wasn't but there's nothing you can do about it now. If you don't go to look for her I shall.'

'If I must,' Tom glared at his mother. 'Give me a piece of that bread to eat as I go. Are you sure she went to her mother's place?'

'It's what she said. If you go there first you may meet her on the way.'

'She'll get a piece of my mind when I do find her.'

Tom pulled on the thick coat he'd taken off and went out. The last thing he needed when he'd finished his chores was to go searching for his wife. If she refused to pull her weight at the farm he'd be better off without her. She might as well go home and he'd find a girl to work for a wage. It was what he should have done in the first place.

The night was bitterly cold as he took a lantern and set off across the fields. There was no point in taking his horse because he might miss her. Besides, he needed light because it was a dark night and clouds had obscured the moon.

Feeling aggrieved by his wife's neglect of her work and her thoughtless behaviour, Tom covered the ground between the farm and her parents' house in good time. He was breathing hard, fighting his temper as he knocked at the door. Mary Jane's father answered it, looking at him oddly.

'Well then, Tom, what are you doing here tonight? Our Mary's not been taken bad, has she?'

'Isn't she here? She told Ma she was off to visit her ma hours ago and she hasn't come home.'

'You'd best come in.' Mr Forrest stood back to allow him to enter the kitchen. 'Janet, Tom says our Mary was coming here – have you seen her?'

Janet Forrest turned round and looked at them, her expression anxious as she wiped her hands on her apron. 'I haven't seen her since Christmas Day and then she only stopped ten minutes afore she was off.'

'She stopped only a few minutes on Christmas Day?' Tom frowned. 'She was late home that evening. She told us she had been with you most of the day.'

'Well, I don't know why she said that but she was only here a few minutes, wasn't she, John?'

'Aye – and I've not seen her since. She always was a contrary lass.'

'You've no idea where she'd be – either of you?'

John Forrest shook his head but his wife hesitated.

'You've thought of something?'

'It's just a chance, Tom – afore she decided to wed you, she was sweet on Jack Dawson. She may have been meeting him.'

Tom stared at her in silence, then nodded. 'She danced with him at the church Christmas do – and she was put out with me. I suppose she might have gone to meet him because she was bored or unhappy.'

'Well, you've only yourself to blame. You neglected her – leastways that's what she told me.'

'I've been busy.'

'The man can't work that farm and run after his wife,' John Forrest grunted. 'Mary Jane always had grand ideas in her head – thought you'd be rich one day, Tom.'

'I might be one day but I have to work for it. I'll go home and see if she's there; if not I'll have to search for her. After what happened to Carrie . . .'

'I'll come with you,' John Forrest said and reached for his coat. 'I've had my supper and I was looking for an early night, but if our Mary's gone missing I'll not sleep a wink.'

'Oh, Tom,' Janet Forrest looked distressed. 'You don't think anything could have happened to our Mary, do you?'

'I hope not, Mrs Forrest, but I can't leave it to chance. I thought she was just playing me up and staying out late to punish me for something, but if she hasn't been here . . .' He broke off because he was beginning to be worried. 'You'd best bring a lantern, John. If she isn't at home we'll need to split up and search for her.'

'Roz.' Julia rose from her chair and came towards her, hands outstretched. 'I'm so very pleased to see you. I was just sitting here thinking that I should drive over to see you tomorrow.'

'Julia, my dearest, I am so sorry,' Roz said and kissed her cheek. 'I have some shocking news for you. I fear it will distress you, but I wanted to tell you before anyone else did.'

'Is it Philip?' Julia's face went white and she sat down abruptly. 'Is he dead?'

'No, very much alive. He came to me earlier this evening and asked for money. He has gambled everything away, Julia. I'm so sorry but there is nothing left for you or Mama.'

'Nothing . . .' Julia stared at her. 'Those wicked people. I warned him but he would not listen. I'm sure they cheated him.'

'Yes, perhaps they did,' Roz agreed. 'I think that is how they earn their living. Madeline blinds the men with her charm and sensuality and Sir Raymond cheats them at the card table. Harry suspected it. He was taken in at first but came to his senses in time. Philip may . . . I'm sorry, but I think he may have had an affair with her.'

'I suspected something of the sort. Her manner was very . . . arrogant.'

'It was the same for me. Harry had a brief affair with her in Paris. No, please don't look like that, Julia. He was upset, angry with me over something. I can't tell you exactly but I didn't tell him something he had a right to know before we married and it hurt him. He realized what the Jensens were when they stayed with us and we made an effort to put things right. We were happy enough recently.'

'Everything is so horrible, Roz. Where is Philip? Why hasn't he been here?'

'I think he means to go away, start a new life.' Julia didn't need to know the worst of Philip.

'Leave me here?' Julia looked stunned. 'He is deserting me knowing that there's nothing left – and your mother too? She will have to leave the dower house. What are we going to do, Roz? I have a small income but it won't buy us a house – at least, not one your mama would consider fit to live in.'

'For the moment you can live with me. Unless you wish to remain here until the lawyers tell you to move out?'

'This is my home. I think both Mama and I should stay put for the time being. Perhaps he didn't lose quite everything.'

Julia was clinging to straws, refusing to believe that Philip had gambled his entire estate.

'I've been thinking. Harry left me a little money and a house in London. I could sell that and buy a house somewhere else for you and Mama to share. If I have a son we could live at Rushden Towers but I may have to leave if I have a daughter.'

'It is so unfair. Philip gambled my money away as well as his own. You may be turned out of your home because your husband left the property to a son or his cousin. I thought better of Harry.'

'He had his reasons, but at least he left me a house and money. Philip took everything you own and wasted it.'

'Where is he? I want to see him.'

'I don't know. He may have gone back to Wisbech or . . .' Roz tried to think. 'It is possible that he might be staying at the cottage.' Seeing that Julia did not understand, she went on: 'It used to be kept for the estate manager but my father dismissed the man because they fell out and after he died Philip neglected to employ a new man. There wasn't much money and he thought he could solve the problem by marrying an heiress. Forgive me, Julia, but you knew why Philip asked you.'

'Where is the cottage?'

'Right at the edge of the estate. Near where Tom Blake's land and another farmer's land meet.'

'Would you take me there?'

'Tonight?'

'I suppose it's too late,' Julia said. 'We could go in the morning.'

'You're upset over all this,' Roz said. 'We'll go tonight – but we'll take a couple of grooms with us. I would rather not drive about in the dark without protection.'

Seventeen

'No, she hasn't come home,' Ellen said when the two men entered the farmhouse kitchen. 'Where on earth could the silly girl be? Staying out until this hour.'

'Mrs Forrest thinks she might have been meeting someone,' Tom said grimly. 'If it weren't for what happened to Carrie I'd leave her to it but she might be hurt or in trouble. We're going to search for her.'

'I'll rouse some help,' Ellen said. 'We need to get men from the village, Tom. There's a murderer out there somewhere. He got away with killing our Carrie. If he's done for Mary Jane as well, no one is safe.'

'I'll do that, Mrs Blake,' John Forrest said. 'You stay here in case Mary Jane comes back. You've got Mr Blake and the babe to watch.'

Ellen agreed and stood staring at the kitchen door as it closed behind them. She'd put Tom's supper into the oven to keep warm but he'd likely be out all night looking for that wretched girl. It was her fault. She'd pushed him into getting married when she'd known he was hankering after the Thornton girl.

A horrible thought crept into Ellen's mind. Tom wouldn't have done anything stupid, would he? Immediately she was ashamed of the thought. Tom had done his best to make Mary Jane happy even though he didn't love her. He was young and strong and a good many in his shoes would go off and find an easier life.

Ellen knew she hadn't been exactly fair to her son of late. If anything had happened to Mary Jane . . .

God forbid! No doubt the selfish girl was just off gallivanting with a young fellow who'd taken her fancy.

There was no moon that night and few stars, which made it difficult to see very far ahead. Roz had ridden this way often when she was a young girl and her father was alive, and she handled the trap easily. Julia's grooms were riding ahead and they shouted out when they saw a horse tied outside the cottage.

Roz tugged on the reins, bringing her horse to a halt. One of the grooms had dismounted and came to help her and Julia down. He looked at her doubtfully.

'It might be best if me and Jem went in first, Mrs Rushden. The door's wide open. It's a cold night to leave the door open.'

'Thank you, Rogers,' Roz said. 'I should be grateful if you will both accompany us. I have a feeling that something is very wrong here.'

Her fingers curled into the palms. Philip had been in a terrible mood when he'd visited her. He needed more money than she could give him. Surely he hadn't done anything desperate?

Holding her lantern firmly in her right hand, Roz offered her left to Julia, who took it. She was shivering and clearly apprehensive.

'Would you rather wait here?'

'No, I'm coming with you.' Julia's eyes were wide and fearful. 'Something bad has happened, Roz. I can feel it.'

'Yes, I know. I feel it too.'

Holding hands and picking their way carefully through the rough grass, they walked into the cottage behind Rogers. A lamp was burning in a room at the back of the house and there was an unpleasant smell that Roz could not place. The groom entered the room ahead of them and then gave a cry of alarm. He turned towards them urgently.

'You'd best not see this, either of you.'

'Please let me pass, Rogers. I would rather know what has . . .' Roz's words drained away as he stepped to one side and she saw that there was not one but two bodies lying on the floor of the small parlour. One was a man with his face beaten to a pulp and the other was a woman. 'Oh my God,' Roz whispered. 'Is she dead too?'

Jem had knelt by the woman, turning her over so that he could see her face. He jerked back with a gagging sound. 'It's Mary Jane Forrest – leastwise, she was a Forrest. She married Tom Blake a few months back.'

'Was she beaten too?'

'It looks to me as if she was strangled,' Jem said. 'She'd been hanging around with Jack Dawson recently. He told me she were fed up being married and . . .' Jem broke off, as if realizing he'd said too much.

'Is it Philip? His face . . . I don't know if it's him . . .' A sob left Julia's lips. 'I think . . . they look like Philip's clothes.'

'Yes, they are. He is wearing a ring Father gave him on the little finger of his right hand. I'm so very sorry . . .' Roz broke off as Julia gave a little scream and fainted.

Jem moved to support her and lowered her into an armchair. Roz went to her, taking her hand as her eyelids flickered.

'I'm so very sorry, Julia. I don't know what happened here. We must summon help.' She looked up at the grooms, who were staring at the body of their late master in evident dismay. 'Jem, please drive your mistress home at once. You must send someone to fetch Sir George Ickleton. He is a magistrate and will know what is to be done here. Also, someone must go to the Blakes' house and tell them that Tom is needed here – and then bring the trap back for me, please.'

'Come with me, Roz,' Julia begged. 'I can't stay here and I don't want to be alone.'

'I have to stay here for the moment,' Roz said and squeezed her hand. 'Rogers can't stay here alone until the magistrate comes. Mrs Monks will look after you, dearest, and as soon as I can I shall come to you. I shall stay with you tonight. Philip was my brother and I owe him this much.'

'Yes, of course.' Julia brushed a hand over her eyes. 'You're always so sensible and so good to me, Roz. I'll do as you ask.'

Roz embraced her. 'You are brave and generous, Julia. The best thing that ever happened to Philip if he'd had the sense to see it.'

'And you are the best thing that happened to me.' Julia kissed her cheek.

Roz went to the door of the cottage and watched as Jem drove her away in the trap, then returned to where Rogers was waiting.

'What do you think happened here?'

He hesitated. 'It looks as if Sir Philip attacked the girl and killed her and then someone found them and went wild. Jack Dawson has a fearful temper when roused, Mrs Rushden. He was always sweet on Mary Jane and got drunk three nights in a row when she wed. If he knew the master had killed her . . .'

'I think my brother killed another girl – Carrie Blake,' Roz said, sensing that the groom she'd chosen to stay was loyal to her. 'If by chance Mary Jane knew something . . . she might have asked him for money and provoked the attack.'

'Maybe he wanted to lie with her and she refused him. He was a bit rough with the women at times – begging your pardon, miss, but that's what I've heard.'

'She must have known that Philip came here – and she came because she wanted something from him.' She knelt by Philip's body and put her hand in his coat pocket. Glancing up, she saw the groom's shocked look. 'I gave Philip some money earlier this evening. He doesn't have it. I think someone knew Mary Jane was going to ask for money and after she was killed he went wild, beat Philip to death, took his money and ran.'

'He didn't take the horse or the ring.'

'Both of which could be traced back to Philip. Whoever did it was scared but he wanted money to get away. I suggest that if Jack Dawson doesn't show up for work we know who the culprit is here.'

'Will you tell the magistrate that, Mrs Rushden?'

'It isn't for me to do his job,' Roz said as she stood up. 'I just wanted to be sure in my own mind.'

'Yes,' Rogers agreed. 'That sounds about right to me, ma'am – but I wouldn't want to get Jack into trouble unless I was certain.'

'We'll simply tell the magistrate what we found and leave it to . . .' She broke off as she heard something in the hall and turned to face the man who had just entered. Her breath caught in her throat as she saw him. 'Tom . . . I'm so very sorry. I sent someone to tell you but they can't have . . .' His face told her that he didn't know.

'I saw the door open and horses,' Tom said, advancing into the room. 'I was looking for . . . Mary Jane!' He shot an angry glance at Roz. 'My wife – what happened here?'

'We aren't sure,' Roz said as he knelt by his wife's side, touching her face gently as he saw the signs of violent assault. Her blue lips, popping eyes and protruding tongue combined with dark marks about her throat pointed to the manner of her death. 'Tom, I'm so sorry. Julia and I came to look for Philip. He has been missing since Christmas Day but he visited me earlier today and we thought he might be here.'

Tom rose to his feet. 'Mary Jane has been meeting someone recently. I thought it was . . .' His eyes held an angry glitter. 'If she's been with *him* . . . Damn his cheating soul to hell! He wasn't satisfied with ruining Carrie – he had to have Mary Jane too.'

'I'm sorry, Tom. I don't know what happened here – but it looks as if my brother may have killed your wife.'

'If he did that means someone else killed him.' Tom nodded grimly. 'The silly girl had been meeting Jack Dawson. I had no idea until her mother told me that's where she might be when she didn't come home this evening.'

'So it's true. I didn't want you to suffer more than you must be already.'

Tom's gaze was fierce as he met hers. 'I should never have married her. She knew I wasn't in love with her. If I'd been a better husband she wouldn't have strayed.'

'You can't blame yourself for this, Tom.'

'What have you done about reporting this?'

'I've sent someone to fetch Sir George Ickleton. He will know what we must do now.'

'You shouldn't be here. I saw no sign of your horse?'

'I drove Julia over in the trap. My groom will bring it back and then collect his horse.' Roz met his furious gaze. 'I shall stay here until the magistrate comes. Whatever Philip is, whatever he may have done, he is still my brother.'

'I suppose I can't force you to leave.'

'No, you can't.'

'Stay then, if you must.'

Tom took the chenille cloth from the table and covered Mary Jane's body, then went into a back room and came back with a patchwork quilt which he placed over Philip.

'There's a table and chairs in the kitchen – and I saw a bottle of wine. Why don't we wait there?' He glanced at Rogers, who had been silent since he arrived. 'I don't know about you, but I could do with a drop of something. I don't know how I'm going to tell Mary Jane's parents. I'm just glad it was me that came this way instead of John Forrest.'

'Thank you,' Roz said as the groom helped her down from the trap. She looked up at the house and saw candles were burning in all the front windows. 'I'm not certain I could've managed this evening without your help.'

'I was glad to be there, Miss Roz.' He paused, then: 'They will be out looking for Jack Dawson in the morning. I wouldn't have said what I know if Tom Blake hadn't said it first — but it seems the magistrate agreed there had to be a third person.'

'Yes, that much is obvious. Mr Blake was very angry over his wife's murder, which is perfectly natural.'

She nodded to him and walked up to the house. Mrs Monks was waiting for her in the hall.

'How is my sister-in-law?'

'In terrible distress, Mrs Rushden. She was hysterical when she came home and I had to give her a little slap. I put her to bed and sent for the doctor. He gave her a sleeping draught and she's settled down now.'

'Poor Julia. She's had so much to bear recently. It was all distressing and I ought to have come with her — but I couldn't leave Rogers there alone. It was important to speak to the magistrate.'

'It's been just as bad for you, ma'am,' Mrs Monks said and pursed her mouth. 'Losing your husband like that — you're both widows now.' She shook her head in distress. 'Everyone is saying that the master did for Mr Rushden.'

'Yes, perhaps. We may never know,' Roz said. She couldn't help thinking that he'd got what he deserved in the end — and feeling guilty because if she'd told someone about Philip long ago Tom's wife might still be alive. 'I should like some tea, Mrs Monks. Do you think you could bring it up to my room, please?' She took a few steps towards the stairs, stopped and looked back. 'Mama! It is too late to send a message tonight. Please have Rogers fetch her in the trap before breakfast. I must stay here for Julia and I would rather Mama heard the news from me.'

'Yes, ma'am. It isn't right you should have to bear this alone.'

'I have no choice.' Roz pressed her fingers to her temples. 'I'm a little tired. If you would bring the tea up yourself, please.'

'Yes, of course, ma'am.' The housekeeper stalled. 'What will happen to the estate now, Mrs Rushden?'

'I imagine it will have to be sold. My brother was in debt, I believe. I shall do what I can for the servants but . . .' She sighed and shook her head before going upstairs.

Alone in her room, Roz undressed and pulled on a satin robe, then sat at the dressing table and took the pins from her hair. Her hair shone; thick and luxuriant it cascaded on to her shoulders. Tears trickled down her cheeks.

How angry Tom had been when he looked at her – almost as if he hated Roz and blamed her for what had happened to his wife.

'I'm so sorry,' she whispered and wiped the tears from her cheek. 'In a way I let this happen. Oh, Tom, what am I going to do?'

There was no one to answer her question. Tom Blake had made love to her once but it seemed so long ago and so much had happened since. How could she even think of a relationship between them now? It was impossible. Philip had caused their family such harm. Even if she had no proof, Roz was certain that he was the father of Carrie's child and he had caused her death, though he claimed it was an accident. Yet he'd deliberately murdered Harry and he must have known what he was doing when he strangled that girl. Perhaps he was so desperate that he'd lost his mind. What she'd discovered at the cottage was clear enough for Roz to be certain in her own mind that Philip *had* strangled Tom Blake's wife.

Even if Tom had truly loved Roz that must be an insurmountable barrier between them.

Roz went to her bed and climbed in as the housekeeper brought in a tray of tea, which she placed across her lap.

'Can you manage like that, ma'am?'

'Yes, thank you,' Roz said. 'Mrs Monks – if the house is sold I shall buy a small house for my mother, and Julia, if she wishes to make her home with Mama. Would you be prepared to take a position with them? It would not be as important a job as here, I'm afraid. I dare say Mama will live quietly.'

'I shall be pleased to accept, ma'am. Lady Thornton is a good employer and so was your mama.'

'Very well, we must see what happens.' Roz smiled. 'Goodnight, and thank you for the tea.'

Sipping her tea after the housekeeper had left, Roz thought about the future. If she did not have a son she would be forced to move out of her home. She did not think she could bear to live with her mother, but if she moved from Rushden Towers she might be forced to do so – or live in a house on Harry's cousin estate. The look in Keith Rushden's eyes at Harry's funeral had made her a little apprehensive of being at his mercy. One unwise marriage had made her wary of another.

'Oh, Philip,' she said as she moved her tray to a bedside chest and snuggled down into her bed. 'Why did you have to do so many terrible things?'

'What has happened?' Lady Thornton asked as she swept into the breakfast room the next morning. 'Is Julia ill again? Where is she? And what was so important that I must come before I've had my breakfast?' Lady Thornton sat down and nodded to the maid. 'I'll have tea unless it is stewed. I suppose it is too much to expect a fresh pot?'

'Please fetch my mother fresh tea, Tilda. I have some bad news, Mama. I fear it will distress you – but I cannot change what has happened.'

'Is it Philip? Has he been gambling?'

'Yes, Philip *has* got himself into trouble with his gambling, Mama – but I fear it is much worse. I am so sorry but I cannot make it easy for you . . . Philip is dead.'

'Dead?' The colour washed from Lady Thornton's face. 'My son is dead? What are you talking about, Roz? It simply cannot be . . .'

Lavender water wafted towards Roz as her mother dabbed at her eyes with a kerchief.

'Forgive me, Mama. Julia and I found him last night at the old estate manager's cottage. He had been beaten to death.'

A moan of grief issued from behind the lace and lavender water. 'Who would kill my son? I cannot believe it – there must be a mistake.'

'I wish it were a mistake, Mama. I'm afraid there is worse.'

'How could anything be worse?' Lady Thornton stared at her belligerently. 'I know you did not care for Philip – but I loved him.'

'Julia loves him, Mama. She is grieving terribly but she knows the truth. Philip was not alone. There was a woman with him in the cottage and she had been murdered.'

'Was it that flighty piece who stayed at your house?'

'No, Mama. It was Tom Blake's wife. We think – it is not certain – but it looks as if Philip strangled Mrs Blake and was then beaten by a third person in revenge for what he did.'

Roz's mother stood up. 'How dare you say such a thing to me? I shall not listen to such foul slander. Whoever killed Philip killed that woman. My son is innocent.'

'Mama, please do not hate me. I cannot change things. I know you loved him but he was not as honourable as you wish to believe.'

'I shall go up and speak to Julia. I refuse to listen to another moment of this foul slander.'

The door closed behind her with a little bang. Lady Thornton would never admit that her son was a seducer and a murderer. She would not listen until it became common knowledge and she was forced to accept it.

The door opened and a maid entered bearing a tray of tea. Roz gave no indication of her feelings as she said, 'Lady Thornton has gone up to have tea with Lady Julia – if you could please take the tray up to them?'

Roz had no appetite for food and pushed her plate away. At this moment all she wanted was to run away as far and as fast as she could. Sighing, she stood up. She had stayed for Julia's sake. However, if her mama intended to move in and comfort her daughter-in-law, Roz would be forced to seek the sanctuary of her own house.

'I wish you would stay until after the funeral,' Julia said. 'I don't feel that I can manage alone.'

'I am near enough to visit if you want me, Julia. It is so difficult here. Mama hardly speaks to me. I think she blames me for what happened to Philip.'

'I've told her she must not blame you. Philip brought his fate on himself.'

'Yes, that is true, but Mama refuses to believe it,' Roz said. 'I do not know what will happen if the worst happens and she is forced to leave the dower house.'

'You must not worry too much. I have spent the past two days turning things over in my mind. Philip sold the house in Bath that was given to us as a wedding gift, otherwise we might have lived there. I think I shall write to my aunt and explain my circumstances. I believe she may offer me a home. She has several properties and I could become her tenant. I should ask Mama if she wishes to live with me.'

'Could you bear that, Julia?'

'Your mama has always been kind to me. I know she can be irritating but her bad temper is mostly directed at you, Roz. I'm quite fond of her, you know.'

'Yes, I do know and I think she would be happier living with you. I have the house in London, which I could sell. If your aunt does not offer you a home I might buy two smaller houses in the country. Mama could spend some time with each of us.'

'You have not yet been forced to leave Rushden Towers, Roz.'

'I shall not until my baby is born, but I am thinking of what might be necessary in the future.'

'Well, I hope you may continue to live in your home in comfort. We shall visit whenever we can, of course, but it will not be quite the same.'

'No, it cannot be,' Roz agreed. 'You have not heard from Sir George yet, I suppose?'

'He wrote a short note telling me that he had the business in hand and would let me know his findings when he was certain of his facts. I believe they will allow us to bury Philip in a few days.'

'It is all so very horrid for you, dearest. I wish I could make it all go away for you.'

'We are both suffering. I do not forget that you have lost Harry,' Julia said. 'Do you suppose that the same person . . .'

'I do not know; it is impossible to guess,' Roz prevaricated. 'Perhaps when Sir George has finished his investigation we may know more.'

'It is frightening.' Julia shuddered. 'Three murders, Roz; four if you count Carrie Blake. No one has ever been certain how she died. You don't suppose they could all be tied together, do you?'

'No, I'm sure they cannot.' In her own mind Roz was convinced of Philip's guilt but she would continue to hide the truth from Julia if she could. 'We must just wait and see what the magistrate makes of it all.'

Roz glanced at her mother as they took their places in the front pew of the church. Lady Thornton was very pale. She had been avoiding her daughter's eyes ever since Julia showed her the letter from Sir George Ickleton setting out his theory. He believed that Philip had strangled Mary Jane Blake and then been beaten to death by person or persons unknown.

It was common knowledge that Jack Dawson had disappeared and people were whispering that it was he who had killed Philip in revenge. An inquest had been arranged for the following month and in the meantime Julia had been given permission to bury her husband.

Roz let her gaze travel round the church. There was no sign of Tom Blake but she had not expected him to attend. Why would he come to the funeral of the man who had killed his wife?

People were talking about Tom Blake too. Rogers had told her that Mary Jane's mother had been heard to accuse Tom of having killed her daughter, but her husband had slapped her and told her to be quiet. John Forrest had made it known that he did not suspect or blame his daughter's husband, but Mrs Forrest's outburst would be enough to set some tongues wagging.

Roz could feel the eyes boring into her back and knew that her husband's murder was also under discussion. So far no one seemed to have put the deaths together, but they had not been privy to her last conversation with Harry. He had intended to search for Philip and she was certain he'd found him; her brother had said as much that night, though it might never be proven, because she had no intention of adding it to her brother's crimes. Julia had enough to bear without making things worse.

She felt like a hypocrite as the vicar asked them to pray. How could she pray for Philip's soul when she knew what he'd done?

Surely this was all a bad dream? She would wake up in her own bed and hear her father's voice calling to the dogs as he set out for his morning ride. If only it *were* all a nightmare and she could wake up.

Julia reached for her hand and held it. How much longer must she endure this torture? She couldn't sing a word of the hymns and the prayers fell on deaf ears. She just wanted it to be over so that she could escape – and yet she knew that there was no escape for any of them.

Roz could hear her mother weeping. Julia was crying silently. Both women had hardly stopped for the past ten days. Gazing through a black veil that obscured her vision, Roz hid the fact that she had shed not one tear for her brother.

'You're not worth it,' the words were in her head but not on her lips. 'You're not worth one of Julia's tears.'

'If she was carrying on with Jack Dawson she isn't worth mourning,' Ellen said. 'It's time you pulled yourself together, Tom. I can't do your work for you and you know it.'

'Have I asked you to? The men are coping with the work. I've talked to Joe Fitch and he says his elder daughter will come in to help with the baby and the chores.'

'Susie's a good girl, I like her,' Ellen said. 'But she won't help with your pa. Mary Jane was good with him. I think he liked her.'

'Next time he shouts just leave him, Ma.'

'He'll lie there and wet the bed if I leave him. I swear he enjoys making more work for me.'

'Well, I'll go up to him before I leave and make sure he's comfortable.'

'Where are you going?'

'I've things to do.'

'You said the men were coping.'

'Does everything in this life have to be about work?'

'I hope you're not going to see that woman. I won't have her here, Tom. The day you bring her into this house is the day I'll walk out.'

'You'll please yourself,' Tom said. 'I might be the one to do the walking, Ma.'

He walked from the room, leaving her to stare after him in

frustration. He was just upset, Ellen thought. He wouldn't really walk out and leave her with his pa and Carrie's baby to care for alone – or would he?

Tom was brooding on something and Ellen wasn't sure what it might be. If he'd seemed guilty she'd have suspected him of having hurt Mary Jane and killing the squire but he wasn't frightened or worried, just deeply unhappy.

He was hankering over the Thornton girl, just as he had all along. Didn't he know that too much had happened? All the scandal and the murders had made it impossible for there to be anything between the pair of them.

Tom stood in the lane that separated his land from that of Squire Thornton and watched the carriages approaching. He wasn't sure why he'd come here, except that he'd known Roz would pass this way as she returned to the house. She was staying with her sister-in-law for the moment, though rumour had it that the estate would be sold in the next few months. Philip Thornton had gambled everything away, including his wife's money.

Tom moved back to the grass verge as the first carriage passed, catching sight of Roz's pale face at the window as she was driven by. She looked in such torment that his heart went out to her. He'd been angry when he'd found her at the cottage but it was for Mary Jane's sake. She hadn't deserved to die like that whatever she'd done – and his anger was with Philip not Roz.

How must she be feeling? Her husband hardly cold in his grave and now her brother murdered too. Tom wondered if the murders were connected but couldn't see why or how that should be.

He wasn't sorry Philip Thornton had got his comeuppance. Tom was certain Thornton had killed Carrie. He was pretty sure that he'd also strangled Mary Jane. There was no veil over his eyes as far as his wife was concerned. Mary Jane was a schemer and if she knew something about Thornton she wouldn't scruple to use it to gain a profit for herself.

Tom had wondered if the child she'd lost had been his. At the time he'd believed her when she declared that she was having his baby, because he *had* taken her down on the night of the church hall dance. Yet if she'd been seeing Jack Dawson before he started taking her out . . .

He would never know the truth and it hardly mattered. Tom had been fond of her in his way, though he'd never loved her as she wanted him to love her. If rumour had it right, Dawson had killed Thornton for what he'd done to her. That meant he must have been in on the blackmail. He must surely have known what a violent brute Thornton could be? If he cared for her he ought to have protected her. Dawson had lashed out in revenge afterwards but it was too late.

Tom felt the anger and frustration build inside him. If Dawson were here now he would thrash him the way he had Thornton.

If Mary Jane had simply run off with her lover there might have been a chance for Tom with Roz. She must hate what had happened – her brother branded a murderer. She probably thought Mary Jane had been having an affair with her brother – the way Carrie had.

It might be that simple, but he was pretty certain Mary Jane had been after money. She must have pushed too hard and something snapped in Thornton's head. Everyone said he was ruined and a man could only take so much.

A feeling of hopelessness settled over him as he walked towards the bottom meadow. Once he'd been filled with ambition, eager to make something of himself – but that seemed an empty prospect now. In time people would stop pointing the finger and the gossips would turn elsewhere for their amusement, but he was sick of it all. For two pins he'd go off and make a new life somewhere else.

Roz went through the motions, thanking people for their kindness in coming but wishing they would all depart. She wasn't sure how much more she could take because everyone was being so polite when all the time she could see their true thoughts in their eyes. What hypocrites they were.

Roz needed to be alone. She'd seen Tom watching from the grass verge as the carriage passed through the lane separating his land from her brother's, and the look on his face made her heart ache. Everything was so awful, so impossible. Not her brother's land for much longer. The lawyer's letter informing Julia that she had one month to leave the house had arrived that morning before they left for the church.

'You know you can come to me,' Roz had told her. 'You have a home for as long as I do.'

'My aunt hasn't replied to my letter as yet,' Julia replied. 'We may have to come to you for a while, Roz. Apparently I can only keep my personal items. All the furniture belongs to the estate.'

'Yes, I imagine it does. I'm so angry with Philip. You gave him a chance, Julia, and he threw it away.'

'I don't care about the money or the estate,' Julia said. 'He thought it was the reason I wed him, but it wasn't.'

'I know you loved him.'

'I still do; whatever he was, whatever he did I can't stop loving him.'

'Mrs Rushden, I wanted to tell you how sorry I was to learn of your misfortunes. Your husband – and your brother.'

Roz turned as the man's voice broke into her thoughts. 'Mr Harcourt. It was so kind of you to come. I did not expect it.'

'Your brother was a friend. I am aware of the scandal, but I do not forget friendship that easily.'

'I think you are one of the few.'

'You bear no shame, Mrs Rushden.'

'You are very kind, sir.'

'I understand Lady Thornton is in some financial trouble. If I can be of assistance . . .'

'I thank you, but Julia has a home with me for the moment. I dare say she will decide to live with her aunt in time.'

'Yes, perhaps.' His dark eyes were thoughtful. 'If I can be of service to you . . . You must know that I always had a high regard for you, Roz.'

'You are very kind, sir.'

'Not kind. I thought it would be inappropriate of me to reveal my feelings at your brother's wedding, but I took too long to speak last time and I lost you. I wanted to make you aware of my regard. It may be too soon but in the near future I should like to call on you. It is my intention to make you an offer.'

Roz sought for words to answer but was rescued by the arrival of Julia and merely inclined her head, feeling stunned.

'Mama needs you upstairs,' Julia said. 'Her head is very bad and she wishes to speak to you, Roz.'

'I shall go up to her at once.' She glanced at Mr Harcourt. 'It was pleasant to see you again, sir. Please excuse me.'

Aware that his eyes were following her, she left the room. Roz could not mistake his meaning. Mr Harcourt had it in mind to make her an offer of some kind, though whether it was to be his wife or his mistress she could not tell.

Eighteen

Roz was in her favourite parlour working on her embroidery a few days later when the housekeeper announced a visitor. She rose to her feet as Julia entered, greeting her with a kiss.

'Julia, how are you, dearest? I was thinking that I might drive over this afternoon if the rain cleared.'

'It is a little wet but I had to come. I wanted to tell you my news at once.'

'Has something happened?'

'I have sad news and also news that will make you pleased for me.'

'You intrigue me. Sit down next to me on the sofa and explain.'

Julia settled herself next to Roz. 'My Aunt Mary died suddenly a few days ago, which is why she did not answer my letter. Apparently she appeared to be in good health and passed away peacefully in her sleep.'

'I am so very sorry. She was a generous lady and I think you were fond of her?'

'Yes, I was. I can only be happy that she did not suffer a long and debilitating illness. If one must die to go in one's sleep is surely the happiest outcome for all concerned.' She hesitated, then: 'Apart from a small bequest to my brother and some servants, Aunt Mary left everything to me. I shall have a substantial income and three houses to choose from, Roz.'

'That is welcome news for you, dearest. I know you must be grieving but at least your financial worries are at an end. Does Mama know?'

'I came immediately to you, Roz, because I knew you were concerned and this will set your mind at rest.'

'I would willingly have given you a home with me.'

'Had Mama not been so unkind to you I should have accepted. Now I can provide her with a home of her own and enjoy my own residence. You will stay with me often, Roz?'

'Yes, when I can. What will you do next?'

'I intend to attend a memorial service for Aunt Mary at her own church. I shall ask your mama to accompany me. Once we have settled the business of the estate I hope to travel abroad. I would ask you to accompany me, Roz, but it would not suit you at the moment. Perhaps in the future?'

'Yes, perhaps,' Roz agreed and placed her hands on her stomach. 'I can begin to feel him here – or her. I'm sure he kicked me this morning.'

'You're so lucky to have the child,' Julia said. 'I would give all I own to have my baby alive and well.'

'Yes, of course you would, dearest. I would offer to come to the funeral with you but I've been feeling a little tired the last few days. I believe it is all the trauma of the past weeks.'

'We've both had a great deal to upset us since Christmas.'

'It may be best for you to get right away. You must try to forget this whole unhappy episode, Julia.'

'I shall not forget Philip. If you truly love a man you accept all his faults.'

'Yes . . .' Roz was silent, then: 'If Philip had been different – a man without an old estate and a title – would you still have married him, Julia?'

Julia looked at her thoughtfully. 'A marriage such as you describe would be a big step to take, Roz. Stepping down from your class is not something to make lightly – yet, if I felt that I was loved as much as I loved, then the answer is yes.'

'You are so brave and wise.'

'I'm not very brave but I know what it is like to love with all my heart – even though I was not loved in return.' Julia gave her an odd look. 'Please think carefully, whatever you do.'

'When did you guess?'

'I was never sure but I thought there might be someone. Is it Tom Blake?'

'Yes – but there is such a wide divide between us, Julia. I don't just mean the difference in class or family – his is better than mine in so many ways. All that has happened . . .'

'Philip ruined your life too, didn't he?'

'It all started with my father's death.' Roz stood up and crossed to the window to glance out. 'There was never any chance for us.'

'At least I can take your mama away. She will not be here to scold and bully you.'

'I am grateful that you care enough.' Roz turned to smile at her. 'One good thing has come out of all this, Julia. We shall always be friends.'

'Yes, we shall.' Julia joined her by the window. 'I should go while the rain holds off. I want to tell your mama the news, Roz. I shall write to you soon and let you know how things go on.'

'Yes, you must,' Roz kissed her cheek. 'Take care, dearest. I shall miss you.'

'I'll visit as much as I can.'

Roz nodded, waiting until Julia had walked from the room. She turned back to gaze out of the window once more.

Tom was forking hay on to a cart when he saw the trap. He stuck his fork into a bale and walked towards it. She was wearing black, her face pale beneath the fine tulle that half covered her face.

'I hoped you might be here at this time,' Roz said as he came up to the trap. 'I wanted to speak to you – unless you hate me too much?'

'Hate you?' Tom gave her his hand to help her down. 'Why should I hate you? You had nothing to do with any of it.'

'We quarrelled earlier that day. Philip was in trouble. He needed money to get away and I refused to give him more than five hundred pounds. He was furious when he left me. Had I been kinder to him he might not . . .' Roz choked back the words. 'You know that they've caught Jack Dawson? I heard this morning that he confessed to killing my brother.'

'I've been told.' Tom led her to the haystack, making a place for her to sit. 'Should you be driving yourself about in your condition? You are with child?'

'Yes.' What would he say if she told him it could be his? 'I don't think I shall come to harm unless my horse bolts – and Dobby is very placid.'

'Unlike the horse that threw you.'

'You haven't forgotten, then?'

'I have forgotten nothing that concerns you.'

She hid her emotion, glancing away as she said, 'They told me Jack Dawson and Mary Jane planned to blackmail Philip because they saw him murder my husband.'

'That was a shock. I thought the blackmail might be to do with Carrie's death. I had no idea that he'd killed Harry Rushden . . . but you did, didn't you?' Roz nodded. 'You didn't tell anyone? Why did you keep quiet about your husband's murder? If you'd spoken out Mary Jane might still be alive . . .'

'Please don't be angry with me. I was concerned for Julia. She had just lost her baby.'

'I'm not angry with you. I just need to know.'

'I couldn't be sure it was Philip. How could I know? Harry went looking for him and something happened between them. Later, I accused Philip of murder to his face. He shouted at me but despite what he said a part of me struggled to believe him, even though I knew he was telling the truth. I didn't want Julia to know because it would hurt her – but I suppose it will all come out now.'

'It's bound to at the trial. I pity Dawson. He was a fool to try blackmail – and an even bigger one to let Mary Jane do it on her own. He lost his head and just went for your brother when he realized that she was dead.'

'Yes. I'm so sorry for what Philip did to your family. I would make it all disappear if I could.'

'We can none of us do that, Roz.'

'I know. I just wish . . .' She caught back a sob. 'Why don't you hate me, Tom? You should.'

'Do you hate me? Dick killed your father and in a sense that started all this business.'

'No, it was before that – when Philip seduced Carrie and told her to blame your father.'

'He was rotten through and through.'

'Yes. I think it was a kind of snowball. When it started rolling he couldn't stop it – things just got out of control.'

'Yes, I dare say.'

'An act of dishonour led to tragedy.'

'Damn his cheating soul to hell!'

'It's all such a mess.'

'That's one way of putting it.'

'Oh, Tom . . .' Tears trickled down her cheeks. 'I shouldn't have come . . . it's too late. You hate me now.'

'Hush, my love.' Tom reached out and drew her to him. 'If my stupid pride hadn't got in the way I should've come to you before this. I thought you must hate me.'

'I could never hate you, Tom. Surely you know?' She lifted her tear-laden eyes to his.

'I can't get my head around that you love me – I've nothing to offer you, Roz.' Tom groaned as he bent his head to kiss her. It was a long, hungry kiss and they were both shaken when they drew apart. 'What the hell are we going to do?'

'I don't know.' She hesitated. 'Rushden Towers is only mine if I have a son. If I have a girl the property and most of the money goes to Harry's cousin.'

'I'm not interested in Rushden's money.'

'I didn't mean that. I just want you to understand.'

'I'd heard something of the sort. It's all one hell of a mess.'

'Yes, I know. People will never let us forget.'

Tom stared at her for a long moment. 'We could go off together, Roz – start a new life somewhere else.'

'But your family – your farm?'

'The house and land still belong to my father, even though Dick and I kept it going for years. If it had been left to Pa he would have lost it years ago, but it is still his legally. I have a small amount of money but no house and no land.'

'What about your mother and Milly?'

'Ma will manage somehow. I've seen to it that she has a girl to help in the house and men in the yard. If she wanted she could run the farm herself.'

'A new life? You would do that for me, Tom?'

'I should never have married Mary Jane. You were the one I wanted – right from the day you caught your skirt on the briars.'

'That seems so long ago.'

'It was another life. I should have swept you up and run off with you then, Roz.'

'I wish you had.' She looked at him sadly. 'I may not have Rushden Towers but I have some money. We might start a little business of some kind.'

'I wouldn't mind running an inn if we could afford it. It would only take a few hundred pounds – and I'll make money for you. I'll give you back every penny.'

'Hush.' Roz placed her fingers to his lips. 'The money isn't yours or mine. It's just there while we need it. We'll think of it as the child's.'

'What if you have a son? Harry's son would inherit.'

'If I was certain it was his.'

He stared at her, stunned.

'You think it might be mine?'

'I'll never be certain. Does it make a difference?' He shook his head in wonder. He'd never thought that he could be the father of Roz's child. 'I wish I could tell you it is your child but I can't.'

'You were married to him. We'll know as the child grows because blood will out.'

'We're going, then?'

'What about your mother? She has to leave the dower house, doesn't she?'

'She will live with Julia. Philip's wife inherited her aunt's property. She took Mama with her.'

'Then we'll go. It's Thursday now. I ought to make sure everything's in place as far as the farm goes. I could be ready by Sunday morning.'

'You really mean it?'

'I'm sure if you are?'

'Yes.' Roz reached up to kiss him. 'I'll bring the trap and come here on Sunday morning. Where shall we go?'

'I've always fancied somewhere near the sea,' Tom said and there was a note of excitement in his voice. 'You won't change your mind?'

'No, I shan't do that. I love you, Tom Blake. If I'd known that I would never have wed Harry.'

'I love you, Roz Thornton. I made a mistake when I married Mary Jane but now we have another chance and I intend to make the most of it.'

Roz's heart was racing as she packed her bags ready for the morning. She'd heard nothing from Tom since their meeting at the hay barn but she was confident he would meet her there on

Sunday morning. It wasn't too late for them. Tom loved her as she loved him. They were going away and they would put the past behind them.

She smiled as she chose the gowns she would take with her. There was no point in selecting her best things because she would never wear her silk evening gowns. She was going to be an innkeeper's wife and the idea pleased her. Her mother would never speak to her again but Julia would understand.

Roz went across to her dressing table and picked up the box that contained her jewellery. The pain was so sudden and sharp that she gasped and bent over, clutching at her stomach. What was happening to her? Roz stared at herself in the little shield-shaped mirror, her eyes widening as she felt the trickle between her thighs and realized what it was. She was bleeding. Was it a miscarriage? Tom had told her she ought not to be driving the trap but she'd felt so well. She hadn't even thought of the consequences.

She must summon help. Turning towards the door she felt a pain much sharper than the first and her head swirled. She screamed loudly and then collapsed on the floor as she convulsed with pain.

She was losing her baby.

'I'm so sorry, little one,' she whispered. 'So very sorry. I didn't take care of you . . .'

The tears were running down her cheeks as the door opened and the housekeeper entered.

'Mrs Rushden. What happened to you?'

'I'm having a miscarriage. Please help me to bed and then send for the doctor . . .'

'You can't leave us,' Ellen said and stared at Tom in dismay. 'How am I going to manage all the work? Even with the girl you hired I've got as much as I can do here. I can't see to the land and the stock as well.'

'Let Pa fend for himself more,' Tom said. 'As for the land – sell it. Sell the stock and just keep a few pigs and some chickens. The money the land brings in will keep you going for a few years.'

'And that's all you care about?'

'It isn't that I don't care, Ma. You know how people talk. I can't ask Roz to come and live here – and I want to be with her.'

'So we don't matter? What happens to your father and Carrie's girl – you can just forget about them, is that it?'

'It has to be this way, Ma. You know I can't ask her here. You told me you'd walk out if I did . . .',

'I didn't mean it, Tom. You know I didn't.' She caught hold of his arm. 'Please don't leave us.'

'It's all arranged, Ma. I'm meeting Roz at the hay barn. We're going off together this morning.'

'Tom, think what you'll be giving up. Everything you've worked so hard for – the land and all the plans you had.'

'It means nothing to me without her.'

'Bring her here. Let people talk. What does it matter?'

'I suppose I could ask.' Tom felt the justice of his mother's plea. 'I'm not promising anything so don't set your hopes too high.'

They heard John Blake calling from upstairs. Ellen threw him another pleading look. 'Please think about it. I must see to your father . . .' They heard the loud thump and looked at each other. 'What's happened now?'

'I'll take a look. It sounds as if he's had a fall.'

Running up the stairs, Tom entered his father's bedroom closely followed by his mother. John Blake was lying on the floor in a heap, his face hidden. Bending over him, Tom looked at his face and made a sound of disbelief.

'I think he's gone. He must have had another stroke or something. By the look of him he choked to death on his own vomit.'

Ellen's face was white as she knelt over her husband's body and checked for signs of life.

'You'd best send someone for the doctor to make sure – and then get off to meet your girl. This makes no difference, Tom. We've known it could happen and you've your own life to think of now.'

Tom was torn two ways. He ought to feel grief for his father but he couldn't. John Blake had been a hard man and he'd killed any love his wife and son might have had for him, but his death made it hard to leave right now.

'I'll speak to Roz. We'll wait for a bit. If I sell the land and give you money you'll be able to move into the village and have neighbours to look out for you.'

'I'll stay here with a couple of pigs and a few hens if it's all the same to you. Fetch that doctor, Tom – and tell your girl she's welcome here if she wants to come.'

Tom nodded and went out. If he didn't get off Roz would already be waiting.

It was as he was about to leave the farm that he saw the young lad waiting by the gate. If his memory served him right, he worked for Roz up at the Towers. He frowned. Had Roz sent to tell him she wasn't coming?

'Tom . . .' Roz's head turned on the pillow. 'I want to see Tom . . . please, I must see him. I must . . .'

'What's that, madam?' The housekeeper touched a cool cloth to her brow. 'If you mean Mr Blake, the lad took your note to him yesterday.'

'Why doesn't he come? I feel so ill. Why doesn't anyone come?'

'Mr Rushden sent a letter to your sister-in-law,' Mrs Martin soothed. 'Lady Julia will come soon. You should rest now, madam.'

'I want Tom. Why doesn't he come?'

Mrs Martin left the bedroom and went downstairs to the front parlour where a gentleman was standing before the fire. He had been staring into the flames but turned to look at her as she entered.

'How is she, Mrs Martin?'

'She is feverish, sir,' the housekeeper replied. 'She keeps asking for Tom Blake.'

'That fellow.' Keith Rushden looked displeased. 'You have my instructions. He is not to be allowed to see her – and she is not to know he called here on Sunday.'

'Are you sure that's the right thing to do, sir? She was crying and begging me to fetch him to her. Would it not be kinder to let him see her just for a while?'

'Her life is in the balance. That man is not a suitable person for her to see. You will please obey me, Mrs Martin – if you wish to keep your position here?'

'Yes, sir. I know you're the master here now that the mistress has lost the baby.'

'I like loyal people about me, Mrs Martin. If you do as I ask there will be a bonus for you when this is over. Remember, I'm only doing what is best for your mistress. I may own this house and the estate but I have no intention of turning Mrs Rushden out, I assure you.'

'Very well, sir. I just want what is best for her.'

'I've heard that Mr Blake's father has just died. I'm sure he doesn't have the time to dance attendance on Mrs Rushden's whims.'

'No, sir.'

'I have business to attend for the moment. I shall return later to see what the doctor has to say when he visits.'

'Yes, sir, of course.'

Mrs Martin stared after him as he went out. She stood for a moment and wondered what to do. He might think he held the whip hand but she wasn't so easily beaten – and she didn't wish to work for a master who thought his word was law no matter what. Mrs Rushden would give her a reference if she needed it and she liked the young woman too much to see her fretting.

Sitting down at her mistress's desk, she took out a sheet of paper and picked up a pen. Her writing wasn't perfect but Tom Blake would get the message and then it was up to him.

Tom looked at the note and frowned. He'd been denied access to Roz on Sunday when he'd gone in answer to her own message. He hadn't been sure why she didn't want to see him and had been on the verge of riding over and forcing his way into the house if he had to. Now he understood why he'd been turned away the last time.

He would have to make sure that he asked for Mrs Martin and that Keith Rushden was not in the house. The man would be gloating now that he had it all, but not satisfied with the money and the house, he wanted Roz too.

'You look as if you've lost a shilling and found a farthing,' Ellen said as she entered the kitchen bearing a basket of clean linen. 'Changed her mind, has she?'

'No, Ma, she hasn't. I told you she'd lost the child. She's ill and wants to see me but Keith Rushden is trying to stop me visiting her.'

'Why would he do that, then?'

'Perhaps he doesn't think I'm good enough for her.'

'What's it to do with him? You're good enough for anyone, Tom. Just because he's richer than you are it doesn't make him a better man.'

'No, it doesn't. I'm going over there now, Ma. If she's well enough I might bring her back here.'

'I'll put fresh sheets on Carrie's bed.' Ellen hesitated, then: 'I'm sorry, Tom. Sorry for the things I've said and done. You've got a perfect right to sell your father's land and go off where you want.'

He nodded, a faint smile on his lips. 'It depends on Roz. I shall do whatever she wants.'

Roz opened her eyes and looked at the man sitting on the edge of her bed. She blinked but when she looked again he was still there.

'I thought you were a dream. I was feeling so ill and I wanted you but you didn't come.'

'They wouldn't let me see you on Sunday. I came yesterday and I've been here all night. Your husband's cousin didn't like it much. I knocked him down and he went off in a huff. Told me this was his house and he'd thank me to get out, but I told him to make me and he couldn't.'

'Oh, Tom . . .' Roz shook her head wearily. 'I must've slept for hours. I was so tired. I feel as if I've been beaten all over.'

'It isn't an easy thing to lose a child, Roz. I'm so very sorry, my love.'

'The doctor told me not to worry because I would have more children,' Roz said, her throat caught with tears. 'He didn't understand. A lost child hurts so terribly, Tom.'

'I know, dearest. I know I can't do or say anything to make it better for you, but I'll be here when you want me.'

'Keith will tell us to leave as soon as I'm able to leave my bed.'

'He won't put you out until you're ready.'

'As soon as I'm well enough to go out I want to leave here.' Roz reached for his hand. 'Mrs Martin told me your father had died?'

'He died on Sunday a short time before we were due to meet. I was going to ask you to wait until we buried him. The funeral is tomorrow morning.'

'You must go, Tom. I'm so very sorry.'

'He was frustrated at being confined to bed. We sometimes thought he was playing us up, but he had another seizure and this one killed him.'

'What will you do now?'

'The farm belongs to me, Roz. I can sell the land and let Ma live in the house until she decides she's had enough and moves into the village. It doesn't have to change what we planned.'

'Your house is not small,' Roz said thoughtfully. 'In time it could be built on, made larger and become more substantial.'

'What are you saying? You wouldn't want to live there?'

'Why not? Why shouldn't we, Tom? I thought I wanted to run away but now I think I prefer to stay. I can be a farmer's wife as easily as an innkeeper's – and with the money I have we can buy more land. In time you might own as much land as my father once did.'

'Would you dare, Roz? You know what people will say? They'll remember the murders and they'll talk behind your back. The people you knew may cut you.'

'There's no one I care about but you and Julia.' Roz held his hand. 'Would your mother have me? Could she bear to have me living in her house after everything that's happened?'

'It would be our house,' Tom told her. His slow smile lit his eyes. 'I reckon she'd be grateful for the chance to welcome my wife home, Roz – if you could bear it?'

'When we first met I was proud and spoiled,' Roz confessed. 'I've been taught a few lessons, Tom. I thought it would be easier to run away, but lying here grieving for my poor baby, I've realized that I'm lucky to have a life. I can make what I choose of it and I don't intend to let a few spiteful tongues drive me away.'

'You're as brave as you're lovely,' Tom said and bent to kiss her. 'I love you and I'll do anything you ask of me, Roz.'

'Then take me to your home as soon as I'm well enough. I was going to take just a couple of bags but now I'll take everything I'm entitled to. We can sell what we don't use and we'll work to make it a good life, Tom.'

'If I have you it will be.'

'I love you, Tom.'

'Did you love me the day you let me win the archery contest?'

'Yes, I think I did.' Roz laughed softly. 'I pulled that arrow deliberately because I thought Carrie was owed the money.' She gripped his hand tightly. 'Can we really forget all the hurt and move on?'

'I don't know,' he said. 'But we'll have a damn good try, Roz.'

Epilogue

Ellen stood watching as Tom came out of the church with his new wife on his arm. It was summer because they'd waited a few months for decency's sake and their happiness seemed to surround them like a golden glow. She couldn't help smiling as Roz looked across at her and winked.

Ellen nodded back. Over the past few months they'd formed a good working relationship. Roz wasn't afraid of hard work, though she'd had to be taught even the simplest of tasks.

'It's what comes of being born a lady,' Ellen had told her when she'd despaired of learning how to bake bread. 'It's a good thing you've got me to show you or Tom would be on short rations.'

'Yes, he would.' Roz laughed. 'You won't tell him how useless I am, will you?'

'You're everything that man ever wanted and he'd starve rather than admit you're not perfect.'

Glancing at Roz's friend Lady Julia, Ellen was glad of the new dress her daughter-in-law had insisted on making for her in a dark blue silk. Ellen had never worn anything like it in her life and might not ever again but she had to admit that it felt good. Lady Julia had been so generous and so friendly, different from Roz's mother who had not come to the wedding and was refusing to have anything to do with her daughter.

Roz didn't seem to mind too much that most of her old friends had cut her. There weren't enough hours in the day to sit and mope because the work never stopped. Roz was happy with her life and she made them smile as she struggled to do all the things a farmer's wife ought to be able to do. She hadn't quite got the hang of the milking yet but she was learning. One of these days she would be as quick and clever at her chores as she was with her sewing and her reading. Ellen loved it when the chores were done for the night and Roz read to them all from one of her many books.

Tom had bought more land and he was talking of building on

to the house soon. Roz needed a parlour of her own for all her bits and pieces and they wanted more bedrooms because there was already a baby on the way and she was set on having a big family.

Most of all, Roz was happy and that made Tom happy too. You could see it in the way they looked at each other as they walked arm in arm towards the wedding carriage. There was laughter in the house now and love, and that was how it should be.

All in all life hadn't turned out too badly, Ellen decided and darted forward to shower the couple with rice and flower petals.